Still Wilde in Outlaw River

by Mike Walters

For my Air Force Brother, Al.
Thank you for so many wonderful
laughs and years of unwavering support.
I am not sure what I did to warrant
such an awesome friendship. Odin
must have been smiling down
on us the day we met.

Chapter 1

Let's Go Hunt Some Clowns

Mitch struggled to maintain his balance. He felt nauseated, and his head punished him with intense pain. Mitch's best friend and rescuer, Jack, steered the watercraft toward the bank. Watching Jack kept him from vomiting. Mitch wondered how Jack knew to drive the damn thing but he didn't have enough energy to ask. He tried speaking, but pain overwhelmed him. Mitch thought of his wife Mabey, and with quiet desperation, wished she were here. Her presence alone would be a comforting salve. His tingling lips felt massive as if he had rubbed mango rind all over them and they'd swelled in an allergic reaction. Jack turned and looked directly into Mitch's eyes. Mitch felt reassured because Jack's eyes seemed familiar. The last few days, ever since Jack had been shot with an arrow filled with Alien juice, Mitch had been waiting to see Jack's normal eyes. It was comforting to see their familiar glint again and he hoped his friend was back for good. At this very moment, Mitch may not have Mabey's warmth and loving touch, but he did have Jack back. Or so it appeared.

Jack started to speak, then stopped. Mitch could see he was struggling with what to say. What came out of Jack's mouth roused Mitch with new intensity, head pain and swollen mouth forgotten in an instant.

"Mitch, I don't know how to say what I am about to say without coming right out with it."

"Spit it out, Jack. I'm not in the mood for games."

"I'm sorry, my brother, but the town of Outlaw River is under some type of an attack, and people are in hiding. We need to get back immediately."

"Sure, Jack, but why so quick?"

"Mabey is missing, Mitch."

As if the cold water hadn't done enough temporary damage to Mitch's manhood, Jack's last comment about Mabey took shrinkage to a new level. Mitch slumped over and fell onto the floor of the craft. He grabbed his head with both hands and carefully squeezed, trying to push the pain away and focus on what he had just heard. He moved his lips back and forth, opening and closing his mouth forcing the movement to quicken the blood and hasten his skin's return to normal. He dropped his hands, rose to one knee, and raised his head in a newfound birth of energy and resilience. He could hurt later; right now, it was time to focus.

Jack roused Mitch from his thoughts with encouraging words.

"Mitch, come on. We'll find her."

Mitch heard Jack and, in a rare instance, had no idea what to say. He was trapped in depressing thoughts.

Jack drove the craft toward the bank, and pointing said, "Mitch, your backpack, and clothes are over by that large outcrop of rocks next to the tree."

"Is that Jasper?"

"Yes, it is. He's the reason I found you. As soon as we get you ashore, get dressed. I don't know how much time we have to get out of here unnoticed. I'm thinking minutes, so the quicker we get in your Jeep and on the road, the better."

Jack was also concerned with the fading daylight but didn't voice the thought. He wasn't sure Mitch was hearing much of what he was saying right now.

"My Jeep is around the other side of the lake, Jack."

"No, Jasper brought it around. It's at the top of the rim, so we need to hustle and get up there as quick as you can manage. So, suck it up, mister. Your wife needs you. You'll have time to hurt later. Okay?"

"Shit, Jack, I can hardly feel the lower half of my body. I'm so cold, I think my balls are completely sucked up inside my stomach."

Jack smiled. "They'll drop, bud; don't worry. If not, then I'm sure Mabey can help you with them."

Jack decided he would mention Mabey as frequently as possible right now to motivate Mitch. Not that his friend – hell, his brother – needed extra incentive, but Jack had read somewhere that adrenaline can be a wonderful elixir. He knew Mitch wouldn't have any issue in cranking out adrenaline now that Mabey needed him.

Mitch replied in what Jack thought was an eerily calm voice.

"You said Mabey is missing, Jack. How do you know she's missing?"

Jack eased the craft the final few feet to shore; Mitch felt it settle and stabilize. Jasper stood on the bank ready to help if needed.

"Mitch, let's get off this thing. Get your clothes on, and we'll hike up to your Jeep. We'll have plenty of time to talk about Mabey on the ride back to Outlaw River."

Mitch grabbed Jack by the arm and steadied himself, finding new strength and stubborn determination in his legs. The sweatshirt Jack had given him to tie around his waist fell off leaving him naked again. He didn't care.

Mitch grabbed Jack with as much force and strength that he could muster.

"Damn it, Jack, tell me what the hell is going on!"

A familiar voice came from the bank.

"Geezus, Wilde, the water was pretty cold, huh?"

Mitch ignored Jasper. "Jack, I mean it. Where is Mabey?"

"We don't know, Mitch, and let go of my arm. We're on the same side. Remember?"

"Are we, Jack? I've seen a lot of weird shit surrounding you the last couple of days. Ever since that fucking arrow dissolved in your shoulder, you haven't been the same person. Am I right, Jasper?"

Jasper kicked the ground. Mitch knew the old guy was searching for words.

"Let's get going, you two nannies. You can verbally cage-fight in the Jeep. We need to get back to Outlaw. We're running out of daylight."

Jack jumped off the craft and headed up the trail. As he walked away he heard Mitch try and yell, with a hint of desperation in a tired voice."Don't you dare walk away from me. How do you know Mabey is missing, Jack?"

Jack stopped and pivoted to face both Jasper and Mitch.

"I found her car in the middle of town with the door open and the keys in the ignition. That's all I know. Now get him dressed, Jasper, and you two meet me at the Jeep. And, hurry, damn it! We'll be lucky to get out of here as it is."

Jasper reached out and took Mitch's hand, helping him off the craft. Mitch watched as Jack moved up the deer trail toward the rim of Crater Lake.

"Come on, Wilde. We need to get you dressed and gone from here. We can talk more on the ride."

As Mitch stepped off the craft, it lifted with a low hum, then spun and started moving away from the lakeshore under its own power. It was as if someone was pulling it.

"Do you see that, Jasper?"

"Yes, Mitch, a whole lot of strange shit is going on right now. This Alien boat can be added to the list."

Mitch tried to smile. He remembered he was naked when he felt a mosquito bite his ass. He swatted at the damn thing.

Jasper guided Mitch toward the rocks and his backpack. He picked it up and handed it to Mitch.

"Sorry, Mitch, I couldn't find your underwear. You'll have to free-ball it. I think most everything else is here, even your shoes. Now hurry and get dressed. You can tell me about it later if you remember. Shit, Wilde, were you sun bathing or taking photos? Your clothes were scattered all over the place. Amazing I found everything but your shorts."

Mitch stood and reached for his pack. He searched his clouded memory. The last image it returned: packing up his camera gear in an effort to get to Jasper as fast as possible to show him the photos of Wizard Island and a ship flying into it.

Mitch struggled to button his Levis. He slid on his shirt, then plopped on the ground to pull on his socks and shoes. His feet were swollen and tender. Mitch stood as best he could, sensing Jasper's impatience.

"Jasper, should we trust him? We both know something has been going on with him."

Jasper patted Mitch on the shoulder, and Mitch soaked up the reassuring gesture.

"Mitch?"

"Yeah, old man?"

"I'm going to be honest with you; you know I'm like that. So, no, right now I don't trust Jack. We don't have much choice, though, Mitch. If it weren't for his showing up and taking that strange Alien boat out to you, tonight would have been your last night on earth. That damn Old Man of the Lake had hold of you and wasn't going to let go. So let's get up to your Jeep, get back into town, and find that wife of yours. For now, we have to trust him."

"Jasper?"

"Geezus, Wilde. Hurry up, will you?"

Jasper stopped and turned. Mitch saw the concern in his face as the old man's eyes pleaded for him to hurry.

Mitch made a weak attempt at running in place. His feet were mushy, and his legs felt like rubber. His entire body itched and felt like dagger tips pricking him from his chest down. He adjusted his backpack, and as he reached Jasper, he grabbed his shoulder to catch his breath and steady himself.

"Jasper, I'm glad you're here. I don't know how I'd be handling this if you weren't with me."

"Good, Wilde. Now, man up, and let's go hunt some clowns."

Mitch smiled at Jasper's reference to clowns. It seemed like so long ago when Jasper told Mitch the story of how his first, and only, wife left him for a rodeo clown.

Jasper grabbed Mitch and started pulling him up the trail.

"I can tell you're laughing a little inside, Wilde, and don't worry, I'm not going to get pissed at you. I feel better now knowing your brain is functioning. Good to see you have some memory working."

Mitch slipped on a rock, and his ankle turned over. He thought it probably should have hurt, but he was still cold, his feet and ankles numb.

The daylight continued to fade, and he wanted – hell, needed – the warmth of the sun. Mitch felt his shoes flex against the gravel on the trail as he worked at keeping up with Jasper. He couldn't remember the last time he'd turned on the heater in his Jeep.

Chapter 2

Mitch, Where Are You?

"Mitch, stop it. You know I hate that. Get up here right now, or I'm turning around and heading back home."

"Oh, all right, beautiful. I wanted to see the flower down here. It's amazing to me how something can want to live so badly. Imagine you're a plant, and the only way you can survive is to grow out of a crack in a rock. It's the ultimate show of strength, courage, and determination. I had to get a photo of it."

"One slip and you're toast, Ansel. I don't care how much of a mountain goat you think you are. If you fall down in the ravine, you're dead. You know there's no way I can lift you out of there."

"Okay, babe, last shot off the trail."

"Why don't I believe you, Mitch?"

"Because I didn't promise you?" Mitch smiled as he slipped and slid backwards. He quickly looked up, and fortunately, Mabey was looking the other way. He'd never hear the end of it if he did fall and hurt himself.

"Come on, you big lug. I want to get to the lake and set up the tent. It'd be nice to get in the water for awhile this afternoon and rinse off some of this trail dust."

"Yes, it would, babe. In fact, you're looking so dusty and wind-blown, I think you'll need to strip off all those dirty clothes to make certain you get *completely clean. I, of course, am more than happy to help, you know, get those hard-to-reach areas."*

"Is that all you can think about, Mitch? God, you exhaust me sometimes. Backpacking is tiring enough. Now I have to worry about performing for you."

"Hey, who said anything about your having to perform? I'll do most of the work, I promise. You can just enjoy our time together."

Mabey laughed and started walking as Mitch grabbed at some roots for the final hoist up onto the trail.

"Wait up, babe," Mabey heard Mitch call out as she turned a corner leaving him out of sight. She knew her photo-seeking husband would catch up to her in less than a minute especially if she made an effort to get out of his sight.

Mabey stirred from her dream, now aware she was sitting as her mind began to focus. Her head bounced back and forth slowly hitting something hard and flat. Her mouth felt as if she hadn't had anything to drink in days. She pictured the Oregon high desert her and Mitch had driven through a number of times. Why couldn't she see? She realized her hands hurt as she reached for her eyes. Her fingernails felt stretched, torn, and painful. One frail and uncharacteristically timid hand reached for the other, cautious of what it might discover.

"What the hell?" Mabey thought she screamed, but her voice was barely audible.

She tried harder to open her eyes, and they both popped; the lids broke free from the crusty dust and dirt that had caked them shut. Peering down at her hands, she gasped at seeing all of her fingernails gone. She started exploring her face. Other than crusty eyes, it felt normal. She rubbed her forehead and felt for her hair. She felt for her hair again. Her hands hurt so bad. The tips of her fingers were badly bruised and torn. Her hands registered skin, and a lot of it. She placed both hands on her head and found only scalp, no hair!. She wasn't sure what to make of the fact she no longer had the auburn hair Mitch always complimented. She wasn't sure if she should cry from the loss of her beautiful hair and the pain or be grateful she was alive. No time to dwell on that right now as new pain registered in her brain: pain coming from her feet. They hurt like hell. In fact, her whole body ached.

Mabey felt deep nausea in her stomach as she became more aware of her surroundings. Sitting next to her, in rows in front of her, and in rows behind her, were dozens of people. Most of them appeared to be unconscious. A few like her were coming around. The person next to her, she thought it was a man, but it could be a woman, was out cold. She witnessed most heads slumping forward, bouncing up and down as the bus creaked over the bumps in the road. It felt like a dirt road to Mabey, similar to the sensations she'd felt so many times in Mitch's Jeep in the mountains outside Outlaw River, Oregon.

Everyone on the bus was dressed in drab gray or beige pants and shirts; Mabey
couldn't tell which in the dim light. She reached for her head again, looking forward and back. She didn't see a single strand of hair on anyone.

"Mitch, where are you?" She said to herself as a tap on her shoulder startled her and caught her attention. She turned with trepidation, expecting something horrible. Her mouth dropped open as she peered into a badly bruised, but recognizable, face. There was no hair on this head either. Cuts laced across his forehead and scalp, perhaps evidence of resistance to the head shaving.

Mabey's head bounced off the window again as the bus hit a hole in the road. She gathered herself, refocused on the seat behind her, and with effort willed her mouth to speak, "Mayor Jenkins?"

Chapter 3

Why Not?

The hike was brutal for Mitch as the sun was fading, and his body needed the warmth right now to help blood flow. In Mitch's mind, he arrived not long ago on the rocky outcrop and was admiring photos he had taken of the sunrise. He was pleased with the new images, happy he had something never before photographed at Crater Lake, which was a minor miracle in and of itself since the place had been photographed so many times over the years.

Jasper reached down, and Mitch grabbed his hand for the last climb over a rock on the deer trail.

Mitch was even more impressed with Old Man Jasper after the climb from the lakeshore to the rim of the crater. With his previously crushed pelvis and all, the old guy and his walking stick motored right up the steep trail. Amazing, considering doctors told him after the logging accident that he would never walk again.

"I'm impressed, Wilde. You'd been bobbing in that water for I don't know how long, and you made it up this nasty trail. Your boys drop yet?"

"Jasper, I was just thinking the same thing about you with your crushed pelvis and all. You moved up the damn trail like an athlete, leaving me in the dust. And yes, my friend, I believe they did. Thanks for your concern."

"Well, pansy-ass QB, it's like I told you: no way was I going to let a falling tree ruin my life. I'm probably requesting too much information but glad your privates are returning to a more familiar feeling. It won't take you long to start feeling whole again."

"Man, have I missed you, Jasper. It seems I haven't seen you for weeks."

"Come on, you two. Let's get the hell out of here. I don't like what I'm feeling right now. I'm probably overly paranoid, but it seems we're being watched." Jack controlled the level of his shout from Mitch's Jeep, affectionately named Black Steel.

Jasper and Mitch moved quickly toward the Jeep. Jack sat in the driver's seat with the window rolled down and engine running.

"I'm driving, Jack."

"No, you're not, Mitch. Can you even feel your feet yet? Don't worry, brother; I'm sure your precious Black Steel won't mind."

Jasper understood Mitch's feelings, but he thought it necessary to chime in.

"Mitch, I agree. Jack should drive. You take shotgun, and I'll sit in the back."

Jasper impatiently jumped in the conversation.

"Damn, would you two quit carrying on like a couple of ninnies."

Mitch knew they were both right, but hell if he wanted to hear it right now. He wanted to get back to Outlaw River as fast as possible, and neither Jack nor Jasper knew his Jeep or the roads back home as well as he did. He reluctantly hopped into the passenger side and closed the door behind him. Jack accelerated up the fire road toward Rim Drive on the way to the highway.

Mitch was certain of nothing now. For some inexplicable reason he had a sinking feeling the road might be blocked. With no real options of circumventing any blockades, he was sweating what might lie ahead.

Jack pushed down the gas pedal hard to get up the short but steep exit from the trail. Black Steel chirped and lurched forward,

14

landing hard on the pavement, screeching the tires. The trio would know in less than five minutes if they were going to make it off the lake's Rim Drive.

Mitch reached over and turned on the heater full blast. He moved his feet forward where he knew the hot air would blast. His feet stung like hell, as did his legs. He could tell, though, adrenaline was returning his body to a more normal state. The challenging hike up the rim was brutal, because of his recent condition, but good in that it got his heart pumping the warm blood through his body. He hoped he would be close to 100 percent by the time they got back to Outlaw River.

"Sorry if it gets too hot, boys, but I think my feet are still numb. You might want to roll down a window or two."

Jack's was already down. Jasper rolled down both windows in the back seat. He got back into the center section of the seat, slapped his seat belt on and directed the first of several questions at Mitch."

"So tell me, Mitch. Do you remember what happened?"

"Why am I so fucking cold, how long until I'll feel warm again?" Mitch directed the question towards neither Jack nor Jasper in particular. He didn't expect either to respond.

"You should feel much better by the time we get back to Outlaw, Mitch." Jasper handed him a bottle of water and four Tylenol.

Mitch turned and looked at Jasper who was tapping him on te shoulder.

"Take these, Mitch, and try to drink as much water as you can. We need to make sure you're hydrated."

Jack braked hard and brought the Jeep to a sudden stop, the newly received pills flew out of Mitch's hand.

"Dammit!" Mitch blurted out. "What the hell, Jack?"

Jack wasted no time responding.

"Quiet. Turn and look straight ahead, Mitch."

Not again! Mitch immediately thought. He remembered the last time someone suddenly slammed on car brakes and said look straight ahead. At least he had on his seat belt this time. Mitch grimaced thinking about his missing Mabey. As much as he hated the word hope, he hoped she was okay.

Jack responded in a firm voice.

"Holy shit, you two. Man, what a magnificent sight! Don't anybody get out."

Mitch spoke aloud while the other two stared.

"Are you kidding me! It's that son of a bitch Shadowfax again."

Jasper piped up, "Don't even try taking a photo, Wilde."

Mitch started laughing before succumbing to a cough. He controlled the coughing and looked at Jasper.

"Why not, old man?"

Chapter 4

Coffee, Tea, or Espresso?

"Mom, what are we going to do?"

"The most important thing we can do right now, Cindi, is to stay calm. Not try to stay calm but actually stay calm." In a methodical and controlled voice, Debbi looked directly at Cindi and said, "Do you understand me?"

"Yes, Mom, I hear you. I get it. Do you think they're going to hurt J.J.?"

"No, I don't, Cindi. Haven't you noticed? They haven't hurt anyone yet, really."

"Well, a few people are hurt, Mom."

"Yes, Cindi, but from falling down and pushing each other when they didn't have to."

"You're right. I didn't even think about that. What do you think they want?"

"I think they want to impregnate all of us with their Alien seed and start another race."

"Penelope, shut the hell up! You aren't helping matters at all." Debbi looked at her flower club friend and frequent Coffee Shack patron and gave her a stare. Penelope bit her lower lip, looked as if she were going to cry, and slouched lower in the booth at the Coffee Shack.

Cindi whispered to her mother. "Mom, if that's true, do you seriously think they would want to impregnate Ms. Penelope?"

"Cindi!" Debbi said with a smile on her face. God, she hoped no one else had heard.

"I don't think they want us at all." Another woman spoke whom Debbi recognized as a regular coffee-drinking patron but didn't know her by name.

"I think they're protecting us.

"Then why lock us in here?" Penelope again.

"I'm sorry. I recognize you for coming in here for Earl Grey tea with soy milk, but I don't remember your name." Debbi stuck out her hand to greet the woman.

"Hi. My name is Delores. I've lived here only a short while. I come in several times a week in the mornings on my way to work. And, yes, tea and soy milk." Delores smiled, appreciating the fact that Debbi did in fact remember her.

"It's nice to meet you, Delores, and thanks for your business."

Debbi watched with curiosity as Delores turned with the grace and ease of a ballerina, stared out the front windows, and lamented:

"Look outside. The Aliens may want us but the Native Americans appear they are here to help. They're talking with the men, not at them."

"You're right, Delores. No one is restrained." Debbi felt her blood pressure calm a little bit with Delores' well-reasoned logic.

"See how they keep pointing in here at us, Debbi? I think they're trying to figure out what to do with us."

"You don't know what you're talking about. That's just a guess." Penelope was still upset, and she was trying to take advantage of Delores' being a newcomer to put her in her place.

"You're right, ma'am. I am just guessing."

Debbi approached Penelope and made a quick mental calculation on how to properly diffuse a potentially tense situation. She didn't want a coffee shop full of women feeding off Penelope's attitude.

"Penelope. I'm sorry, but saying things like 'impregnating us' is not going to help anyone. Can I get you some coffee or something?" Debbi had only so much patience with Penelope to begin with, and it was, with speed, wearing thin. Panic was one thing nobody needed right now. She felt a bit bad for snapping at Penelope but bickering wasn't going to help either.

Debbi turned and took her daughter's hand.

"Come on, Sweetie. Help me out, will you?"

Debbi led Cindi around the counter, put on an apron, and handed one to Cindi.

"Is anyone hungry or thirsty? We may be here awhile. Sandwiches and drinks are on the house."

"How generous, Debbi. Do you two need some help? I've run an espresso machine or two over the years."

"That would be great, Delores, and thanks. There're some more aprons in back. Cindi will show you where they are."

There were about thirty women in the Shack, Debbi counted. There was also a recognizable uniformed man, Sheriff Gunther, slumped over a table next to the front door. As most of the women left their booths and headed to the coffee bar, Gunther appeared to be waking. Knowing him all too well, Debbi didn't feel like dealing with him right now – if at all. Cindi returned with Delores decked out in a Coffee Shack apron and her thick dark hair pulled back in a ponytail.

Debbi smiled at the two, caught Delores' eyes, and mouthed the words,

"Thank you."

She turned back around and clapped her hands together, leaving them clenched after her final clap. She faced the long line of women who clearly needed some distraction.

"Okay, what can we get for you: coffee, tea, or espresso?"

Chapter 5

An Obnoxious Cling

"What the hell!" Gunther shouted.

Everyone in the Coffee Shack froze. The remaining noise in Outlaw River's only coffee shop came from the whistling of the espresso machine.

Debbi broke the silence, then everyone turned their attention back to the free coffee, tea, and espresso drinks being served.

"Sheriff Gunther, can I get you something?"

Gunther recognized the voice, but he wasn't sure he could respond.

He wiped a little drool from the side of his face. Looking around, he realized where he was. His forehead felt pressed in like a tire holding a car off the pavement. His mouth was dry, and he was thirsty. He felt out of sorts, as if he weren't himself. This feeling seemed to be subsiding, though, as his awareness increased. His head started to throb, and the noise from everyone – it appeared from a quick glance they were all women – pierced like an ice pick through his temple.

Someone sidled up to the table where the Shack's only male visitor slouched.

"Sheriff Gunther, my mom asked if you would like anything? Are you feeling okay?"

"Um, yes. Could I have some water, please, a lot of water? I'm pretty thirsty, and thanks."

"Sure, Sir. I'll be right back."

Cindi worked her way back through the women to her mom.

"He said he wanted some water was all. Something is wrong, though, Mom."

Debbi grabbed another couple of coffees and set them down on the counter for the ladies.

"Why is that, dear?"

"Because he said please and thank you in the same conversation. If I didn't know any better, I would think he's an impostor."

Debbi laughed. "According to J.J., his head slammed into his cruiser's airbag pretty hard. I imagine he has a slight concussion. We'll have to keep an eye on him. Take him a couple of bottled waters, will you, Cindi?"

"Sure. I'll be right back to help with the sandwiches and pastries."

Cindi grabbed a couple of waters from the chiller and walked them over to the sheriff.

"Here you are, Sheriff Gunther. Anything else? Are you hungry?"

"Thanks." Gunther opened the first water and guzzled it down. He then opened the second and finished it off in no time at all. Cindi just stood there and stared; he drank so fast. Cindi felt as if she were at the local fair watching a pie-eating contest.

"I don't suppose I could get another one, young lady?"

"It's Cindi, and yes, Sheriff Gunther, I'll be right back with a couple more."

Cindi headed back behind the counter and worked her way between Delores and her mother as they continued to serve the women. She grabbed more water and returned to her thirsty patron out front. He continued drinking, but more slowly. Cindi figured his stomach must be filling up.

"Thank you, Cindi. I feel a little better. I should see what's going on outside. I'm not sure how much the water is, but here." Gunther dug his wallet out of his back pocket. He had several twenty-dollar bills and some smaller bills. He grabbed a twenty and set it on the table.

"Um, don't worry about it, Sheriff. My mom says it's on the house."

"Nonsense, young lady, I pay what I owe. A twenty should cover it, I think. Keep the change, and thank you very much."

Startled by the normally gruff sheriff, Cindi quickly recovered from her disbelief and replied, "Um, okay."

The shop owner's daughter and weekend barista stood there with her mouth open as the Sheriff exited the Shack to the familiar sound of cling, cling, cling.

Cindi grabbed the twenty off the table and laughed. As she went back to the counter, the door opened again to the familiar clinging Cindi thought one day might drive her insane, or at least out of Outlaw River. Sheriff Gunther popped his head in and commented.

"By the way, tell your mom thanks for the water. I appreciate it."

The door closed to the hated and obnoxious sound. Cindi chuckled in disbelief, hoping the trauma to Gunther's head lasted. She liked this Sheriff much better. Cindi went back to the counter to help her mother. As she walked, she decided before the summer was over, that she was going to destroy the maddening bell.

Chapter 6

Chosen

Gunther exited the Coffee Shack and walked down the street toward the large crowd. He worked his way through the gathering of people to the front of the group.

"Excuse me, I hate to interrupt, but could someone fill me in on what's going on here?"

"Sheriff Gunther, good to see you up and about. We were just getting ready to move this little get-together into the theater. Come over there with me. There are more than a few people I think you should talk with."

"So from hardware store owner to town speaker: moving up in the world, Parsons?"

Gunther was referring to Ralph Parsons, co-owner of Parsons Hardware on Main Street.

"Not really, Sheriff. You were temporarily incapacitated; the Mayor and Deputy Mayor are nowhere to be found, and since I am on the town council, it just made sense."

"He has a loud voice and more hot air than the rest of us."

Sheriff Gunther heard someone yell from the back of the rather sizable crowd. There were probably a hundred men in the street group, the sheriff estimated, a large gathering by Outlaw River standards.

There was a round of light laughter from the last comment. Perhaps a cheer thrown in as well, Gunther wasn't sure.

"Okay, very funny. Was that you, Dave?" Parsons was referring to Dave Marble, also on the town council and owner of one of the local gas stations in town.

"Okay, everyone, let's walk over to the theater. They're waiting for us. Sheriff, would you mind walking with me. I need to get you up to speed."

"Absolutely, Ralph. What in the world is going on? You said the Mayor is missing?"

"Yes, along with a bunch of other Outlaw River citizens. One of your deputies is missing, Pat Finnegan isn't around, I can't contact Major Piele, Janene is missing, and Mabey Wilde. I'm sure there are others missing as well. We're trying to get some kind of a count, but it's nearly impossible.

"Geez, Ralph, your sister – and Mabey Wilde? What about Mitch? Is he around?"

"Well, according to Debbi Howard, he was on a photo shoot at Crater Lake when everything happened, so Jack Jenson went there to try to find him and get him back here. There's more we don't know than what we do know. Does that even make sense? Anyway, first things first. Do you remember seeing an Indian on horseback and getting shot at with an arrow?"

"That really happened? Shit, I was hoping it was a dream."

"No, it wasn't a dream. Come on; pick it up, folks. Let's get over there. They're waiting, and we don't know how much time we have. Doesn't your shoulder feel sore?"

"Is that why there's a hole in my shirt?" Gunther reached up, and with his right hand felt the hole in his left shoulder sleeve.

"Who's waiting, Ralph?"

"The Indians, including the one who shot at you."

"I believe it's preferable these days to say Native Americans, Ralph."

Gunther's voice tailed off after the last statement as his brain registered he was being nice. Something didn't quite compute. His headache lingered, and he was beginning to wonder just how hard the hit to his head was.

"We're going to go over there and chat with them, Ralph. That's all."

Gunther reflected on being shot at by the horseback warrior and reflexively reached down to touch his gun. He realized he was scared as his fingers touched nothing but a holster. The gun must be in his car; at least he hoped like hell it was in the cruiser.

"I'm not so sure I should be going in there, Ralph. What in the world is going on?"

"Well, Sheriff, I am not going to sugarcoat this for you. Apparently, we're under some sort of an Alien attack. The Ind..., I mean Native Americans, are working at negotiating a peaceful transfer of power with the Aliens. At least, that's what they're telling us. They seem genuine and want to help. They aren't holding any of us against our will or telling us what to do at this point, just making recommendations."

Sheriff Gunther looked around as if someone might overhear before replying.

"Ralph, how do you explain their coming after me while I was in my police car and taking a shot at me with an arrow?"

"From what I can gather, Sheriff, they thought you were a potential threat. The arrow they shot at you couldn't do any serious damage apparently. The tip, filled with some sort of Alien technology, is harmless. If the person shot has Native American blood, the arrow can allow the person a special power of sorts. Not sure what exactly. Jack Jenson knows more about it, and you can ask him when you see him. Or if you feel like it, you can ask one of the Indians in the theatre."

"And what about those who don't have Native American blood pumping under their skin?"

"From what I remember, they said the wound would hurt like hell, and then the person would feel healthier, different somehow, with a quick recovery and a boost of energy like a drug. Luckily, the arrow didn't actually hit you, though."

Sheriff Gunther contemplated the thought of being hit, wishing it had happened. He frankly couldn't stand himself, and the thought of his having a chance to be healthier and different was appealing. He reached down and found his holster empty again. He wondered where his gun was. He wanted to get back to the cruiser.

"One of the things I do know, Sheriff: some of the people that are missing, probably most of them, have been abducted by Aliens or whatever the hell they are. They are alien to us, right?"

"Geezus, Ralph. Seriously, how long was I out for all this to have happened?"

"Well, it's been going on awhile. You were out only about an hour or so. We put you in the coffee shop to keep you out of the way and near people in case you needed anything. We probably should have taken you to the hospital, but Doc said all your vitals were good and you should be fine. He said you would have a bad headache for awhile.

Ralph held the door to the theater open, and the last citizen, save him and the Sheriff, entered. A handful of others took off running away from the theater and down Main street.

"Come on, Sheriff. Let's get inside and see what they have to say. They should get you up to speed and help us with a plan of attack or a plan of defense."

"I'll join you in a minute, Ralph. I'm going over to my car to see if my gun is there. I can see that no one has moved the cruiser from against the building."

"We've certainly had a bit on our minds. Moving your car didn't seem to be a real priority at the moment."

"No, that's fine and makes sense. Where the heck are the other deputies, though? Do you know?"

"They're either missing or on patrol trying to keep people from looting and causing a ruckus."

Ralph looked up and down the deserted street and closed the door behind him, leaving Sheriff Gunther standing on the steps of the theater, alone.

Chapter 7

Just Curious

Jack brought Black Steel to a complete stop on the road. He angled the vehicle in a way so the driver's door was nearly perpendicular to the Native American on horseback. The horse stood rock steady under his rider as the Jeep came to a stop. The horse and rider blocked the Jeep from passage. Jack knew he could take Black Steel off road and go around, but he didn't feel the need at the moment.

"You two stay here, and don't do anything stupid. I can handle this."

Jack jumped out and headed straight towards the mounted rider, giving neither Jasper nor Mitch a chance to discuss the situation..

Mitch noticed there wasn't much daylight left, and it worried him. Part of him felt as if the absence of daylight would mean the absence of Mabey forever.

Mitch looked back at Jasper.

"Is there something I should know about, old man?"

"Remember when your buddy got shot by that arrow?"

"Yeah, why?"

"Well, Jack speculates that the arrow was meant for you, but it hit him instead. Jack will have to explain more, but apparently it allows a person to communicate with the Indians."

"Meant for me? Communicate with the Indians? What in the name of Odin are you talking about?"

"Well, when fancy lad gets back, he'll have to explain. That's about all I know. I haven't had much of a chance to talk with him. Take these, Mitch, and hang onto them this time. You'd think for a quarterback; you'd have better hands."

Mitch smiled in recognition of Jasper's smart-ass comment, reached out and took more Tylenol. He tossed them in his mouth, took a healthy swig of water, and swallowed the pills. He fumbled with the water bottle lid, having to concentrate more than usual to put it back on. He was frustrated because he didn't want his nerves getting the best of him. He stared out the windshield watching Jack approach the rider.

"How did Jack get up here anyway?"

"Hell, Wilde, I don't know. Now that you mention it, I never asked him. He appeared while I was searching for you and trying to figure out things when he showed up with Park Ranger Rick. Add that question to the long list we have for him."

"Look at him out there carrying on with Geronimo, Jasper. He looks as if he's in his element. Damn, he's still as quick as he was in college, even on a bum knee."

Mitch was referring to the sudden burst of Jack's speed as he sprinted back to the Jeep, away from the horse and rider.

Jack jumped in the Jeep and slammed the door.

"Let's go. I'm told there won't be any more road obstacles on the way back to town. We need to get to Outlaw as fast as possible. Apparently, there are Alien plans to empty the town of as many people fitting their criteria as possible, along with folks from a number of other small towns in the area."

Mitch grabbed his head, briefly noticing what felt like a small crust of dried blood on his forehead, as the pain surged once again. He wasn't sure if the current pain was more from the fall and subsequent stint in the lake or from serious worry over Mabey.

"Jack, what in the hell is going on?"

Mitch paused as Jack looked out the driver's side window. He either saw something or was avoiding answering. Mitch figured it was the latter.

"Jasper, I know you have some answers as well. None of what has happened the last couple of days seems to surprise you at all."

The trio looked forward as Jack got the Jeep into gear and accelerated on Rim Drive.

Mitch looked in the side-view mirror. The Native American on horseback was gone.

"How in the hell do they just disappear like that? This is the exact same thing Mabey and I saw the other night on the road, the disappearing, that is." Mitch winced and took a deep breath.

Jasper jumped in, eager to provide some insight. "Well, Mitch, my guess is that they are kind of place-jumping. Like on *Star Trek*. Beam-me-up-Scotty-type shit. Or something like that."

"You're pretty close to dead on, Jasper. I don't understand the science behind it myself. But if they concentrate properly and enter into a certain state of consciousness, they can move between places through their spirit world. They claim we all can do it, but our minds are so filled with clutter and negative energy, it's all but impossible. Now I have that ability, for a time, since I was shot with that arrow. It's how I got up here. It has something to do with the liquid in the tip of that damn arrow that pierced my shoulder. It helps clear the mind."

"Okay, Dr. Von Däniken. So I'm to believe you can think hard enough about somewhere you want to be, and poof, you'll go there?"

"In a sense, yes. The catch is I must have a need to go there, and I have to be totally focused and sincere. I can't just go jumping around from place to place all willy-nilly."

"Now there's a phrase you don't get to hear enough these days," Jasper chuckled in the back seat.

Jack brought Black Steel around the final corner before getting on the main highway leading back to Outlaw River.

"Um, Jack, if you can spirit jump, why not pull over, and you leap back to Outlaw River. Then Jasper and I can meet you there within an hour or so?"

"I actually thought about that, Mitch. In fact, the Native American I just spoke with wanted me to port back and let you two drive back alone. However, if anything should happen, I'd need to be here to help. I wish you'd been shot with the damn arrow and not me, Wilde, as was supposed to happen."

"Me too, Jack. Perhaps then I'd be with Mabey now, and she wouldn't be missing. Has anyone tried calling her?"

"Yes, Mitch, I did. Jasper asked me the same thing. There's no answer, and the phone goes straight to voice mail."

"Does anyone have any idea where she might be?" Mitch directed his stare at Jack.

"Not yet, Mitch, but we'll figure it out. I'll start asking a lot of questions once we get back to Outlaw."

Jasper cleared his throat in the back seat as Mitch reached over and turned off the heater.

"You got something to say, old man?"

"I think I know where Mabey might be, Mitch. Yes, I have something to say. You ever know me not to speak when I want to?"

"Well then, speak, damn it."

"I think the staging ground, one of them anyway, might be right here near Crater Lake. It has something to do with the spacecrafts' hitting lakes and slamming into mountains. We just have to figure out which one Mabey would be taken to."

"Jack, what about Junior? Where is he?"

"He's back in town, probably at the Coffee Shack or theater. Knowing my son, he's trying to stay as near as he can to that new girlfriend of his. He can fill us in when we get back there."

"Thank goodness. I'm sorry I didn't ask sooner, Jack. You know how important Junior is to Mabey and me."

31

"Shit, Mitch. It isn't like you haven't had a lot on your mind. No worries, thanks for asking, and yes, I know how much he means to the two of you."

"Okay, you sweethearts. I would think that the two of you were married the way you carry on. Can we focus here?"

Silence filled the cab of the heat-blasted Jeep as Mitch and Jack both thought about reaching in the back seat and whaling on Jasper.

A couple more miles passed as all three thought about events and what to talk about next. Mitch spoke first.

"So as long as there is a sincere need to get someplace, you have the ability to move around in this spirit world, Jack?"

"Yes, for the most part, I guess. Again I've used it only a couple of times now, but so far, so good. I'm told that if there isn't a need, then it won't work."

"Well, shit, what constitutes a need?"

"Hell, Mitch, I don't know. Something to do with the mind and clarity, being close to and one with nature. Some shit like that anyway."

"And it was because you got shot with that arrow?"

"Evidently the arrow is tipped with some type of Alien technology that was shared with the Indians thousands of years ago. If the shit penetrates a human's bloodstream, it will last a couple of days or weeks apparently. And it won't work on everyone, they say. It has something to do with a person's character and state of mind. They also said that if a person has Native American blood, it's all but guaranteed to work because of their being closer to Mother Earth. That damn arrow at the BBQ was obviously meant for you, Mitch. Wasn't your grandmother half Indian?"

"Yes, she was. No side effects or health concerns?"

"Not yet. Painful as hell at first. I could feel it coursing its way through my veins. Once it was done, I haven't felt much different, other than feeling energetic with really clear thoughts. I haven't been sleeping much, but it doesn't seem to affect me. A bit of a rush doing the spirit travel, and I get light-headed, but it isn't bad. I know I drink more water than I ever did before, but that is a good thing. Why, Mitch?"

"No reason really, just curious."

Jasper had a good idea of exactly what Mitch was thinking. Mitch looked back at Jasper with acknowledgement. No words had to be spoken.

Mitch remembered his dog, General, had found such an arrow at the river. He thought about Mabey and his need to find her. Then he turned his thoughts back to the arrow still locked up in his safe. He had plans for it now.

"Step on it, Jack, will you? I need to get home."

Chapter 8

More Freud, Huh?

"Mayor, do you have any idea what's going on and where we are?"

Whispering, with slow and attentive effort, Mayor Jenkins replied.

"Uhhh, Mabey, ummmm, please call me Larry. I, ummmmmmmm, don't have any idea. And I don't know what the hell is going on. I..." another long pause as he gasped to fill his lungs, "I know my fingers hurt like hell, and I haven't felt this bald," rubbing his head with his nail-less right hand, "since I came out of my mother's womb five decades ago."

"My hands and feet feel as if they've been put through a meat-grinder. I can feel each one of my fingers and toes with every beat of my heart."

A few more people started waking up. Both the Mayor and Mabey started to say hi to several of them. Most of the faces were recognizable to the Mayor; he just didn't know the names. Mabey recognized only a handful.

"Mabey, what's the last thing you remember?"

"Mayor Jenk..., I mean Larry, I'm not sure. I think I was driving to the Coffee Shack before going to Medford for a physical therapy session."

Mabey paused and gathered her thoughts. "Yes, I was driving, and just outside of town, my car died. I rolled to the side of the highway and was getting ready to call AAA. When I looked down at my Blackberry, it had no signal which is strange because I always have a signal in town. Anyway, I remember getting out of the car."

Mabey paused, desperately trying to remember.

Mayor Jenkins impatiently jumped in.

"Then what?"

"That's it. I remember getting out of my car and then nothing."

"Well, kind of similar for me. I was going to the Sheriff's office when my car stopped. I remember thinking that I couldn't believe a brand new Mercedes could possibly be having any issues. That's it for me. I don't even remember what street I was on."

Mabey turned facing forward now and looked out the window. She couldn't decide if she was more scared, or pissed, as she faded into fond memories with Mitch.

"Mitch, why in the world would you act like that around those people; they were just asking questions."

"You can never be too sure, Mabey. One of the few things my father taught me that I actually think makes sense is that it's better to be pissed than to be scared. He said, and I think his father taught him this: if you ever get in a situation where you aren't sure of an outcome, stay focused by staying angry. He always felt that when people are angry, they're on their toes ready to act or react. If they're scared, though, they're less likely to be able to respond properly, if at all. He felt it had something to do with being timid and then trapped in your own indecision because of fear."

Well, okay, Freud, but backpacking on a trail where you are asked for directions?"

"Perfect place when you think about it. You and I are alone out here relaxing and hiking. All of a sudden, and it was sudden, two guys show up from a side trail and start hammering questions at us. We don't know anything about them. I got a bad vibe off them. I'm with a beautiful woman, no one else around

35

for miles, and they could probably overpower me with my loaded backpack on. They had very light daypacks by the way, if you remember. Anyway, if we start talking with them and I am soft, unsure, and act timid in any way, they get confident and think we are easy pickings."

"Seriously, Mitch?"

"Hear me out, babe. So suddenly they come out of nowhere , and I immediately take a defensive position in front of you and act as if I have a chip on my shoulder, and you had better not fuck with me, so help your god. Which do you think is better for us in the end? Safety or the fact that we won't make two new friends and will never exchange holiday greetings. We would never have done that anyway."

"Well, I do see your point, I suppose. However, it just seems that we could all be a little nicer. The world would be a better place."

"I agree we could all be nicer. Nevertheless, I am not willing to take that risk when I'm out enjoying some backpacking with my gorgeous wife. Do you feel safe and secure, by the way?"

Mabey chuckled, "Yes, I guess I do, now that you mention it."

"Well, good. I don't relish the fact that I have to be an ass sometimes, but I would never forgive myself if something happened to you that I could have prevented by being one."

"You know, Mitch, some people get ratcheted up by others' being aggressive."

"You're right, but I was in no way being aggressive. I was being defensively confident. They surprised us, remember? By the way, people who usually are ratcheted up by someone's being aggressive are usually already cranked up and are looking for an excuse to do something. I think that they're much more likely to go after someone who appears weak rather than confident."

"More Freud, huh? I didn't realize you were such a deep thinker, Mr. Wilde. I hope like hell, Mitch, I never piss you off."

"I love you, Mabey. Now let's get down to that lake and get you cleaned up. You look like you could use a good cleaning."

"Mitch, you are exhausting me."

"Not yet I'm not, but I hope to be soon."

"Geezus, Mitch!" Mabey started laughing.

Another bump in the road and the side of Mabey's head slammed the window of the bus, snapping her back into the here and now. She rubbed her head and looked out the window. The terrain looked odd, but familiar. She didn't know why, but she could swear that somewhere in the recesses of her mind, she'd been on this road before.

"Mabey, can you tell who's driving the bus?"

Mabey felt a hand gently squeezing her shoulder.

"Mabey, can you tell who's driving the bus?"

"Oh, I'm sorry, Larry. I was thinking. Um, no, I can't say that I can. Whoever it is, though, has on the same outfit and a shaved head like the rest of us. Almost looks as if the person isn't driving, though, just holding onto the wheel."

"Okay, I noticed that too. But I wanted to see what you thought. I also see several more buses in front of us and behind us. I think I'm going to try to get off this damn bus."

"What? Like jump?"

"Yes, exactly."

"How? Out the back door?"

"Well, I was thinking about the back door, but it's too risky with another bus behind us. It would be tough to roll out of the way in time. We could pop out one of these windows and hang out the side. Still a little risky because of the drop and the possibility of rolling an ankle or falling under the bus."

"Why not just walk down the aisle, open the front door, and jump out that way?"

The Mayor, Larry that is, took a couple of deep breaths and tried to get more oxygen to his brain. His shortness of breath was getting better, but he still was having to work too hard at speaking.

"Mayor Larry, what are you doing?"

Mabey saw the Mayor stand up and start walking down the aisle. He got about two rows from the front of the bus, near the driver, and just stood there. People who had come out of their slumber were whispering and pointing at the Mayor. Mabey surmised they probably recognized him. The Mayor spun around after a minute or two and walked back. He gently lifted the person sitting next to Mabey and placed him in the seat behind. He slid in next to Mabey.

"Mabey, I'm going out the front as you suggested. The driver didn't even look at me when I was walking down the aisle. You're right; he's in some sort of trance. His hands are on the wheel, but he isn't driving. I see where the button is for the door. It should be easy enough to press, once we're up there. There's an electronic gadget on the dash, and wires appear to be running down to the accelerator and brake. I'm guessing that whoever put us on this damn bus has them rigged up and are remotely running them. Notice how our speed hardly fluctuates, and the distance between the buses is exact? It never changes."

"No, I hadn't noticed, but I'll take your word for it."

"I have no idea what's going on or where we're being taken, but I don't want to wait passively and find out. What about you?"

Mabey again thought about Mitch, and she wished he were here with her.

"You always have to be prepared, Mabey. Don't take anything for granted, and mentally stay in a place where you're in control. Always be thinking of what to do next. Stay active, never passive. And for fuck sake, if you ever have a chance to run, then take it. I say better to die trying than probably dying anyway by sitting around waiting and hoping."

"So, Mabey, what do you say? We might not have much time left. We can use the darkness to our advantage right now. I'm going, and I think you should go with me."

"What about all these other people, Larry? We can't just leave them."

"Well, Mabey, we can, and we must. If everyone on this bus gets off, then I'm certain there would be a problem. If only a handful of us get off, I think it's less likely that the buses stop. And besides, I am not going to stop anyone. If they want to get off, they can."

Mitch's words echoed in Mabey's head.

"If you ever get the chance to run, Mabey, then take it."

"Okay, Mitch. I'm sorry, I mean Larry, let's go."

The Mayor chuckled, "No offense, Mabey. I wish it were Mitch here with you."

The Mayor noticed more people around them were starting to stir, and their awareness level was increasing. He and Mabey needed to get off this bus now. He also noticed that the driver moved his hand off the wheel and, like a robot, pressed a switch attached to the electronic box he had noticed before. Smoke vapor or something started rising from the floor.

"Let's go and fast. This can't be good. We'd better cover our mouths and noses."

"Right behind you, Larry." Mabey already had a hand over her face.

The Mayor eased down the aisle with Mabey closely following. With caution, they walked toward the front of the bus, steadying themselves on seat backs and an occasional shoulder. They made it to the front, and the driver hadn't even flinched. The vapor was rising higher and higher. People previously stirring were starting to nod off again. The Mayor looked back to make sure Mabey was still with him then reached down and pressed a button, and the door swung open. There was still nothing from the driver. The mayor stepped down and perched himself on the edge, surveying the ground below. He guessed they were doing about twenty-five miles per hour or so. Damn, he should have looked at the speedometer. A corner was coming up. Just then he felt Mabey, he hoped it was her, tap him on the shoulder. He turned, and Mabey was pointing at the driver who was now staring at both of them. He appeared to be reaching for something on the dash.

39

"I think he's going for the door switch, Mabey."

Unlike the Mayor, Mabey didn't hesitate.

As quick as a trap snares a mouse, she saw the small window closing on their chance to run. She pushed the Mayor hard and then launched herself as the door started closing. The Mayor's hesitation almost cost him. He was starting to feel light headed just before he received a big push and tumbled off the bus into the ditch between the road and the woods.

Mabey rolled, landing among some large ferns on fairly soft ground. She lay flat, motionless, as the last bus went by on the dirt road, kicking up a hurricane of dust. Her ankle throbbed. She lay still until the sound of the buses was a distant echo. With great care and concern, she felt her body piece by piece. Her brain signaled only an ankle hurt from the fall. She stood, testing it out. Yes, it was sore, but she could walk without too much pain.

"Mayor, are you here?" No reply. Mabey walked a few more paces. "Larry, can you hear me?" Perhaps he was on the ground hurt. There, Mabey saw him lying face down not too far off the road.

"Oh, great, is he dead?" Mabey whispered to herself.

She went to him, grabbed him by his shoulder and side, and rolled him over. He appeared to be breathing. She grabbed his wrist. Good, he had a pulse. Shit, he must have breathed in some of that gas, whatever the hell it was.

Mabey sat down on a stump to gather her thoughts. She noticed the thick woods surrounding them and was thankful for the cover the ferns and deciduous trees provided. She was cold and hungry. She had no food, no water, no hair, no fingernails or toenails, and no idea what in the world was going on. Her thoughts turned to Mayor Larry. How long was he going to be out, and could he walk when he awakened? Man, what she wouldn't give right now for some "exhausting" talk from Mitch.

Chapter 9

Take it From Me

"So Jack, one more time please. You're telling me that you have the ability to place travel or port travel, whatever the hell you call it?"

"Yes, Jasper. I know it sounds whacked, but yes. I've done it a couple of times already."

"And you're telling Mitch and me it's a result of the arrow you were shot with?"

"Yes, Jasper. Jesus, you don't think I just woke up one morning with the ability, do you?"

"Don't get smart with me, young man."

Mitch, listening but consumed in his own thoughts, sat there contemplating his next move. He knew what he wanted to do, what he'd have to do. He first had to get back to Outlaw and home. He chuckled as Jasper continued hammering on poor old Jack. Mitch felt bad for his best friend; he knew what a sharp tongue the old guy had, and he was unrelenting when he latched onto something.

"I could tell you more than a few things, mister. Things I'm sure you have no idea about, including everything occurring around us right now. You may have been shot with an arrow infused with Alien technology that allows you to place-jump, but need I remind you the arrow was intended for Mitch?"

Poor bastard, Mitch thought.

"Listen, Jasper, I don't care if it was intended for someone else at this point. The fucking thing hit me, and I'm stuck with the responsibility now, not you and not Mitch. And for the record, it isn't time-jumping; I can't go forward or backward in time. I can go from one location to another and only under certain circumstances. I don't fully understand them yet."

"Well, didn't someone tell you about the circumstances, you numbskull?"

"Well, yes, but it all doesn't make much sense to me."

"It must have if you were able to help Mitch."

"Will you get off my back, Jasper, or I'm going to pull over and throw your ass out."

"Try it, pretty boy. I ain't got nothing to lose. I'll take on your clown ass any day you want."

"Whoa, you two. Enough. Both of you stop fighting over me, and remember we're working together. Let's get back to Outlaw so I can figure out how to find Mabey, and then maybe the three of us can also save our little town."

On cue, as if orchestrated, the "two" looked at Mitch and replied "Fuck You, Wilde!"

With another thirty minutes or so before they reached Outlaw River, a couple of seconds passed in silence as the Jeep roared down the highway. All three of them started laughing. Mitch's head, for a few seconds, lost its pain, and he enjoyed the moment. He returned his thoughts to his wife, and he could not hide his concern.

"Have either of you ever read *Jonathan Livingston Seagull*?"

Jack stared at Jasper, then back at Mitch, and then back to the highway.

Neither responded, so Mitch took that as a no.

"Never mind. I'm sorry I asked. Jack, do you know anything at all about Mabey other than her car's being found?"

"Not really, Mitch."

"What do you mean by 'not really'? Do you know something else?"

"No, just speculation by the Native Americans."

"What's the speculation?"

"They're saying the Aliens have been coming here for thousands of years taking humans and using them for various things back on their home planet, primarily for labor but also for scientific experimentation and reproductive testing. The Native Americans have been dealing with the situation for centuries. All you have to do is look at the cave paintings throughout the world to see documentation of Aliens visiting this earth."

"So do you think Mabey was taken? Is she gone then?"

"Yes, Mitch, unless she's hiding somewhere, she has been taken."

"Do you know exactly when?"

"That we don't know, Mitch. According to the Native Americans, every so often, the Aliens come back for a mass gathering when they take thousands of people at once. Apparently the last mass gathering happened hundreds of years ago."

Mitch spoke up. "Well shit, you make it sound hopeless Jack."

Silence filled the Jeep for a minute before Jack continued.

"There is documented proof of whole tribes of people going missing. One day they're there, and then the next they're gone. Ever hear of the Anasazi?"

"Whole tribes, as opposed to only a few at a time?" Jasper chimed in from the back seat.

Jack, in his comfort zone now with a chance to speak about one of his new interests, wasted no time in responding.

"I have been doing a bunch of reading the last couple of days, and from what I understand, most of the missing-people reports we've become accustomed to over the years are not only missing from their homes and neighborhoods; they're missing from the planet."

Mitch was tuned in and listening as close as possible blocking out the road noise from the Jeep's tires.

"No shit, Jack. And they're being abducted by Aliens?"

"Exactly Mitch. The Aliens take just enough to suit their needs but not so many as to raise alarms where our governments would have to start looking at ways to protect their citizens. But if I understand the situation correctly, the Aliens have asked the Native Americans to help round up thousands of new people to take back. They evidently had a mass virus outbreak of some kind that all but wiped out their entire supply of human slaves."

Jack flipped the blinker on and turned right onto highway 234 accelerating rapidly.

Jasper sat back in his seat, pounding both fists on the seat. Mitch didn't need to turn around and investigate Jasper's body language to know how upset his friend was. He heard it clearly in his voice.

"Damn! Governments already know and are too afraid to do anything about it. They, in typical Washington fashion, are too concerned about not offending a foreign force, rather than putting their collective feet down and stomping American boots right down on their Alien throats."

Jack nodded his head in agreement the entire time, Mitch noticed. He wished he could move his head like that without total discomfort. The pain was subsiding, he realized, just too damned slowly. He looked at Jack and showed agreement in his eyes. Jack reached over and patted Mitch on the leg and responded to Jasper.

"I'm sure you're right, Jasper."

Jasper cut him off. "The major role of any government is supposed to be protection of its people – first and foremost."

"Jasper, you're preaching to the choir here. Ask Mitch how I feel sometime."

Mitch straightened in his seat. "Please, would the two of you get off the conspiracy theory shit for now? We have more pressing issues to deal with. Wouldn't you both agree?"

Silence from both told Mitch they did in fact agree; however the more he thought about it, perhaps they were humoring him because Mabey was missing.

"Just so you know right up front: I will do anything and everything to find Mabey and get her back. Whatever it takes. Do you both understand?"

"Mitch, take it from one who's had a woman stolen, may have been by a rodeo clown, but she was taken from me just the same. I'm right there with you, son. Do you understand?"

Mitch felt a warm rush of care flood over him. He paused before replying.

"Thanks, Jasper."

Jack guided Black Steel off the highway and exited into Outlaw River.

Mitch held back his emotions. Losing his own dad too early to an aggressive cancer was in its own way having him stolen. He didn't want to go through something like that again. Having Jasper's support and being called "son" meant more than the old guy could ever imagine.

Chapter 10

Not Much Time

"Delores, thank you so much. Cindi and I would have been here for quite a while longer if you hadn't stopped in and helped."

"Don't mention it, Debbi. I'm glad I could help."

Debbi untied her apron, folded it and set it on the counter. She stood there wondering what to do next.

"So, Delores, what do you want now that we have a few minutes for ourselves?"

Cindi spoke up.

"I would be glad to make you something Delores, what would you like?"

"How about a small iced soy chai latte; I love the chai mix you serve. I stopped in several weeks ago in the morning and tried the hot one. An iced one sounds good now though."

"One iced chai coming right up and thanks. It's a recipe I found online a couple of years ago. I love it."

"Cindi, I'm going to go in the back for a minute and sit down. Call me if you need anything."

"Okay, Mom."

"So, Cindi, how long has your mom owned this place?"

"She bought it about eleven or twelve years ago, I think. It was a couple of years before her husband left."

"Oh, she was married before? Wait, that can't be right. You have to be at least seventeen or eighteen, right?"

"Yes, I'm eighteen. Hard to explain and talk about, but her first and only husband was also my father. He left during my tenth birthday party. Never came back."

"Oh, I'm so sorry. I didn't mean to pry. I was curious and making conversation."

Cindi noticed something odd about Delores's eyes. She wasn't sure, but it looked as if they glowed.

"Her husband, he wasn't your father?"

"That's okay. Mom and I are tight, and we have friends who're family to us, like Aunt Mabey and Uncle Mitch. Mom always said family is what you make of it and being on our own made us tougher and more resilient. Technically, he was my father, but like I said he left on my birthday, and I haven't referred to him as father since."

"Well, that's certainly a positive way to look at it. Remarkable job your mother has done with you, I think. And she runs her own business too."

There again with the eyes. Cindi was certain there was something odd about them. She stood and looked directly at Delores, who turned her head away.

"So I have to ask, Delores, why Outlaw River of all places? Don't get me wrong. I love it here, but we don't see a lot of new people move into town."

"I started teaching at Southern Oregon University last fall and lived in an apartment for the first four months while I was house hunting. I fell in love with Outlaw River and really like the size of the town. I was never much for cities, and I didn't want to live in the same town as the university."

"The river certainly is beautiful. Cool, SOU huh? I've thought about going there so I can be close to Mom. What do you teach?"

"Yes, it is, and I like the quick access to the river so I can shoot the rapids in my kayak."

"Oh man, I've always wanted to try a kayak. My best friend Shontey and I have been down a bunch of times in rafts but never in a kayak."

"You should try it. I'd be glad to teach the two of you this summer, if you want, once we get through all this."

"Thanks, Delores. What do you teach?"

"Oh I'm sorry I didn't answer. You already asked that. I suppose I should listen better," Delores flushed and smiled.

"No, it's okay; I have a habit of asking too many questions at once. Mom's always telling me I have diarrhea mouth. I never give anyone a chance to answer them all. It's a nervous habit."

"No worries, Cindi, I understand. I do the same thing sometimes. I teach anthropology. Southern Oregon is rich in Native American history. My ancestors were Takelma. When the opportunity came for me to teach at Southern Oregon, or SOU as you call it, I jumped at the opportunity.

"Here's that iced chai you asked for. Wow, so you are part Indian. You think we'll get through all this, Delores? Oh, shoot, I am sorry. It isn't polite to say Indian, is it? I didn't mean anything derogatory by it, Delores. I should have said Native American."

Delores started to say "no biggie" to Cindi, and "yes, Native American is now preferred," but the sound of the door opening interrupted the discussion.

Cling, cling, cling. "Shontey! Speak of the devil." Shontey entered and wasted no time as she made her way behind the counter and grabbed Cindi.

"Delores, this is my best friend Shontey who I just mentioned."

Cindi peeled her eyes away from Delores and turned back towards Shontey who was nervous and upset.

"Man, am I glad to see you. I've been texting like crazy but no reply."

"Where's your mom, Cindi?"

"She is in back. What's wrong?"

48

"Can we go see her please?"

"Excuse us, Delores."

"No problem, Cindi. I'll watch the front."

Shontey dragged Cindi and burst through the door to the back office.

Debbi, who had been sitting down trying to call her best friend Mabey Wilde, jumped and almost dropped her cell phone.

She didn't hesitate and put her phone in her back pocket. She grabbed for Shontey, squeezing her shoulders.

"Shontey, good, one of our two worries accounted for now. Are you and your parents okay?"

Shontey slipped from Debbi's grasp, slumped to the floor, and started sobbing.

Cindi dropped to the floor with her.

"Shontey, what's wrong?"

Cindi had a depressing idea pop into her head when she saw Shontey walk in alone.

"Shontey, honey, come here. Sit in this chair. Now what's wrong? Has something happened with your parents?"

Cindi helped Shontey off the floor. She clutched her shoulders guiding her to the chair her mother had pulled out.

Shontey got her sobbing under control, enough to speak and be understood. Her voice shook, but she got the words out with effort.

"They took them. My mom and dad are gone. They took them."

The door opened, and Delores walked in.

"Debbi, do you have somewhere the four of us can hide? Now! We don't have much time."

Chapter 11

Something's Wrong

Black Steel and the three cohorts seated inside approached Outlaw River on the state highway. The heater was still blasting, and Jack was sweating. Mitch was starting to feel all his body parts again. He never wanted to feel that cold again. He contemplated life near a beach with Mabey.

"Jack, don't turn here."

"Mitch, I think we should go into town first."

"Are you fucking kidding me? Take me home."

"Better yet, Mitch, why don't we let Jack go into town so he can meet up with his son. Then you and I can take the Jeep over to your place? It shouldn't take more than five extra minutes."

"Okay. You okay with this, Jack?"

"I would like us to stay together, but I understand why you want to get home."

"Good. Where did you find Mabey's car, by the way?"

"Oh, yeah, how could I forget? It was on the side of the road on Pine. Not too far north of Juniper Street. Here are the keys."

Jack repositioned himself in his seat, got the keys from his back pocket, and handed them to Mitch.

"They were in the ignition Mitch. I wanted to move it but the battery was dead. So I locked it up okay."

Jack half-expected Mitch to complain for some reason. Mitch sat in contemplative silence so Jack continued.

"How about you and Jasper meet me and Junior in an hour at the Coffee Shack?"

Mitch fidgeted in the seat. His head felt much better, and his blood was flowing through his legs. He popped his neck, and stretched his fingers out straight, just as he had done to prepare for high school football games all those years ago. He took a couple of deep breaths.

"Jack, I don't suppose you have my cell phone?"

"No, Mitch. Jasper and I didn't find your phone. It doesn't matter anyway. There's no signal, hasn't been since this morning. The cell towers have apparently been disabled."

"Best way to control the ants, my boys, is to figure out a way to stop them from moving easily and from communicating. I'd be willing to bet we won't be able to drive much longer either. They can probably disable the electronics in our vehicles if they wish, unless they already have what they came for and have hightailed it out of here."

"God, please don't say that, Jasper."

"Listen, Wilde, this is no time to get all soft with the facts, hard as they may be to hear."

Jack pulled up outside the theater and brought Black Steel to a stop.

Outlaw River felt like a ghost town. There was no movement in town and very few lights. It looked as though the entire main street was a movie set, and there was no filming going on.

"Man, I've never seen this town so empty. This is creepy."

"Yes, it is, Mitch. Okay to meet in an hour at the Shack?"

"Wait a second, Jack. Take this." Jasper tossed him a walkie talkie. It looked familiar to Mitch.

"Hey, Jasper, that looks like the one you gave me."

"It is, dumb-ass. You left the damn thing in your Jeep. No wonder I couldn't get hold of you this morning."

"Uh, yeah, they work better when you have them with you for sure."

"Just keep it on channel 10. Press this to talk. When you're done speaking, let up so you can hear the reply. If anything changes, give us a call, and we can discuss options."

"Sounds good. How're you feeling, Mitch?"

"Better, Jack, and thanks. I just realized I never thanked the two of you."

Jack left the door open and hollered over his shoulder on the way into the theater, "Don't mention it, and see you in an hour."

Mitch started to get out of his seat.

"Don't bother, Mitchy. I'll drive. You'll need to drive Mabey's car when we find it."

Jasper jumped out of the back seat and crawled into Black Steel's pilot seat.

"Nice rig. Almost as good as mine, Wilde."

Jasper had a big smile on his face. He buckled up and backed Mitch's Jeep out of the parking spot in front of the theater.

"I mean it, Jasper. Thanks. I would probably be dead right now if it weren't for you. Man, am I glad you wanted to go to Crater Lake with me."

"No problem. I got pretty worried when I saw one of those anomalies I've been showing you slam into Wizard Island."

"No shit, are you serious?"

"Yep, sure as shit, looked almost identical to the footage I have of St. Helens."

Jasper slowed at Juniper Street where Jack said he'd parked Mabey's car.

"There it is, Jasper. Whip a U-turn and let me out?"

"You okay to drive, Mitch?"

"I'm fine; see you at my house in five minutes."

"Let's make sure it starts first."

"Oh yeah, good thinking."

Mitch unlocked Mabey's driver door and climbed in. He got the key in the ignition, but it wouldn't start. He opened the door since the window wouldn't lower.

"I think the battery's dead, Jasper. Pull up in front of me, and let's jump it."

"Do I dare ask if you have cables, Wilde?"

"No, you dare not, old man."

Mitch went to Mabey's trunk and opened it. He pulled the mesh netting back and took out a canvas pouch with a pair of jumper cables in it. He briefly reflected how he'd taught Mabey to use them many years ago.

He stood with a hand on the trunk lid drifting off into thought.

Jasper snapped him out of it.

"Wilde, you okay?"

Mitch came to realize he was standing at the trunk of Mabey's car holding the cables.

"Oh, yeah, sorry, Jasper; I was thinking about the time I taught Mabey how to jump start a car. I have to find her."

"Let's get her car started and back to your place. We'll figure it out."

They had the car going in a few minutes. Mitch put the cables back into the trunk and got in the driver's seat. Jasper had climbed back into the Jeep and pulled up alongside Mitch.

"Let's go, Jasper. I'll be right behind you."

Jasper nodded and gave a two-finger salute from his forehead.

Mitch put the car into Drive and checked both directions before pulling onto the road. Not that it would have mattered. He hadn't seen a single moving car since he returned to town. As Mitch pulled out, he felt something blocking the accelerator. He blindly reached down, feeling around while keeping his eyes on the road, barely seeing over the dash. His right hand found the problem. It was Mabey's Blackberry.

53

Good, he thought, a first clue at least. He really didn't know where to start. He was hoping there would be something at their house, but he knew there was probably nothing except for the arrow in his safe.

In less than ten minutes, Jasper guided Black Steel into Mitch's garage. Mitch, only a minute behind him pulled Mabey's car in next to the Jeep and hopped out.

He got out of the car and raised his hand in the air so Jasper could see what he was holding.

"I found Mabey's Blackberry on the floorboard, Jasper."

The door into the house from the garage opened, and Mitch's heart briefly took pause.

"Mitch, is that you?"

The voice was familiar, but it wasn't the one his ears or heart had hoped for. It was Mabey's sister, Michelle.

"Shit, Wilde, she about gave this old man a heart attack. I thought perhaps our work was done before we even got started."

"Jasper, this is Mabey's younger sister, Michelle. Michelle, this is our neighbor and my good friend, Jasper."

"Nice to meet you, young lady."

Jasper extended his hand as he approached Michelle. She eagerly shook it.

"You the guy with all the antennas on the roof across the street?"

"Yep, proud to be guilty as accused."

She had heard wild rumors from people talking about him at some of Mabey and Mitch's barbecues. He seemed harmless enough. Michelle remained apprehensive but relaxed as she felt security and trust with him through his handshake.

"Nice to meet you, Jasper."

Mitch turned on Mabey's Blackberry, bringing it to life. He searched for, found, and selected the voice recorder application Mabey loved to use. She constantly made herself reminders which auto populated her calendar. Mitch gave her crap about it, saying she just liked to hear the sound of her own voice. Mabey always replied that he was just jealous for not being as organized as she was, and she was right. He scrolled through to her last entry with no title, just a time stamp. He turned up the volume pressed play.

Jasper and Michelle continued to talk until Mabey's voice, booming now from her phone, called for their immediate silence.

"Mitch. Something is wrong. I am trapped."

Chapter 12

Those Damn Little Hairs

Sheriff Gunther sauntered down Main Street toward his recently wrecked cruiser. From a distance, the damn thing looked drivable to him. The way the car was jammed up against the building gave the appearance of serious damage, but not major. Regardless, Gunther knew the Mayor's office would complain about the repair costs. They always did. The Sheriff tried focusing on the bigger picture rather than worrying about what his estranged, currently missing, friend, the Mayor, would say.

Gunther felt odd. The town was eerily quiet. As much as he always complained about how busy the little town could be, he realized his ears would welcome some traffic noise and bustling streets right now.

"Hey, Sheriff, what the hell is going on? Where is everyone? Do you know what's happening?"

Sheriff Gunther crossed the middle of the street. Someone approached unheard from behind. He recognized the face but had no name to put with it.

"I'm not sure, but if you want to get a better idea of what's going on, go to the theater. A bunch of Outlaw residents are there right now. I'll be along myself in a few minutes."

Sheriff Gunther watched as the young man looked up and down an empty Main Street. He lifted the ball cap from his head, pushed his hair back, and then repositioned the hat. He broke into a fast-paced walk toward the theater.

"See you in a few minutes, Sheriff. Thanks."

Sheriff Gunther uncharacteristically smiled, finding a new sense of appreciation in one of the town's residents. Prior to today, he would have been irritated and, without a doubt, would have ignored him. If he didn't ignore him, he would have found something to snap at him about. He reached up and felt the bump on his head as he approached his police cruiser.

The cruiser door was open, and the back end of the car rested against the brick building. Formerly a candy factory, the town's most recognizable building was now the community center. Gunther sat down in the driver's seat and looked out the front window at a very quiet town. He looked over his shoulder and saw his shotgun lying across the back seat. A quick look in both the front and back didn't reveal his sidearm. He lay down and reached around under the bench seat with his left hand. He wasn't too worried about anything disgusting since this was his car, and he kept it very clean.

"Your car is your office," he told his deputies, *"so treat it with the respect it deserves. If I find one of you with a dirty office, discipline will follow. You have to share cars with other deputies, and none of you wants to sit in a pile of filth, so keep them clean."*

Gunther didn't have to share his car, fortunately: one of the few perks of being the Sheriff. Share or not, he kept his car spotless.

Finding nothing under the seat he sat back. He wiped the sweat and oil from his forehead, and then pushed his palm down his pant leg to dry it. Although the dark pants showed no residue, he would put them in the wash as soon as he got home. He gazed out the front windshield in awe of the empty city. A chill ran down the back of his neck. It felt as though a breeze blew across the fine hairs which grew too quickly as he advanced in age. He rubbed his receding hair and neck with his newly cleaned hand and then exited the cruiser grunting as he searched for his balance.

The Sheriff walked around to the back of the car and looked more closely at the damage. Not so bad, he thought; it looks to be drivable, no doubt about it. Okay, a little doubt.

He walked around the front of the car and ran his hand along the hood of the car feeling the smoothness of the paint. The texture, although smooth, revealed a few patches without wax. He would ask the body shop to repaint the whole thing or, at the very least, do a proper waxing and buffing. He wanted, and expected, the vehicle to glisten when he drove through town.

Gunther regained focus as he removed his hand from the hood. He reached the passenger door and opened it. His S&W model 19 revolver fell to the grass at his feet. He must have lost hold of it when he rammed the car into the building, and it fell down between the seat and door. Gunther picked up the gun and examined it carefully. He felt comforted by the cold texture of the metal. The cylinder was fully loaded. Pleased with his find, he slid the gun into his holster. God, did he love the feeling of hard leather against steel.

Sheriff Gunther's mind raced as he started to feel more like his old self again. Townspeople liked to say he was a mean, vindictive prick, but Gunther knew it was his edgy attitude that set him apart. A certain toughness was necessary for a good sheriff. He picked up a chunk of brick from the ground. It must have come off the building when the cruiser rammed it. He looked around and then threw it as hard as he could towards the community center. A window pane shattered as the brick piece flew inside. Gunther smiled, pleased with his aim. He looked around, disappointed there was no one to see his accuracy.

He slammed the car door shut, walked back around to the driver's side, and slid in. He adjusted the rear-view mirror making sure he could see the outline of the back window equally on both sides. He grabbed his hat from the seat next to him and put it properly on his head as he admired himself in the mirror. Gunther turned the key in the ignition, and his beautiful little darling roared to life. He put the car into Drive and, creaking a little, the cruiser moved off the grass, dropped off the curb and planted its rubber firmly back on Outlaw River asphalt.

Gunther accelerated down the street wondering where a certain black Jeep was and if the damn taillight was fixed yet. If not, he would write a very expensive citation to one Mr. Mitch Wilde, hoping he would get some kind of reaction from the town's favorite citizen. It was about time he put Mitch in his place.

Sheriff Gunther slowed, parking the cruiser in front of the theater. After he exited the car, he went to the rear bumper and bent down to look at the damage. It wasn't bad at all, he thought, probably repairable with no need for a bumper replacement. His knees creaked as his legs powered him to an upright position. He turned up the sidewalk toward the theater door.

Gunther grabbed the door handle to enter when a loud scream pierced his ears. Those damn little neck hairs ruffled again, and he spun instinctively toward the sound while his eyes and brain calculated the noise's whereabouts. Without hesitation, he moved his right hand toward his gun. His left hand released the door handle as he refocused his eyes across the street. He heard the theater door shut behind him as he started toward the Coffee Shack.

Chapter 13

Don't Move

The Rabbit Moon looked majestic as it highlighted the towering pines standing tall and firm. Mabey was hungry and emotionally shaken. Physically she felt decent but not great like she was used to. Her hands and a tender ankle were her biggest concerns at the moment. She knew resting a bit more would put her in a better state mentally. Mabey held out hope a break would also help her gain insight as to which direction to go. She hunkered down among some thick ferns in a bed of pine needles. Lying on her side, she made a pillow of her slightly swollen and sore hands. She was cold, but not shivering, and knew sleep would give her body the needed strength to recover.

Then her head reflexively raised off her hands. The noise coming down the road started as a low growl, and as it got closer, the vibrations in the earth confirmed something was coming.

Mabey made sure to keep her body low and hidden from view. She was at least fifty feet off the road. One by one more of the old school buses passed. Ten of them she counted, and all of them looked full. She saw no eyes, only slumped over bodies, and shaved heads bouncing against the windows.

She put her head back down on her hands and faded off again. She must be dreaming.

Mitch would wake her soon with a warm kiss and a promise of some hot tea. She smiled and dozed off.

Bad dreams or a growling stomach woke Mabey. She didn't know which. What she was sure of; she no longer had nails on her hands or feet, her head no longer was home to her auburn hair and she was cold, hungry, and somewhere in the woods. Her whereabouts seemed oddly familiar. The full moon tried to help, but the trees were so thick, they blocked much of the moonlight's usefulness. Somewhere in the deep recesses of her mind, she felt the pull to go the same direction as the buses, not really logical, but maybe a good choice. Yet, she stumbled alongside the dirt road in the opposite direction the buses traveled. She realized one good thing about the pain in her hands and toes: she wasn't noticing much pain on the bottoms of her feet. Man, what she would give for a pair of hiking boots or running shoes right now. Hell, a pair of dress flats would be a welcome sight.

"Geezus, what should I do? Oh shit, the Mayor."

Mabey had completely forgotten about the Mayor when she fell asleep. She turned around and went back. He was gone.

"Shit!"

Perhaps she was dreaming.

"Psst, over here."

Mabey turned, hoping the noise she just heard was the Mayor.

"Mabey, it's me. Over here."

She thought about calling him Larry, as he asked, but it still seemed odd. Even as she guided him in his physical training sessions, she called him Mayor. But things had changed so dramatically now; the formality of a title did seem pretentious. The moonlight pierced its way through the grand old pines and glistened off the shaved head of Mayor Larry Jenkins.

"Shit, Larry. I thought you wandered off, or I was dreaming the whole damn thing and was out here alone. Are you okay?"

"Yeah, still a bit woozy from the gas or whatever it was filling the bus. My shoulder took quite a hit when you pushed me and I hit the road, but all things considered...."

Mabey kept walking and approached the Mayor.

"Sorry, Larry. But I figured the damn driver was reaching for the door switch, and if we didn't get off, we were going to be stuck."

"Please don't apologize, Mabey. If it weren't for you, I would still be on the fucking bus, asleep on the steps, going Lord knows where."

"I'm glad you're okay. How're you feeling overall?"

"Like I said, a little woozy, and my fingertips and toes hurt like hell, but all things considered, okay. I wish I had some shoes, but I suppose I should be grateful at this point to be alive. Where in the hell are we? Do you have any idea?"

"I don't know for certain, but I think we're north of Outlaw River near Tiller. Mitch and I backpack up near here at a place called Fish Lake. I'm almost certain of it. I won't know for sure until daylight. Hell, even then I might not know for sure unless we stumble onto one of the trails we hike."

"Should we follow the road or head through the woods?"

"If we're going to walk tonight, we need to shadow the road. It's too dangerous going through the woods at night even though the moon is full and bright. Last thing we need is to break a leg because we can't see."

"Okay, makes sense. Should we walk at all during the night then?"

"I don't know. Part of me wants to follow the buses, but I think we should get as much distance as we can from where they're going."

"Mabey, did you hear that?"

"No, what?"

"There it is again. Like a whirring sound. It seems to be getting louder. There."

Mabey, whispering now, "Okay, I heard it. Let's get down."

Larry and Mabey found cover and got as flat as they could on the ground under dense ferns surrounded by large rocks and towering pines. The noise was getting louder and louder and sounded foreign. It was coming up the road.

"What do you think it is, Mabey?"

"I don't know, but it isn't like anything I've heard before. Sounds like an electric lawn mower."

A light, now visible, swept back and forth across the road. It appeared to penetrate about fifty feet on each side of the road.

"I think it's looking for something, Mabey."

"You're right, Larry. Has to be. Want to bet what it's looking for?"

"No, Mabey, I don't."

It was a disc-shaped vehicle about the size of a small compact car. It had no wheels that either of them could see, and it was now even with their location on the road. Mabey hoped it would be past them in another thirty seconds. It stopped and rotated, directly facing them. The Mayor let out a little squeal. Dammit! Mabey thought to herself. If this damn thing heard the squeal, she was going to kill Larry, that is, if the craft didn't beat her to it.

The light got brighter and penetrated the woods, falling short of them by about twenty feet. Another intense beam penetrated the space overhead. This one was a different color. It pierced the woods, cracking and hissing as it slammed into the top of a nearby tree. Something, now falling, noisily bounced off tree limbs, ping-ponging its way down to the ground. Mabey thought she knew what it was, but she wasn't sure until the large, once beautiful, owl landed with a thud only a few feet from them. She cautiously peered back through the ferns at the disc. It continued hovering. After the frightening laser display, they couldn't run for it. She knew without any doubt it could take them both out.

It started moving towards them.

Mabey carefully rolled so she was pressing up against the Mayor. She could see his eyes, and they were wild with fear. Mabey squeezed his arm gently and whispered in his ear.

"Don't move, and don't you dare run, or we're dead!"

Chapter 14

We're All in This Together

Jack worked his way down the theater aisle until he spotted Junior. Catching Junior's eye, he smiled and gave a subtle nod. Quietly excusing himself, Jack made his way down a crowded row to sit next to his son. He directed his attention to the voice coming from the stage. He saw five Native Americans in full battle regalia on stage with Ralph Parsons. One of them was speaking to the crowd in a booming authoritative voice.

"They have asked us for help in procuring your peoples. But we will not. They leave us alone because they think it is unwise to attack the land's native people. Our sons and daughters have taken to hiding. They will not be found unless they choose, or until the collection is done. We have never had, or sought to have, the means to fight with them. Previously, they have taken only what was needed, and we have always thought a few bodies were what the Star People desired. Now that our sons and daughters are so few, we feel differently. Despite our love of the land and our determination, we have dwindled beneath your strength. To lose any more of my brothers and sisters to these beings from beyond the stars is no longer acceptable. We will not go quietly into the stars.

"We recommend you resist if you can, or they will return again and again and take what they need whenever they want – much the same as your forefathers did with my people. The Star people will attack smaller towns and regions of your people in order to minimize attention. They believe your leaders will be less likely to attack or defend if they don't approach large cities and if they stay away from the strength of your armies. So, small towns such as yours will be aggressively targeted. Hide if you can. Run if you desire, but you cannot outrun them. Again, they are very hard to see. Your mind can feel them, but your eyes will betray you. Learn to trust your mind. Your women and children are prized most. Protect them if you can. Some men will be taken, mainly the strong, for fertilization purposes. Once they have taken what they need from the men, their lives will be discarded. So this is the counsel we give. We will continue to do what we can, but battling an entire force of the star people is neither wise nor possible.

Pastor Steadmeyer of Outlaw's First Baptist Church stood up shaking his head. In a deep, rich Southern Baptist voice, one that didn't disappoint even a heathen's ears, the pastor spoke.

"Brothers, this presence in Outlaw River is evil incarnate. We must get down on our knees and pray. The Lord will deliver us from the evil hanging like a cloud over our city. We must repent of our sins and pray. These Native Americans are heathens and not of the Lord Jesus Christ, and He will not approve. As the Lord commanded in the book of Exodus, Chapter 20:4:

"You shall not make for yourself a carved image, or any likeness of anything that is in heaven above, or that is in the earth beneath, or that is in the water under the earth. You shall not bow down to them or serve them, for I the LORD your God am a jealous God, visiting the iniquity of the fathers on the children to the third and the fourth generation of those who hate me, but showing steadfast love to thousands of those who love me and keep my commandments."

There was silence in the crowd. Many men stared at the stage and the Native Americans. Many men stared at the pastor. Several were chuckling to themselves including Ralph Parsons who was fighting to hold in what he really wanted to say to the pastor. He considered his words carefully as he spoke.

"Um, Pastor, I consider myself to be a religious man, but frankly, I have a lot of doubts right now about a lot of the things I believe. These Native Americans are not asking us to worship them. I am certain they would rather be somewhere else right now."

Parsons looked at the group of Native Americans on the stage with him and nodded. He felt his gesture was important in keeping them on stage and engaging the group.

"I say we listen to them and see what we can learn. Something is going on whether you want to face it or not. I don't see Jesus standing here with us. I do see five very impressive, and willing to help, Native Americans."

"You're right, Parsons," someone yelled out from the crowd.

Another Outlaw River citizen added his two cents.

"Sit down, Pastor, or leave. We don't have time for this."

"Come on, folks, let the pastor speak."

"Thank you, sir. Now I am leaving and heading to the church to pray. I am certain God will protect those of us who trust and have faith in Him. He will send help."

"Hey, Pastor Steadmeyer, how do you know God didn't send these Indian Warriors to help us?"

"Because the Bible doesn't say anything about them; that's why."

"The Bible speaks of angels, doesn't it?"

"Of course it does, my son."

"Well then, Pastor, how do you know these Indians aren't angels?"

In an effortless, booming voice and pointing toward the exits, the lead Native American spoke again, directing his words toward the crowd but locking his eyes on the Pastor.

Jack thought the Pastor looked more than a little afraid and figured he might wet his pants.

66

"Those of you who do not want to listen with open minds, please leave. We have little time to waste."

Pastor Steadmeyer spun and headed out the door. A handful of men followed.

Once they were gone, the Native American spoke again.

"You must prepare; you have little time."

Jack turned his attention briefly to Junior, and Junior whispered,

"Glad to see you back, Dad. I was starting to get a little worried. Is Mitch okay?"

"He's fine, Junior. Pissed off and scared like most of us but as fine as he can be under the circumstances."

"Where is he?"

"He and Old Man Jasper went to get Mabey's car, look for clues, and head to his house. We're planning to meet at the Coffee Shack in about forty five minutes."

The Native Americans exited the stage and quietly left by the side exit. Everyone watched in respectful silence until the door closed behind the last one.

Ralph Parsons stood alone on stage, watching the graceful exit like everyone else.

Rumbling in the nervous crowd started to pick up again. No one really knew what to do.

"Everyone, I see Jack Jenson has made it back safely. Glad to see you, Jack. Can you possibly come up here and answer a few questions? It seems you may know more about what's going on than any of the rest of us."

Jack stood up and told Junior, "I might as well get this over with. We have our own shit to worry about."

"What do we have to worry about, Dad? It's just the two of us."

Looking back over his shoulder, Jack replied, "Mabey, ace, Mabey."

Jack left his son's side, making his way to the stage.

"Ralph, I'll be glad to answer what I can. I don't know much, but I do suppose I know more than most of you schmucks."

A few, knowing Jack's sense of humor, laughed out loud. The light-heartedness was welcomed.

"Has anyone seen the Sheriff?" Ralph Parsons held his hand above his face blocking out the bright stage light as he looked out over the crowd.

"I think it would be good if he could join us."

Jack replied, "I left him outside, Ralph. He was going to check on his cruiser. You know the one which somehow found its way into the side of a building while he was behind the wheel. I'm sure the building will be getting a ticket in the mail soon for failure to yield the right of way."

This comment had everyone laughing.

Jack approached Parsons on stage.

"Okay, everyone, please quiet down, and let's get going. I'm certain we all want to get back to our loved ones, and for those of us whose loved ones are missing, start searching for them. Let's see if Jack can shed any light on just what the hell is going on. How about we raise hands, and I will call on you one at a time so we aren't shouting over each other."

Several hands shot up in the crowd, and Ralph Parsons scanned the group trying to decide whom to pick first. It came down to familiar faces and names he knew so he could call them out. Everyone would get a chance, he thought.

Pointing down in the crowd, Parsons called on longtime Outlaw River resident Delbert Oliver.

"Delbert, what's on your mind?"

"Thanks, Ralph. I have a question for Jack."

"Okay, Delbert, go ahead."

"Can you help me find my wife and daughter? They were taken sometime during the night or this morning. I don't know. But they're gone."

Jack looked at Ralph Parsons before turning his attention back to Mr. Oliver.

"Delbert, I'm so sorry, but I don't have any idea where any of the missing people are."

"Then why are we here if you can't help us?" came an unsolicited response from the crowd.

"Look, everyone." Ralph Parsons interjected. "We're all in this together, like it or not. We all don't know much, but I figure the more of us thinking things through, the better off we'll be. None of you has to be here, remember, and can leave whenever you want."

A couple of guys in the last row got up and walked out.

Unsolicited questions jumped out from those who remained in the crowd.

"What do we do then?"

"My son is missing."

"My wife is missing."

Parsons put his hand up in a pleading position of stop.

"Everyone, please. Please quiet down. Let's see what we can figure out and quickly so we can get back out there."

"Jack, I'd like to defer to you if I may. Not to put you on the spot, but I know you were shot several days ago with a weird arrow, and from what I gather from Junior, you've been reading up on things. Perhaps you could get us going?"

"Sure, Ralph, I'll try."

Jack stood on stage for a minute looking at the crowd. He really wasn't sure what to say or how to say it. He didn't want to cause a panic of any kind with the group, but he sure as hell didn't want to give everyone a false sense of hope either. Silent anticipation held the air in the crowd. Jack could sense that not only were they desperate for answers, but for someone to give them hope. The way Jack was seeing things right now, his immediate concern came down to a handful of people. Junior, of course, the Wildes – Mitch, Mabey and her sister Michelle – and local coffee shop owner Debbi and her daughter Cindi.

They were dear friends of the Wildes, and Junior had recently started dating Cindi. Other than these people, Jack felt he didn't owe anyone anything. He wanted everyone to be okay and for Outlaw River to return to normal, but he knew this wasn't going to happen anytime soon. He decided he would give this crowd a few minutes, and then his focus was going to be on his core group. Jack took a breath, searched for a phrase, and directed it towards the men of Outlaw River.

"Look, I don't want to startle anyone, but this situation, as you all know, isn't good. I've done a lot of reading the last day or two, spent some time listening in on conversations between the Native Americans and Star people, and to put it bluntly, and forgive me, everyone….."

Jack paused and scanned the crowd as he searched for the right words. He cleared his throat. He wasn't sure what he was going to say until the words exploded from his mouth.

"This town is FUCKED!"

The words pierced the air, as the crowd remained silent.

Chapter 15

It's too Late

"Seriously? What are you talking about, Delores?"

"I don't know how to explain. Just listen to me, please. I can sense trouble is coming. We need to run or hide, and hiding is the best option."

"Mom, what is going on?"

"I don't know."

Shontey stood from the chair with newfound strength and wiped her eyes dry as best she could.

"I hid in our basement. Mom was out gardening, and Dad was in the kitchen. He grabbed me and told me to go the basement and hide. He said he would get Mom and be right down."

Shontey fought to hold back the tears as her breathing became erratic again. Cindi put an arm around her.

"Except they never came down."

Delores looked out the small window in the office door and turned back to Debbi.

"Do you have anywhere to hide? If not, we should go out your back door and find somewhere to hide, and I mean right now!"

"What about all the other women out front? We can't just leave them." Debbi thought about some of the women out there she knew well.

"What in the hell is going on, Delores?"

"Mom, we can hide in the basement with all the supplies. It isn't very big, but the four of us can get in there."

"Good, Cindi, where is it? Your mom and I will join the two of you."

Cindi passed her mother, keeping hold of Shontey as they walked toward the back.

"It's right around the corner here."

Delores was right behind both of them anxious to get out of sight.

Debbi moved the opposite way toward the door to alert the others. Alert them to what, she didn't know, but she did get the sense from Delores that an impending threat was real and imminent. They couldn't all fit in the storage basement though. This much she knew. They would be lucky to get the four of them in there with little room to spare. Leaving all the other women out there without warning seemed unfathomable.

"Debbi, I know what you're thinking, but we can't save them all. If we don't hide, we'll be taken."

Debbi paused at the door looking out the small window as women were eating, drinking, talking, pacing, and waiting.

"Can't we warn them somehow?"

"Well I suppose we could tell them to run, but will they believe us? And for those who do believe but won't run, they will be back here with us trying to hide in the basement. It doesn't sound as if the basement is big enough. If that happens, none of us will make it. I'm sure this is harder for you since you know some of those ladies out there, but we need to hide."

Cling, Cling, Cling.

Debbi heard the front door of her beloved Coffee Shack open. She changed her viewing angle to see who was coming in, hoping it was Ralph Parsons with some instructions. She started to walk out the door for a better view when Delores grabbed her arm holding her back.

"Don't go out there. You have to trust me."

Debbi did not want to hide. She pushed Delores's arm away and turned to go out the door. She only opened it a crack when she noticed there was a mist, spraying wildly all over the room. Women were grabbing their faces, trying to cover them with shirts, jackets, napkins, whatever they could find. Debbi closed the door and stared in horror as women started dropping to the floor. Her stomach knotted up, and a chill ran over her entire body as she wished she'd selected a door without a window.

Delores grabbed her again, this time with more force, and pulled her away from the door whispering,

"Come on, Debbi; it's too late. There's nothing we can do. The gas will probably penetrate here within seconds. We have to hide in the basement and now."

Chapter 16

Don't Stop

Mabey and the Mayor buried their faces in the ground, desperately hoping the damn thing didn't spot them. They could hear it getting closer, and Mabey could feel the heat from the light. She decided to heed Mitch's advice yet again and "run." Whispering to the Mayor, she made her play known.

"Larry."

"Yeah?"

"I get the feeling if we're found, we are going to be killed. It doesn't look like a transport of any kind, but a hunter, if you know what I mean."

"Shit! I wish we'd thought of that a few minutes ago. We have less of a chance of making it now, that is, if you're thinking about running."

"That's exactly what I'm thinking. If we dart and move, it'll be much harder to be hit. Because of its size, it won't be able to maneuver its way through the pine trees easily. They're too thick."

"My legs are fine, but your ankle looks sore. Are you going to be able to run?"

"Believe me, my adrenaline will kick in, and I'll be fine. I might not stop though, and we might get separated."

"The assumption is I can't keep up with you."

Mabey smiled thinking this is the guy who should be talking to the people of Outlaw River, not the political jerk he so often was.

"Don't forget, Larry, I'm your trainer, and I know what you can and can't do. Outrunning me is not on the 'can-do' list of yours. Trust me."

Larry smiled back and said, "Let's go!" He jumped up and took off running. Mabey sensed his energy had mentally prepped him for bolting. She was up in an instant and knew she could overtake him in a few seconds.

CRACK! A beam of light pierced the night again and ruptured a pine tree in their path.

SNAP!

Mabey was about to overtake the Mayor when she thought she heard a voice other than his.

"Yee-haw! I got it! I got the damn thing!"

Mabey knew it wasn't Larry's voice. He was off to her side and in front of her, and this voice came from a distance behind them.

She dropped to the ground and got behind a giant pine tree. She saw Larry dive to the ground and scramble behind his own tree.

"What the hell was that, Mabey?"

Mabey peered from behind the tree in the direction of the craft.

"I don't know, but the thing is gone. I still see lights, though. Did you hear the voice?"

"I did. It was definitely human. Not sure what it said, but it was human. Let's go check it out."

"Uh, let's not, at least not yet. Can you see anything?"

An intimidating bank of lights bounced up and down in an almost rhythmic motion. The lights looked familiar in some way to Mabey. There was smoke coming from the craft, or drone, or whatever the hell it was. The bank of lights stopped bouncing, and Mabey could now see why they were familiar. They were similar to the lights Mitch had on top of his Jeep, Black Steel. She chuckled to herself as she thought about Mitch and his need to name his Jeep. Men and their silly love affair with vehicles. God, she missed her husband!

Larry and Mabey looked at each other sensing the other's need to stay put for a while longer.

A man jumped from the back of the old Jeep pickup. Mabey watched as a second man, climbed out of the driver's side and approached the downed craft.

"I told you I'd get it, Billy."

"Shut the fuck up and get over here. Bring your shotgun, and be careful. There may be something inside it."

"You think so? It doesn't seem big enough to have anything inside."

"Quiet, dumb ass, and come on."

Mabey watched from a safe distance as the two men moved through the woods toward the drone. They were about thirty feet off the road. Mabey felt the need to stay put, and if these two yahoos started heading towards them, she was taking off, with or without the Mayor. She started realizing now why Mitch was so leery of strangers while they were in the woods. He always said there was no way anyone would ever make him squeal like a little piggy. He'd die first. Mabey now had to agree.

"Billy, it's toast. God damn, the rocket took it down and hard."

"How many more shells we got, Dusty?"

"Two more in the Jeep. I think we got another ten or so back home. Plenty to do lots of damage."

"Enough to win a war?"

"What are you talking about, Billy? You think there are more of them?"

"I think there's going to be a lot more of them."

Billy relaxed as he lowered his shotgun and started kicking at the drone. There didn't appear to be any doors or windows. It was strange. It was as if it was invisible or cloaked. Billy thought he could see through it, in a way.

"I think I found what it was after. Look at the size of this owl.

At least what is left of it. Hah! Damn, it was a big one. Must have an eight or nine foot wing span. Head's been blown clean off.

"Dusty, get over here."

"Okay, Billy, be right there. I am going to bring this owl with us. The feathers on this thing will be great for tying flies."

"Leave the damn bird, and get over here. You can get it in a minute."

Dusty dropped the owl and jogged over to the craft.

"What's up, Billy?"

"Dusty, what color do you think it is?"

"What do you mean?"

"What color? It's a pretty straightforward question. Geezus, you can be so damn stupid."

"I don't know. Doesn't look like it has a color to me. Why?"

"Why? Because I want to make sure I'm not going crazy."

"Whoa, Billy, what's that? What's it doing?"

"Quick, Dusty. Back to the Jeep."

Mabey could see the two hightail it out of the area. She couldn't tell what was happening, but the smoke was gone from the drone, and it appeared to be glowing. Mabey heard a loud crack which sounded unnatural and was frightening. She watched as the men hopped into their pickup and accelerated away from the craft.

Turning to Larry, Mabey wasted no time in speaking her mind.

"Larry, we need to get out of here. Run!"

Mabey was off and running as fast as she could. The Mayor was in hot pursuit. Mabey pushed her legs hard and noticed the air felt cool on her scalp. She also noticed that the woods were all of a sudden eerily quiet. All she could hear was the pounding of her feet and the deliberate push of air from her lungs as it exited her body. Mabey dived behind a big clump of boulders. She focused on controlled breathing as she steadied herself on all fours, peering around the edge of the large rock. She heard an enormous CRACK and saw a path of destructive light moving quickly toward her. She saw the Mayor slowing. Mabey watched in fear as the woods seemed to cry out in agony. Trees were shredded and disintegrating. The destruction moved toward her. She wasn't sure they'd be safe behind these boulders, but she knew for a fact they wouldn't be safe in the open. These massive rocks were their only hope right now.

Mabey yelled out, "Larry, faster! Don't stop!"

The Mayor dived behind the rocks, landing hard on Mabey's legs as the two of them buried their heads against each other and closed their eyes.

Mabey felt a warm heat envelope them.

Chapter 17

I Have an Idea

"Mitch, what is Mabey talking about? Where is she?"

"You mean you don't know, Michelle?"

"Know what? What on earth are you talking about?"

"Have you been here all day, Michelle?"

"Yes, Mabey said she thought she'd be late and for me just to hang out, and she'd have a drink with me when she got home. She didn't think you'd be home from your photo shoot until late tonight."

"Did you get any calls or texts at all from Mabey today, Michelle?"

"No, and, as a matter of fact, I have texted her a couple of times with no reply. Now I know why. You have her phone. And, Mitch, you drove up in her car. It didn't hit me until just now. What the hell is going on, and where's my sister?"

Mitch looked at Mabey's phone as if it were going to give him some answers. Jasper interrupted Mitch's incoherent thoughts.

"Wilde, I'm going to go check my house. See if I have any messages, new information, recordings, or whatever. Come get me when you're ready to go back down to the Coffee Shack. I want to go with you."

"Mitch, where is Mabey?"

"Just a second, Michelle."

"Sounds good, Jasper. Give me about thirty minutes or so, and I'll be over."

Jasper grabbed his pack and hiking stick from Black Steel and headed for his house across the street.

"Michelle, walk with me will you? There's something I need to tell you about Mabey."

General begged for attention as Mitch guided Michelle with his arm around her shoulder to the backyard shed. He noticed Michelle stiffen when he touched her. They'd hugged many times before, but Mitch never experienced this feeling with his sister-in-law until now. He knew she was picking up on his current state of fear and apprehension. He was worried sick, fearing for Mabey's safety. He didn't want anyone to know how much, especially Michelle. Mitch let go of Michelle, and she stayed right next to him stride for stride as they reached the shed. Silver labs, General and Delilah, were bouncing up and down as they continued trying for attention. Mitch gave the two a few pats on their heads and 'good boy' and 'good girl' but he wasn't feeling it. General settled down; he knew something was wrong. He fell in step with Mitch and whimpered. Delilah continued bouncing for a while longer.

"Are you going to tell me what's going on, Mitch, or are you going to take me to your shed and lock me up?"

"Mabey is missing."

"What do you mean, Mitch?"

"I mean her car was found on the side of the road with the door open and the keys in the ignition. I found her phone on the floor."

"So the voice message you were listening to…"

"Yes, it appears to be her last message, and she sounds scared and in trouble."

"Jesus, Mitch. What in the world is going on?"

"Have you heard the radio or TV or been on the internet at all today, Michelle?"

"Not really. Slept a little, listened to music, played with the dogs, and did my laundry. Who took Mabey, Mitch?"

"Michelle, I don't know. I think Aliens, but I just don't know."

Michelle stopped and laughed nervously. She remembered the

feeling she had in her apartment a day ago when it was ransacked. She knew at the time what she saw wasn't human, but her mind didn't allow her to take the leap toward Aliens, until now.

"Very funny, Mitch. But this isn't a time to joke."

Mitch unlocked the door to his shed and stepped in. Michelle followed, and General lay down outside the door. Delilah just stood there with concern on her face. She tried barking at General to get him up and then started licking her brother's head.

"Michelle, this may sound like a load of crap, but I promise you I'm not making it up. Outlaw River, hell, all the Pacific Northwest and perhaps the U.S., is under some kind of attack from Aliens."

"What, like illegal aliens, Mitch? Hell, that's been happening for the better part of thirty years or longer. Tell me something I don't already know. Are you saying Mabey was taken by illegal aliens?"

Michelle desperately hoped Mitch would say yes, but she knew damn good and well what he really meant.

"Geezus, Michelle, really? First off, there is no such thing as illegal aliens, you should know they are undocumented, seasonal, or transitional residents. Now I know you never listen to or read the news."

"Very funny, wise ass. Mitch, what in the hell are you talking about? God damn it, where is my sister?"

"Let me see if I can put this in terms you will understand. What's your favorite *You Tube* show?"

Mitch knew the answer to this already because he always heard her talking about it with Mabey. He'd jump into the conversations from time to time because he liked the original show from 1998. He decided his method of reference might resonate with Michelle more quickly than normal lest they be stuck in an Abbott-and-Costello routine for the next several minutes.

"*X-Files: A New Chapter.* You know this, Mitch."

"Aaaaaand?"

Mitch drew 'and' out as long as he could in an exaggerated tone.

Michelle needed to come to this on her own.

"What the....? Are you serious, Mitch? You aren't shitting me?" Michelle looked around as if she were about to be punked on the internet. She sensed the truth; she'd already come to the conclusion on her own, but she just didn't want to admit it.

"Do I look as if I'm joking in any way, Michelle? You know I like to screw around and be a smart-ass, but have you ever seen me play a prank like this? Especially about Mabey's being missing?"

Michelle dropped to her knees and started sobbing uncontrollably.

"Oh, my God, she's dead. I'll never see her again. Mabey doesn't deserve this."

Mitch didn't know what to expect, but this emotional display wasn't even on the list of possibilities. It caught him completely off guard. He stopped turning the dial on his safe, turned around and knelt on one knee next to Michelle. He put an arm around her and handed her a clean rag. Michelle took it, wiped her face, and quickly stood up.

"What do we do now? Do you have any idea where she is? How do you know it's Aliens, Mitch?"

Just as quickly as she had broken down, she found some inner strength. Michelle, for the first time ever, at least any time Mitch had seen, showed a glimpse of the Mabey strength he had become so accustomed to over the years. He was going to remember this moment, when everything was over, and tell Michelle this was how she needed to act toward the losers in her life. When she did, she would be a whole new person with a plethora of possibilities.

"Wow, Michelle, I like the fire I see in you. Listen, I'm as worried as you. You know how much I love Mabey. I, or rather we, are going to find her. Mabey's going to need both of us to be strong. And I don't know it's Aliens with 100-percent certainty, but it adds up in light of what's going on in town. But first..."

Mitch lowered himself back to his gun safe and opened it. He extracted a couple of pistols and several boxes of ammo, setting them on the workbench. He then grabbed what he really came for and with deliberate care laid it on some clean rags. It was still in one piece and still had the liquid encased in the tip. He sighed with relief. Without it, he thought he had no chance of finding Mabey.

"Mitch. Mitch. Have you heard a word I've said? You look as if you've been in a trance."

"Michelle, I'm sorry. I was just thinking about the first time I saw your sister at college."

"I've heard Mabey tell her version of your story a dozen times probably, Mitch. Not sure if I've ever heard yours."

"When this is all over and your sis is back, I'll be glad to tell you. But first..."

"But first what, Mitch?"

Mitch came out of another self-induced day-dream and brought his attention back to Michelle.

He reached over and flipped a switch, turning on the floodlights, filling his backyard with something close to daylight as the sun had started its daily retreat. He turned back to Michelle.

"I'm sorry, Michelle. I was thinking about Mabey. I have an idea for starters. I will die trying to find her, and I'll kill if someone gets in my way. But first, do you know how to shoot a bow and arrow?"

Chapter 18

A Seed of Doubt

Delores stopped by the sink, turned on the faucet and soaked a coffee-stained towel from the rack at the edge of the sink.

"What's the towel for, Delores?"

"To seal the bottom of the door from the gas. I don't think it will penetrate all the way back here, but I don't want to take any chances either. Can you grab some tape?"

"Sure, right here in my desk."

"Come on, Debbi, we need to hurry."

Debbi grabbed the scotch tape out of her top desk drawer, hot on Delores's heels as they entered the supply room. Cindi and Shontey were already sitting on some bags of coffee beans. Shontey had stopped crying, but she still didn't look good.

Delores closed the door behind her, dropped the wet towel on the floor and pushed it as tightly as she could to the bottom of the door. "That's going to have to do it."

"What's the towel for, Delores, and why are you holding tape, mom?"

"Delores asked me to grab it, but I'm not sure what it's for, honey."

"If the gas penetrates this far, I'm hoping the towel will keep it out of here. I soaked it just to give it some weight and help it to stay in place. The tape? Are there any vents in here?"

"Yes, there's one right there," Cindi said, pointing over Delores's head.

"Okay quick, is there any paper in here?"

"Mom?"

"What, Cindi?"

"Something's coming out of the vent. Oh my God! Is it gas?"

"Quick, Debbi, rip some cardboard off one of those boxes, and hand me the tape."

Delores slid a box, firm enough to stand on, under the vent. She climbed up making sure she could reach the vent.

"Here, Delores. I think this is big enough." Debbi handed Delores a piece of cardboard she had torn off one of the supply boxes.

"Debbi, take the tape and start tearing off some pieces. I wish you had some heavier tape."

"Cindi, grab the tool box off the shelf. I think there's some duct tape in there. Hurry!"

Delores pushed the cardboard hard against the vent, putting the tape in place. She was hoping like hell there was duct tape in the box because the Scotch tape was too weak.

"Here, Mom."

Cindi handed her mother the duct tape.

"Thanks, Cindi. Here, Delores. Let me know when to stop." Debbi handed a long piece of the duct tape to Delores who immediately used it on the cardboard. No stick problems for this tape. Within another minute Debbi and Delores had the vent covered.

"Any other vents, ladies?"

"That's it. I know because I'm constantly having to adjust the opening on it so I can keep it cool in here. I don't like the beans to get hot and sweaty."

"Okay and good. We should be safe as long as they don't try to come in here. Let's push something heavy in front of the door, and we all need to be quiet. In another couple of minutes, they'll come in the

85

shop and take out the women."

Debbi and Delores grabbed one of the storage shelves and awkwardly pushed it in front of the door. They added some coffee bags from other shelves to give it more weight.

"You think they'll come in here, Delores?"

"I'm hoping they'll be satisfied with the number of women in the main area. If they look in the back door and don't see anyone on the floor, they probably won't come in here. They have to hurry. Someone could show up outside at any time and interrupt their plans."

"You sound as if you've been through this before."

"No, I haven't. Purely speculation on my part."

"How did you know they were going to gas us out there then?" Shontey asked with some suspicion in her voice.

"I didn't know exactly what they were going to do. I could just sense a dark cloud that entered the Coffee Shack, and I felt something bad was going to happen. Something told me we needed to hide or run. Hiding seemed like the best thing to do. We really should stop talking for a while. Let's be quiet."

Shontey looked at Delores with suspicion and rolled her eyes at Cindi.

Cindi noticed the look but figured Shontey was just upset over her missing parents. Delores seemed okay to Cindi and more than willing to help them.

"Okay, I agree. Shontey and Cindi, let's all keep it down. We'll have time to ask Delores questions once we know the danger has passed."

Cindi whispered and directed her stare at Delores. Delores didn't have to look too close to see Shontey had planted a seed of doubt in Cindi's mind about her credibility. She thought to herself, no worries. In time she would gain their trust. Her future depended on it.

Delores was now whispering, "Debbi."

"Yes, Delores."

"If we are taken, don't resist."

Chapter 19

Lewis or Clark?

"Larry, are you okay?"

"I think so. Son of a bitch, that was close. What the hell happened?"

"Two of Oregon's finest used their weekend warrior shit, and the drone exploded. It sounded like a bomb went off."

"One hell of a defensive mechanism. Think it's military?"

"Hah! Larry, you're asking the wrong person. Mitch would have a better idea, and our neighbor, Old Man Jasper, could probably tell us who built the damn thing."

"I don't know about you, but I don't think it's our technology. Our government wouldn't make something that would self-destruct and potentially kill innocent victims. At least I don't think they would."

"Again, not my purview. I have to admit, Larry, I don't spend a lot of time watching the news. Other than major headlines or what is splashed across the screen on my home page, I just don't pay attention. I probably should, but I feel we're all just along for the ride. D.C. doesn't give a damn about us. It's all about a lust for power and doing whatever is necessary to keep it. Politicians do what they want when they want and then have the gall to stand in front of a camera and lie to us. They make me sick. Present company excluded, of course, Larry."

"I hear you and completely understand, Mabey. Funny thing is I don't really consider myself a politician. I pretty much ran for mayor because of my dad and the whole legacy thing. It isn't a bad job, but I would rather be a car salesman, I think."

"You might get a chance next election. Mitch says he is going to run against you."

"Seriously? Wow! I'm sure he'd get a lot of votes. People really have a lot of respect for him. He could play the local-sports-hero angle. His platform could be based around the idea of building a wall around the earth to keep the unwelcomed visitors out."

Larry smiled and Mabey laughed trying to hold the loudness in.

"Don't worry, Larry. He isn't serious. He just says it every time he gets mad about events in town. And it's almost exclusively about Sheriff Gunther. He would like to see a new sheriff in town."

"What's the deal with those two, Mabey? I've asked Gunther a number of times, but he won't talk about it. He always just says your husband is a fraud. He gets so angry at times I know there's much more there. Did you know he broke Mitch's tail light on his Jeep?"

"Mitch guessed as much. Now I have confirmation. I think I'll keep the tail-light incident to myself the next time I see Mitch. He might go off and demand Gunther pay for a new light."

"I'd like to keep making small talk, Mabey, but we kind of have some more important stuff going on. What the hell are we going to do?"

There was a pause as they sat on the ground with neither having any idea what to do next. Mabey broke the silence.

"Well, I was hoping we wouldn't have to do anything. Simply sitting here chatting won't accomplish anything, though. I just don't know what to do. I wish I had a better idea of where we are."

"I don't think following the road is smart, at least not as close as we were. That drone or ship thing probably isn't the last one. And even if it is, I don't know if I would feel much safer around those two guys in the Jeep. What did you call them, 'Oregon's finest'?"

Larry let out a belly laugh and then quickly covered his mouth hoping to choke off the noise.

Mabey smiled and looked around as if someone, in fact, had heard.

"Those survivalist types scare the shit out of me, Mabey."

"Me too, Larry, especially when Mitch isn't around. Not that I don't have faith in you, but Mitch gets an attitude about him that most people don't want to mess with."

"I've seen it, Mabey, and no offense taken. I don't have faith in me around them either. One of my strong suits definitely isn't survival in the outdoors. Hell, if it weren't for you, I'd probably have already died or be on one of those damn buses with the rest of the zombies."

"Mitch practically forced me to pay attention out here when we took photo treks around the woods. But strength-wise I would be no match for Jethro and Bobby-Jo or whoever the hell they were. They probably wouldn't be looking to probe you the same way they would me, Mayor."

"Now that I could handle, Mabey." The mayor said with a smile on his face.

"Another speculation of Mitch's and mine turned into a confirmation. My, you are chatty, Larry."

"I guess shaving me bald and ripping off all my fingernails and toenails has that effect. Do your hands hurt, Mabey?"

"I don't know what hurts worse: my hands, my feet, or my ankle. I'm with you on the 'at least we're alive' part. I think we should hide out and get some sleep if we can. We're going to be more effective hiking during the daylight hours, and perhaps by then I can get a better sense of where we are. Not here, though. Take a leak, and then let's get some distance between us and the exploded drone in case anything unfriendly comes looking for it."

"Okay, Mabey. I'm with you. You know much more about the outdoors than I do. I'll be right back."

Larry walked a whole twenty feet and took care of business behind a tree keeping Mabey in sight. Mabey noticed and could sense

89

the fear coming off him. She figured he was feeling much the same as she, and she was glad he stayed in view.

"Okay, Mabey, where to?"

"Let's head this way, should be south, back towards Outlaw River, unless I'm completely turned around."

"Okay, Sacajawea, sounds good to me."

Mabey rubbed her tender ankle trying to sooth it. She pushed her elbows back and straightened her back. She reached over and patted Larry on the back. "Let's go, Lewis, or would you rather be Clark?"

Larry smiled, enjoying the playful banter with Mabey. Barefoot he stuck close behind Mabey, looking over his shoulder with frequency. He tried, without success, not to think about his painful fingers and feet as the two headed farther into the towering pines bathed by the moon.

Chapter 20

Don't Give Up Yet

The door to the theater burst open, and several men led by Pastor Steadmeyer came running in shouting.

"The Coffee Shack is empty. All the women are gone."

Several men jumped up from their seats. Jack couldn't hear exactly what each was saying, but it was all pretty much the same thing.

"I told you we shouldn't leave them there."

"Great job, Parsons, I hope you're happy now." A reference to Ralph Parsons' recommendation that the women stay together in the Coffee Shack while the men tried to figure out what to do. Obviously, a mistake, he now realized.

Jack yelled out, "Wait, we should all go together: strength in numbers."

Most left the theater for the short walk down Main Street to the town's social palace. Several men were running. Jack got off the stage and caught up with Junior.

"What in the hell, Dad? This is crazy. Is this ever going to end?"

"At some point, Junior, it will. I think the better questions are what will our town be like, and will there be any of us left by the time it ends. Come on, let's go with them. We're supposed to meet Mitch there anyway in another twenty minutes."

Jack and Junior were side by side at the rear of the pack. Jack, like everyone else, didn't know what to do. He'd watched enough of the

History Channel over the years to know it's almost impossible to fight a battle against unknown enemies who can cloak themselves. He wanted, hell, needed, to talk to the Native Americans again. He had so many questions to ask them. He wasn't sure how much longer his transport ability would last. As badly as he wanted to go track them down and get more information, he wasn't about to leave Junior alone under the circumstances. Perhaps when Mitch was back.

"You know, Dad, we could just go hide somewhere and wait this out."

"I thought about that, Junior. Hell, I'm still thinking about it. Where would we go, though, and how long would we have to hide?"

"I was thinking about going down the Outlaw River Trail towards Galice. Great trail and plenty of rugged spots with creeks and mine shafts; we could disappear for quite a while."

"I sure don't feel like sitting around here, Junior, waiting to be taken, but we aren't going anywhere without the Wildes,." Jack said.

"They'd do the same for us, son."

Jack slapped Junior affectionately on the shoulder.

"Definitely, Dad, and I agree. I'm just scared. So much for pro baseball."

"Let's not give up yet, Junior. Perhaps this will all blow over, and everything will be back to normal in no time."

Jack didn't believe at all what he just spouted to Junior and felt a rush of shame in the white lie.

Junior stopped in the street. Jack stopped and turned.

"What is it, Ace?"

Junior stood there in silence trying to block out the noise of all the men entering the Shack and rambling around in the street.

"Not sure, Dad. I thought I heard something down the alley, but I guess not."

"Okay, Ace, let's see what happened inside, and then we need to meet with Mitch and Jasper and see what our next plan of action is. I do know one thing; I no longer think we're safe running around town. We need to be stealthier."

"Shit, Dad, I hope Cindi and her mom are okay. I knew I shouldn't have left them there alone. I should have stayed there."

"No, you shouldn't have stayed there. I'm not losing you as well. None of them should have stayed. We should have all stuck together or spread out and made it more difficult to capture us. Really not very smart of Parsons, but, shit, I might have done the same thing I suppose."

The first couple of men left the Shack as Jack and Junior arrived.

"They're all gone except one lady. She's passed out or dead in one of the booths."

"God, Dad, I hope it's Cindi, and she's alive."

"Come on, let's go in and look."

Jack and Junior pressed their way through the pack of angry men expressing everything from panic to anger to remorse over leaving the women behind.

Cling, cling, cling. Junior passed his dad and went through the door first. The Shack was entirely empty save one woman slumped over in a booth. Junior recognized her from around town but didn't know her. His heart dropped when he saw it wasn't Cindi. The feeling sucked and reminded him of seeing his mother dead, lying on the pavement behind the fucking garbage truck. Different, but similar. He didn't understand how he could be so attached to Cindi already. He had to think about it some more. Perhaps he wasn't attached, and it was just the stress of everything going on around them. That or his raging young-man hormones. Thinking about it now, she looked amazing in her tight jeans and tank top wrapped in a classic Pendleton shirt.

"Dad, you know who she is?"

"I think her name is Penelope. The town gossip. She's in the garden club with Mabey."

"From the looks of her, she probably sits more than she walks."

"Junior, I thought I raised you better." Jack said with a sly smile on his face. He had little patience for gossips. He let it slide by realizing he had much more important concerns right now than Outlaw River's town spinster.

A couple of men were hovering around the unconscious Penelope. One of them was a doctor, Junior was guessing by the way he was grabbing, poking, and prodding. If he wasn't a doctor, the guy was a pervert.

"Dad, do you care if I check in the back?"

"Shit, Junior, you don't have to ask. I'll go with you."

Junior led his dad behind the counter and through the swinging door to the back office. "Shit, Dad, there's no one back here." Junior walked through the office and peeked out the back door into the alley.

"They could have run out through here, Dad."

"I don't think anyone made it that far. They could have though, I guess."

"Dad I really like Cindi and her mom."

"I can tell, Son. I like them too. Don't give up yet. We haven't seen anyone get killed, just taken."

"Where in the hell are they being taken?"

"That, son, is the question. Come on. Close the door, and let's get back out front. Mitch should be along soon, and we need to come up with a game plan."

Wham! Junior slammed the door hard. He was frustrated and pissed and felt the energy boiling up inside him. The partial release slamming the door felt a little satisfying. He needed more, though. A good day of pitching is what would really do the trick. Man, what he wouldn't give to be on the mound right now, holding onto some red seams.

"Shit! I can't believe all this is happening right now."

Junior started moving back towards his dad.

"Dad, I'm going out into the alley for a second."

"Okay, Junior, I'm going out front to watch for Mitch. Join me when you're done."

"Okay dad, I'll be right there."

Junior pushed the heavy metal door open to find the Sheriff looking quite tattered, smelling of the distinct marking odor that came from a canine. Junior thought he looked as if someone had rolled him in the alley and then pissed all over him.

The Sheriff grunted a few nasty words at Junior and quickly moved down the alley.

Junior shrugged off the encounter as Sheriff Gunther's being nothing more than his charming self. He pivoted and went back into the coffee shop to meet his father.

From his new perspective, Junior noticed a door tucked around a corner partially hidden by some shelving.

Junior approached the door, grabbed the handle and pushed. The damn thing wouldn't open. He pushed harder this time with his shoulder. He could have sworn he heard a faint voice. He stopped and listened more intently. Nothing. He called out.

"Cindi, are you in there?"

There was no response, so Junior tried again.

"Mrs. Howard? Hello."

Junior let go of the door handle, disappointment showing in his body language as he turned to join his dad. After a step or two he knew he heard something. Turning with hope, Junior grabbed the door handle again."

This time it flew open.

"J.J., is that you? Oh thank God! We were scared to yell for fear of being taken."

Chapter 21

Fever Dreams

Sheriff Gunther rolled from his belly to his back. He heard crunching and felt hard lumps grind his head as he turned. The street lamps flickered, piercing his sore, tired eyes. The light from the lamps, hell, even the moon, pissed him off, but later he would be grateful. His eyes throbbed with intense pain. They felt thick and mushy, not his own, as if they were borrowed from a stranger. Perhaps someone put these eyes into his head while his were being cleaned. Outlaw River's Sheriff grabbed his head trying to make sense of the scattered thoughts. They reminded him of his childhood and the fever dreams he had that were incoherent, totally random in nature, and absolutely terrifying.

A German Shepherd licked his face, and the sheriff slugged it trying to scare it away. The dog growled, and lifted his leg. Gunther recoiled, frightened at the dog's anger and confidence. He felt a warmth on his right leg and ankle as he lifted his head enough to see the beautiful dog pee all over his once pressed slacks and polished police-issued loafers. A tear moved down Gunther's cheek as he sat up grabbing the back of his head watching the dog jog away. Gunther was sure the damn thing was laughing. He stared around the alley trying to remember how he got there. The last thing he recalled was standing in front of the theater when he heard a scream and had instinctively put his hand on his revolver while heading toward the noise.

He sat for a moment searching for some equilibrium as his ass was firmly planted on the asphalt in the alley. His head was wet and sore, and his trousers were torn in both knees. He could hear people around the storefronts at the end of the alley. Noisy but nonsensical voices. Gunther wanted to stand, but he was coming to his senses enough to know it would be a foolish attempt right now. He wondered if he had blacked out.

With care, Gunther reached up and rubbed his scalp. He noticed right away there was blood, but not a lot. The blood from the cut had already started to coagulate, and his hand showed red but not an oozing liquid red, just a dusting of a once bleeding wound. His hand reflexively returned to the scalp and felt for serious damage. There was a tender knot and what felt like a rising bump. He stayed on the ground breathing heavily. Gunther wondered for an instant if this was how his dad had felt when he was on the receiving end of a Mitch Wilde pass. Anger grew inside him as he rose and balanced himself on one knee. He took some controlled breaths and stood on both feet, bending over at the waist with his hands on his knees, his stomach pushing towards his ribs. Sour vomit burned his throat as it left his mouth.

He looked around with relief, glad that no one had seen him. He wiped his mouth, then tightened his belt, adjusted his holster and felt his gun. Gunther lifted his right foot and rubbed the top of the shoe along the backside of his left leg. He repeated the motion with his left foot along the back of his right leg. Neither shoe would pass his rigorous daily inspection process, but at least most of the vomit was gone. The pee, well, he decided not to think about it lest the shoes go in the trash right now and he would have to go home barefoot. Gunther took one step, then another, and made his way down the alley back towards his car. He wanted to get home and in the shower. He couldn't let the people of this town see him in this condition. The Sheriff knew they would make fun of him and never elect him again. He couldn't let a little blood, pee, and vomit keep him from being sheriff. Being a sheriff was all he had.

Making the way down in the protection of the alley, he looked to have clear sailing to his cruiser when a door. Out popped Mr. Baseball himself.

Chapter 22

Steve Rogers and Oliver Queen

"Mitch, you're crazy. I could never hit you. I'd probably shoot you in the face or something. Mabey would never forgive me."

"If you don't shoot me and we never find her, it won't matter."

Mitch pleaded with his sister-in-law.

"Come on; take another shot. You can do this. Pull back slowly and focus on your breath. Keep the string close to your face, but make sure your nose isn't sticking out in front. If that string rips by your cheek, it will hurt like hell. Pretend you're Katniss, if it helps. Just don't put it up against your cheek as tight as she does."

"Ooh, I liked those movies," Michelle replied excitedly, and Mitch was frustrated with himself because he distracted her.

Twang - - - Whoosh. Another arrow gone to the river.

"Shit. Are you even trying, Michelle?"

She started crying. Again.

"Crap. I'm sorry, Michelle. I just want to get Mabey back. I don't know what else to do."

"Making the young lady cry isn't going to help, Oliver Queen."

Mitch turned. The unexpected familiar voice startled him. Old Man Jasper had returned with a fresh shirt. Mitch looked into his friend's eyes. They oozed excitement. He swore the old guy was in his element. Mitch didn't know if he should feel disturbed right now or grateful the old guy wasn't more nervous.

"Damn, old man, I was about ready to draw and put a couple of caps in your ass."

"Not in this life, Wilde. I would have ducked, dodged, and darted my way around them."

Mitch laughed. He felt a little guilty laughing right now with Mabey missing.

He turned back around to Michelle. "I'm sorry, Michelle. Don't worry about it. This was a bad idea from the start."

"No, I'm sorry, Mitch. I want my sister back just as bad as you do. I shouldn't be such a baby."

Mitch took the bow from Michelle and patted her on the shoulder. He then realized she deserved – hell, probably needed – more than a pat. In a tender way he grabbed her and gave her a hug. Michelle responded and hugged Mitch back.

She held back more tears.

"We'll find her, won't we, Mitch?"

Mitch let go and looked directly into Michelle's eyes. From his confident eyes, Michelle knew the answer, and she believed. Mitch wouldn't have had to say a thing.

"We'll find her, I promise you. As clichéd as this sounds, I will bring her back or die trying."

"Who is Oliver Queen, Jasper?"

"He was a super-hero, Michelle. I think Jasper spends a lot of his waking hours coming up with new nicknames for me."

Mitch smiled looking at Jasper.

"I have to admit, Jasper, that was a pretty good one."

"I thought so, Wilde. I'm chuckling inside my head right now repeating the phrase. I'm so impressed with myself."

"I was more of a Steve Rogers fan as a kid, but I did have my share of Green Arrow comics, old man."

"Oh, Green Arrow. You mean Jeremy Renner, though; don't you, Mitch?"

Mitch chuckled. "No, Michelle. Jeremy Renner is the actor who plays Hawkeye in the *Avengers* movies. Wrong super-hero, wrong name. Close, though. Oliver Queen was the man's name in the actual comic book. He was some filthy rich dude who became the Green Arrow. I'm surprised you know that, though, Jasper."

"Well, Mitch, when you aren't married and have no real friends or pets, you end up with a lot of time on your hands. I read a lot, and I've always had a soft spot in my heart for the American mythological comic book genre. Besides I could read an entire issue while on the throne."

"Okay, Jasper, TMI."

"What is he talking about, Mitch. Throne?"

"Michelle, honey, you've got to get out more."

"Listen, Wilde; when this is all done, I'll show you my collection of comics. I have some great ones. I have a Captain America or two I think you'll like. But for now we need to get down to the Shack."

Almost as if on cue, the two-way radio in Jasper's hand squawked.

"Mitch, you there? Come in, Mitch or Jasper."

Jasper brought the device up to his mouth and pressed the talk button.

"We're here, Jack. We're getting ready to leave and head that way. What's up? Over."

"A lot to talk about, but we need you all down here. All the women in town who were at the Coffee Shack have been taken. Most of them anyway. Over"

"What in the hell is he talking about, Jasper."

"Not sure, Wilde. Let's go find out."

Jasper turned his attention back to the radio.

"We should be down there in 30 minutes. Over."

"Okay, hurry. Junior and I will be at the Coffee Shack as planned. Over and out."

101

"Let's go, Wilde. I'm thinking about taking my Jeep as well, in case we need to spread out. What do you think?"

"I think it's a good idea. But first, Jasper, and hear me out before you say no."

Mitch took a couple of steps away from Michelle and toward Jasper. He grabbed him carefully by the arm and led him further away talking quietly as they walked.

"I agree. Let's do it. But we have to be smart about it."

"Are you serious? No argument. No trying to talk me out of it?"

"What are you two talking about?"

"Just a second, Michelle."

"Green Arrow wants me to shoot him with the arrow just as he wanted you to do. For some reason, he thinks I can shoot a bow."

"Can you, Jasper?"

"No, Michelle, I've never touched a bow and arrow in my entire life. Strike that. I actually shot them in high school a few times. I wasn't any good, though. I much prefer a rifle or a handgun. So the correct answer is not in over fifty years and never as an adult."

"Well, Mitch, this is no good then."

"Don't worry, Michelle. I have a better idea. The main reason I went over to my house was to prepare for this very thing."

Jasper reached into the backpack slung over his shoulder and pulled out a plastic bag. Inside were some cotton balls and a syringe, among other things. That much Mitch and Michelle could tell.

"Are you thinking what I'm thinking, Jasper?"

"Hopefully you are now thinking what I've been thinking all along, Wilde, now that I've shown up with the necessary tools. We're going to have to be careful, though. We'll get one shot at this. If we make a mistake, game over. You won't get your chance, and any teleportation or port jumping is out the window."

"Follow me, and I'll get the drill."

Jasper and Michelle followed Mitch back into the shed. Mitch grabbed the drill and handed the bits to Jasper.

"What size do you think we should use?"

"That's crucial, Mitch. We have to be careful not to crack the tip and spill the liquid. I'm going to try this thirty-second-inch bit. The needle can easily slide into the tip and extract the juice. Less chance of cracking it, I think, if we use a smaller bit."

Jasper inserted the drill bit into the drill and tightened the chuck. He goosed the switch slowly, checking the variable speed.

"Nice drill, Wilde."

"Yes, it's a good one with plenty of power, so be careful."

"Okay, Wilde. I'm going to try to drill inside this plastic bag, so if the tip does crack, the liquid will stay in the bag and we can extract it."

"Sounds like a good idea, Jasper. Just be careful."

"Hey, you two, what if the stuff can't be exposed to air. You know, the air contaminates it or something?"

Jasper looked up from the drill briefly at Michelle and then over to Mitch. Jasper could see a flicker of doubt in Mitch's eyes. He held the same doubt himself now, thanks to Michelle's question.

"Well, young lady, we'd better hope the air doesn't affect it negatively, or we'll have to go to plan B."

"Plan B, Jasper? What's Plan B?"

Mitch asked, reassured, not surprised Jasper would have a back-up plan.

"We try to get you taken, Mitch."

"That's your back-up plan? Hope I get taken and then hope I somehow can find Mabey, and hope and hope and hope. I should tell you what I think about the word hope, Jasper."

Jasper smiled, nodded in agreement, slid the arrow inside the plastic bag and gripped the drill with care.

Chapter 23

Channelling Mitch

Mabey wasn't certain, but she figured they'd been walking about an hour. The Mayor was struggling to keep up even though Mabey herself had slowed her pace considerably since they began. Her ankle was swollen, and she knew she needed to get off it. She wanted to find a creek or lake to soak it. There was no gas station or market for ice, so one of these high mountain bodies of water would help, if she could find one.

The moon was full and glistened on the tattered duo as they trudged on. Mabey was about to give up on any immediate relief for her ankle when she swore she heard something familiar in the distance – the undeniable trickle of life-giving water working its way toward a river.

Mabey stopped and turned to face the Mayor. It took him a couple minutes to catch up.

"Not sure I can go much farther, Mabey. And I realize how disappointing it must be for my physical trainer to hear me say this, but so be it. I said it."

Mabey smiled, a thin slightly upturned attempt with her mouth, and grabbed the mayor by the arm.

"Larry, I'm impressed both of us have done as well as we have the past hour. By the way, this little hike will count for at least 5 sessions together, I figure."

"You aren't going to charge me for them, are you? If you do, can I at least get a discount for the fact I'm doing this barefoot?"

Mabey chuckled.

"Come on, Larry. Only another minute or two. I hear a stream ahead. We'll call it a night there. We can soak our feet and hydrate."

The Mayor made a weak attempt to wet his lips with his tongue. He couldn't remember his mouth's ever being this dry. Now that Mabey mentioned it, he realized how thirsty he was.

"Damn, Mabey I didn't think I was thirsty until you mentioned it. I hope like hell you're right, and there's a stream ahead."

The two trudged another fifty yards or so before they came to a creek, a good-sized one with the water flowing rapidly from the sound of it. Mabey felt a flicker of hope as they approached.

"Let's get our feet soaking and drink as much as we can. Both of us are close to dehydration, I'm guessing. And as you know, dehydration is not good."

"How about we drink first, Mabey, and then soak our feet? I don't want to drink downstream from our feet-soaking water. My dogs are filthy, not to mention raw, and the dirty water couldn't be good for us."

"I'm with you there, Larry."

Mabey released her arm which had been supporting Larry the last few minutes. Larry dropped to his knees and buried his face in the stream. He raised his head like a crazed man as if it were the first time he had tasted anything so spectacular. Water dripped from his chin.

"Shit, this is good, Mabey. What's wrong? Aren't you going to join me?"

Mabey turned her head back and forth scanning the woods all around them as best she could in the moonlight.

"Good and yes. I thought I would let you get your fill first, and then I'll take a turn. Call me paranoid, but I like the idea of keeping an eye out when possible. I guess I am channeling Mitch."

The Mayor had his head close to the water, ready for another gulp. "Okay and thanks. A couple of more swallows, and I'll give you a turn."

The Mayor rose after what seemed like an eternity to Mabey. She was thirsty and could almost taste and feel the cool creek water on her swollen lips.

"Thanks, Mabey. Your turn. And please do keep channeling Mitch. I feel much safer if I know he has my back."

Mabey nodded in agreement and bent down to take a drink. Then she heard a loud thwack and boom ring through the woods.

Chapter 24

General's Smile

Mitch tapped his left foot on the floor of the shed. His concern for Mabey grew with each unsuccessful turn of the drill bit and every tap of his foot. He was certain he could be doing a better job than Jasper and was about to say something when Michelle got to the gate first.

"Why is it taking so long? I thought drilling was straight-forward and quick?"

Jasper stopped drilling and set the drill down on the work bench. He moved his wrist back and forth to get the blood flowing again.

Mitch grinned knowing Jasper would be irritated.

"What did you say, young lady?"

"She wants to know why it's taking so long, Jasper. I'm wondering myself, old man."

"Well, for starters, fancy pants, I'm trying to go slowly so I don't crack the damn thing, and second, I don't think the bit is actually cutting the glass at all, or whatever material it is. Take a look."

Mitch looked at the arrow tip. The old coot was right. The damn thing didn't appear to have a scratch on it.

"Wilde, I have some nice cobalt-carbide tips, brand new, at home. I'll be right back."

"What's so special about carbide, Mitch?"

"Hell if I know, Michelle. They certainly sound impressive, though."

Mitch picked up the arrow and looked as closely as possible at the arrow tip. He touched it and rubbed it back and forth. He jumped a little and pulled his hand back in a sudden move that Michelle couldn't help but notice.

"What's wrong, Mitch?"

"I don't know. I could have sworn the arrow tip got warm and started to melt on my finger. It was a strange feeling for sure."

Mitch looked at his fingers and then back at the arrow and made a decision. He didn't want to wait for Jasper to get back. Every lost second could mean the difference between life and death for Mabey. And too many precious ticks of the clock had already passed by.

"Michelle."

"Yes, Mitch."

"Please go in the house, get as many bottles of water as you can, and come right back. I'm going to try something."

"Are they in the refrigerator?"

"Yes and some in the garage too. Bring back at least six. And if I should need them, there are probably a few more in the small refrigerator over there."

Mitch pointed across his man-shed to the adult-beverage refrigerator.

"Just look behind the beer okay?"

"Got it, and I'll be right back."

Michelle jogged to the house. Mitch figured she'd return in a couple of minutes max. Jasper might be back before then.

He sat down and called General who without hesitation licked his face and wagged his entire body. Mitch loved his dog's smile.

"Good boy, General. Dad's going to do something stupid right now. You keep an eye out for me, okay?"

Mitch gave General a kiss on the head and rubbed both sides of the lab's head. He looked around, then lay down on the wood floor. His head was two to three feet away from everything once he was lying flat.

Good, he thought to himself as he sat back up.

Mitch took a towel off the work bench and put it on the floor where he thought his head would be if he fell back. He rolled up a shirt sleeve and rubbed his left shoulder trying to identify a soft spot thinking it would hurt less for some reason. He laughed at himself thinking it was hard to find a soft spot on a body of steel. He smiled knowing if he said this out loud to Mabey, she would get a big smile on her face and then poke fun at him and his ego.

Mitch grabbed the arrow with his right hand about six inches from the tip. He saw Jasper coming across the yard, so he took a deep breath, clenched his teeth for the impending pain, and then plunged the arrow deep into his shoulder. He felt an immediate rush of adrenaline, or Alien juice, as his body tensed and collapsed backwards. His head hit the hardwood floor missing his strategically placed shirt. He thought of Mabey and his desire to hold her as his eyelids closed and his heart stopped beating.

Chapter 25

Drained and Defeated

The office door of the Coffee Shack burst open, and Cindi wasted no time in burying her face into Junior's chest. Junior wrapped his arms carefully around her and squeezed with what he thought was the appropriate amount of pressure for this early stage of their relationship. He wanted to squeeze harder, but Ms. Howard was standing right there.

"Junior, am I glad to see you! Are you alone?"

Ms. Howard, Shontey, and an unknown lady walked past Junior and Cindi with deliberate caution.

"No, Ms. Howard. My dad's out front, and there're a bunch of other men from town in your shop and on the street. Why?"

"Just curious. Did you see anything?"

"No, Ma'am. Someone came running into the theater and said something about an attack, so we all ran for the Shack. By the time we got here, everyone was gone. No trace whatsoever. Just some lady passed out in one of the booths."

Cindi lifted her head from Junior's chest and looked at her mom. They said at the same time,

"Penelope."

Junior, this is Delores, one of my customers and a professor at

Southern Oregon University. She's also an expert on local Native American tribes and is part Native American herself. She's been a big help and saved our asses. If she hadn't been here, we'd all be gone with the other women.

With affection, Debbi touched Delores on the shoulder. Delores smiled and extended a hand to Junior.

"Nice to meet you, Junior. Are you the same Jack Jenson who pitches for the Dodgers single-A team in Medford?"

Junior smiled, and Cindi answered.

"He was, Delores, but he's been called up to the Chattanooga Double-A team because he's so awesome."

Junior flushed, and Debbi smiled. As a parent, she felt warm seeing her daughter so affectionate towards someone. The warmth came from seeing her happy, yes, but knowing Junior was a decent young man intensified the feelings.

"Wow! Congratulations. I've seen you pitch a couple of times, and I'm not surprised. I was at the game the other night where you gave up only three hits I think and fanned at least ten batters. I saw you strike out the Giants' Housebender who was rehabbing. Great stuff."

"I don't suppose it really matters, but it was eleven strikeouts that night. Right, J.J.?"

Cindi stressed the 'J.J.', knowing everyone else called her boyfriend Junior.

"Even better," Delores smiled

"Hi, Shontey. How're you doing?"

Junior looked at Shontey with concern. He could sense something was wrong with her beyond the current situation. He figured it had something to do with her parents, but he'd leave it alone for now.

Shontey straightened up a little and tried to smile.

"Hi, Junior. We're really glad to see you."

"Okay, Junior… or Delores. What's the game-plan now?"

Debbi projected with confidence, as much as she could under

the circumstances. She was glad she was with her daughter but scared out of her wits right now and had no idea whatsoever what to do. The only thing that popped into her head was hiding. And she knew hiding was not a real solution.

"Well, Dad and the others are out front. The Shack is all clear right now, so we can see them for starters. The group will have a plan, I'm sure, and if not, my dad and Mitch will think of something."

Debbi spun towards the door with renewed faith hearing Mitch's name.

"Mitch is out there? What about Mabey?"

Debbi started a quick walk to the front of her coffee shop, and everyone followed, with Junior bringing up the rear.

"Not sure if Mitch is here quite yet, Ma'am. If not, he will be soon. He went to his house looking for Mabey. Apparently she's missing."

As soon as Junior said his last statement, he regretted it. He wished he had said it differently, knowing that Debbi and Cindi were so close with the Wildes.

All the good feelings that Debbi had felt mere seconds ago disappeared, leaving her feeling drained and defeated again as she pushed through the door into the main room of her beloved Coffee Shack.

Chapter 26

What Will Save This Town?

Gunther tucked in his shirt and straightened his belt. He gathered himself the best he could under less-than-optimal conditions. He looked like crap, and he had to do something about it. His breathing shortened, and he felt close to hyperventilating. He wanted the security of his home. It was as if he were a boy again in the comfort of his closet hoping his father would go past his bedroom on returning from the bar every Saturday night. These fucking people in this straight-laced town couldn't see him like this.

Gunther's hopes of being unseen now gone, he proceeded down the alley towards the cruiser hoping no one else saw him. Once home, he'd shower, grab a clean uniform and then get back down here and set things right. This damn town had serious issues right now and needed a leader to fix things.

He looked around for the damn dog hoping he could give it a good kick. Shooting it was out of the question as the chance of being seen was too great. He loved animals, but nothing pissed on him and got away with it.

Just a few more feet to reach the safety of his car. Gunther kept his head down and stayed focused on the cruiser.

There were no other encounters of Outlaw River citizens fortunately as Gunther reached his car and got behind the wheel. He could see some of the townspeople coming towards him wanting to talk. He started the car, slammed it in reverse, and eased back onto the street with his head turned backwards so he wouldn't make eye contact. He whipped the wheel, spun the car around, and drove back through town away from his home. He'd circle back once he got a block or two away from the mother-fuckers.

He checked his rear-view mirror and saw a couple townspeople waving at him, but he pressed the patrol car forward. He caught a glimpse of his disgusting self in the mirror. A tear appeared ready to fall from the corner of his right eye. He wiped it away with the back of his hand, shook his head, and cleared his throat.

Gunther slammed his right fist repeatedly on the seat as hard as he could and screamed at the top of his lungs until he could barely breathe. He accelerated through town until he was able to back track unseen and go to his house. He'd take a quick shower, put on a clean uniform, and search for some courage to return. There was nothing like a clean uniform and a raised chin to help him demand respect. Something, which could save this town; Respect for the law.

Chapter 27

Silver Surfer

"Don't worry, Kiddo. Let's just stand back. He should be fine in a few minutes and quite thirsty from what I hear. Good thing you got the water."

Michelle had just returned from the house with the water Mitch had requested only moments earlier. She found Mitch twitching on the ground looking damn near dead. She panicked at the distorted sight of him and dropped the water. The plastic bottles scattered on the shed floor. Jasper was standing over him with a cell phone capping off some photos with an intermittent chuckle or two.

"Why are you laughing, Jasper? What the hell happened? Is he okay?"

Jasper couldn't believe someone could talk so much, the only thing he didn't miss about his ex-wife. The woman never stopped talking.

Jasper handed Michelle the phone. "Here, take a couple of shots with me and Mitch, will you? I'm going to give him a hard time with these babies when it's all over."

Michelle reflexively reached for the phone thinking Jasper was nuts when Mitch suddenly sat up and grabbed Jasper by the wrist, yanking him to the ground. Mitch's eyes looked as if they were full of

115

silver and glowing. He blurted out, "sat'waaYi ʔis, paused for a second and then shouted, san'aaWawli ʔan ʔambo…" gibberish as far as Michelle was concerned. Jasper, on the other hand, had an idea after many years of listening to Native American language about Star People and Alien legends. He pried Mitch's hand from around his wrist and placed it gently behind his neck supporting him. Looking up at Michelle, he spoke calmly.

"I think he wants some water. Hand me one of those bottles of water you dropped, young lady. Take the top off, please. I want to keep my hand behind his neck."

Michelle picked up the closest bottle to her, took off the cap and handed it to Jasper. She then backed away as if Mitch might attack her.

Jasper held the water up to Mitch's mouth, never taking his eyes off the silver, glowing ocular cavities that once held blue eyes. Jasper hoped they'd return to normal. He wasn't sure he'd be comfortable around the Silver Surfer.

Mitch grabbed the water and drank as quickly as his body would allow.

"Hand me another bottle, will you?"

Michelle opened another bottle and handed it to Jasper.

Mitch's eyes danced around, and to Jasper the silver appeared to be fading. Michelle could see some of the blue coming back, and the whites of his eyes were returning to normal. Jasper handed Mitch the second bottle and gestured to Michelle for a third.

"Just keep 'em coming, young lady, until he stops drinking."

Chapter 28

Speechless

Why are his veins and eyes all silver, Jasper? God, he looks like a freak! I hope the two of you know what you're doing. If we find Mabey, and something is wrong with Mitch, I had nothing to do with it. This reminds me of an episode of the *X-Files: Internet Edition* where Mulder got hit with something in the woods and started acting all strange. Scully was concerned, but Mulder acted as if she were nuts, and he had never felt better and...."

"Hey!" Jasper raised his voice and snapped his fingers trying to get Michelle to look at him.

"Sweetie, I know you must be worried about your sister and Mitch, but please, and, I'm close to begging, could you put a zipper on that mouth of yours for five minutes? That's all I'm asking, five minutes. Let's focus on Mitch, okay?"

"You didn't have to say it all nasty."

"Jasper, my heart feels as if it's going to burst through my chest."

Jasper took the fifth bottle of water from Mitch's hand and tried to comfort him. He placed his right hand behind Mitch's neck with affectionate care. Then Jasper almost reflexively pulled his hand away. It felt as though his hand was going to sear, Mitch's neck was so hot. He had wisps of steam coming out from around the edges of his eyes and from his ears.

Mitch lay flat with his head on a towel Michelle had placed as Jasper lowered his head. Mitch grabbed Michelle, and, of course, she shrieked. Jasper laughed and thought the little filly needed to get laid. She was excessively uptight. He figured he had pushed his limit of frankness with her for a while, so he would leave it alone.

Michelle tried to pull away, but Mitch wouldn't let go.

Mitch gasped for air and flopped around. His behavior reminded Jasper of a fish out of water, struggling for air, longing for water, and hanging onto life.

Mitch sat upright and held Michelle with a firm grip. He started to speak again.

"Michelle, I'm fine. I know I must look like hell, but I'm starting to come around. Just give me another minute and some space."

"Okay, Mitch. Can you let go of my wrist? Please. It feels as if you're going to break it."

Mitch released Michelle's arm and put his right hand on his racing heart. He hoped to slow it down somehow. He focused on controlled breathing and the peaceful running water of Outlaw River. He could picture the water as it flowed by the rocks to find its way to the Pacific.

"One, two, three, four, five, six...."

"Why is he counting, Jasper?"

"For God's sake, young lady! Shut it! Let the man catch his breath."

"You're an asshole, old man."

"Listen, Honey, I may be an asshole, but I sure as hell know when to put a cork in it."

"Well, I never..."

"What, never learned to put a cork in it? I know; that's what I'm trying to tell you."

Jasper was proud of his last come-back. Michelle actually smiled a little, knowing she walked right into some humble pie. The two had been so busy bickering, they lost track of Mitch who leapt to his feet.

"Okay, you two pansy-ass whiners. Will you both shut up! All I could hear the whole time I was at death's door was the two of you going on and on. And Michelle, my beautiful sister whom I love to death, Jasper is right. You need to learn to quit talking so much."

"Oh, so both of you are going to pile on now, huh? You wouldn't talk to me like that, Mitch, if Mabey were here."

"You're right I wouldn't, but I would be thinking about it. Have you ever noticed you always have to have the last word? And don't answer. Just think about it."

Jasper gently grabbed Mitch on the shoulder and looked into his eyes.

"Okay, Alien-boy, now what? You feeling okay?"

"God, Jasper, I've never felt better! A little hot still, but I feel I could bike around the rim of Crater Lake in an hour and not even break a sweat."

"Well, good, because you're going to need all the energy you can muster. Things are just getting going, I'm afraid.

Mitch grabbed another bottle of water and chugged it. He opened the door, and there were the two silver Labradors, General and Delilah, with very concerned looks on their faces.

"Hope you don't mind, Wilde, but I closed the door. Didn't want them thinking Michelle and I were doing something to you and have 'em get all pissed."

"No worries. Probably smart. Come here, boy. Good boy. Good girl."

Mitch patted both of them on their heads and knelt down allowing General to lick his face.

"Okay, I want to swing into the house and get something to eat, and then let's get down to the Coffee Shack and figure out how to find

Mabey. God, I am starving. Michelle, please feed these two and quick, okay? Do you want to stay here with the dogs or come down to the Coffee Shack with us?"

Jasper jumped in before Michelle could answer.

"Mitch, if it is all just the same, don't you think she should stay here in case Mabey calls, or comes home?"

"No, I want to go with you two. I promise not to talk so much."

Mitch rotated his head, popping his neck. He felt his blood surging with energy. He needed some fuel, though. He grabbed Michelle by both shoulders and looked directly into her eyes.

"I need you to stay here. Keep the dogs with you in the house if you like. Just stay here and listen for the phone and keep the radio on. Not sure if there is any broadcasting you can get right now, but the emergency channel is most likely working. Anyway, Jasper is right. We need you to stay here."

Michelle didn't want to stay, but she knew the two of them were right.

"Okay, but don't keep me in the dark. Let me know what's going on. Please."

"We will. Okay, now for some food, and then let's get down to the Shack."

Mitch broke into a run for the house. The dogs raced to keep up.

Jasper looked at Michelle standing there with her mouth open. For the first time since Jasper had met her, she didn't say anything.

After watching Mitch move so quickly, Jasper had to admit that he was speechless himself.

Chapter 29

Fresh Pants

"No, damn it, we may need both vehicles. I'm driving my Jeep."

"Don't you mean Black Steel, Alien-boy?"

"Whatever, Jasper. I'm in no mood for any of your shit right now. If you don't want to take your Jeep, then fine, ride with me. I'm driving."

Jasper let out a big sigh while clenching his fists. He didn't want Mitch driving. Jasper's caring reaction touched Mitch for a second, but he had to focus. He put Black Steel into gear, easing out of the garage in reverse. His chest felt as if it were on fire. Still thirsty, he decided to put a pause on drinking for a time. He had already downed at least a dozen bottles of water. He felt as though he should pay close attention to his subconscious as his thoughts became increasingly clear with each passing moment from his Alien-juice injection. Mitch steered his Jeep behind Jasper's. The position of Mitch's vehicle at the end of the old guy's driveway held Jasper's Jeep at bay for the moment.

"Hey, old man, you need a ride the rest of the way?"

"Very funny, silver freak."

"Okay, you riding with me or driving yourself?"

"I hate to admit it, but you're probably right. We may need both vehicles. I'll be right behind you. I have to see a man about some business first, and then I'll leave."

"Seriously?"

"Yes, Wilde, all this commotion has me a little backed up, but..." Jasper looked around, as if someone might hear, before finishing his thought.

"I think watching you go all Alien on me and seeing your eyes float in silver jarred things loose."

Mitch chuckled and shook his head in disbelief, thinking this is too much information, then blurted out,

"No shit, old man?"

"Well, you scared the shit out of me. I need some clean shorts and may as well put on some fresh pants as well. Not sure when we'll get to shower again."

Mitch burst out laughing, put his Jeep in gear and started to pull away from Jasper, who stopped and turned. Mitch looked in the rearview mirror and saw his dear friend standing in the driveway with his right arm up, giving him the bird. Mitch placed his left arm out the side of the Jeep and waved at Jasper to let him know he saw him and then continued to laugh as Black Steel lurched forward into second gear chirping the tires.

Chapter 30

Ground Control

Mitch turned on the radio, and there was nothing. Dead static air. The digital radio scanned and scanned in a never-ending loop. Mitch switched over to his USB drive and searched through the folders hoping to find something that would brighten his mood. He felt energetic and ready to take on the world or if not the world, then the bad-ass Aliens, or whoever it was who had stolen his wife. Mitch felt a calm peace when he thought of Mabey. Somehow he knew she wasn't in immediate danger. He had a sense she was under stress and needed help but not in a life-threatening way. This sensation helped him to cope with his anxiety some, but not enough.

While the Jeep tires ground out the space between his home and the Coffee Shack, he wondered if his mind was simply trying to mitigate the fact Mabey was missing. Mitch felt in the front pocket of his jeans to make sure he had her Blackberry. Mitch continued to hunt the music folders for something to listen to. His mind drifted as his eyes deliberately moved between the radio and road.

"Mitch, why do you want to marry me? Don't get me wrong, I'm excited you asked me and flattered, but that isn't enough. Why do you want to marry me?"

Mitch had what he could only think was a dumb, bewildered look on his face. Mabey threw out a question he hadn't expected. He figured she would simply say yes and throw her arms around him and kiss him. At least that is what he he'd hoped for. When he asked Mabey that night at the art exhibit on campus, he thought he had run all the possible scenarios through his head. None of them had included this question. A mistake, too, because as soon as the words penetrated his brain and he was able to digest them, it made all the sense in the world. This was exactly who Mabey was: a beautiful, thoughtful, intelligent and deliberate woman who wasn't going to be satisfied with making do with life. This woman had expectations and a deep desire to make a difference on the planet, not in some deep, pretentious way, but on the smallest of levels. She always told Mitch, "You never know, Mitch, what an interaction, even the smallest one, can mean, not only during the moment but down the road. So this is why I try to be thoughtful and aware of each and every situation. Like the Butterfly Effect." The way she said things was one of the reasons Mitch loved her. She was so empathetic and genuine. She kept Mitch grounded, and he loved her for it. His reply, which he replayed over and over in his head through the years, was one born out of trust and a genuineness he had never shown until Mabey came along. He was emotionally safe with her, and he loved her even more for it.

"Wow Mabey, I didn't expect that question. I suppose I should have."

Mabey stared at him, not wanting to give him an out. She could wait through the uncomfortable silence, and Mitch knew it. He also knew his response would set the tone for the rest of their evening and, possibly, their marriage. He took his time. He didn't feel as though his response would be make-or-break for her saying yes or no, but it would say a lot about the strength of their relationship. He rolled the dice and started to speak.

"Why do I want to marry you, you ask? Well, a good question, dear."

"Quit stalling, you big goof-ball, and answer the question if you want to marry me."

"Why? Because of the question you asked."

"What does that mean?"

"Give me a second, okay. You caught me a little off guard. Now sit *there, drink your wine, enjoy your Tiramisu, and let me answer."*

Mabey smiled. A good sign, Mitch thought.

"I could say I want to marry you because you are thoughtful, caring, considerate, intelligent, empathetic, and beautiful. All of which are true, but that's too easy."

Mabey set her wine glass down and nervously spun her fork as she picked at her dessert.

"You don't settle, Mabey. You are deliberate and methodical. You have a vision for what you want your life to be. You want your life-partner, your spouse, to be able to stand on his own."

Mabey smiled and laid her fork down across the plate and leaned towards Mitch with focused intent.

"Keep going, mister."

"When I first met you, I, of course, was mesmerized by your beauty. Mabey chuckled and looked around the restaurant to see if anyone was listening.

"But I quickly got over my shallow thoughts and fell even harder for how beautiful you are on the inside. I've never known anyone who had so much fire and desire for the world to be a better place. Someone so willing to do her part in making a difference without being pretentious. You're the real thing, and I feel better about myself and my situation, not because of you, but because you encourage me to be myself. You want me to be nothing other than what I want and who I think I am. It's so freeing and confidence building; I feel as though the world can be ours for the taking. So, in short, why do I want to marry you? Because you expect more out of life than just a yes or no. You want to know the why behind the yes or no, and I love you for that."

Mitch felt a tear in his eye and took a quick drink of his Malbec to cover up, hoping Mabey couldn't see. Mabey reached over and gently wiped the side of Mitch's face. Mitch's heart fluttered; he swallowed hard.

"A beautiful, unexpected answer, Mitch. I would have said yes no matter what, but I just wanted to see you squirm."

"You little..."

Mabey laughed and said, "I will, Mitch."

Mitch steered the Jeep into a parking spot across the street from the Coffee Shack to avoid all the commotion. He put the vehicle in park and reached over to turn the radio off. He laughed to himself at the lyrics coming out of the speakers. He evidently had selected a song during his flashback, although he didn't remember making the choice or hearing any of it until he parked. He left the key in the ignition and sat back in his seat for the remainder of the song. Bowie blurted out, "Ground control to Major Tom…"

Chapter 31

A Little Crow

Mitch closed the door to the Jeep. He grabbed Mabey's Blackberry from his pocket and stared at it as if he could somehow speak with her. He replayed her last message again, hoping to pick up on some type of clue. Nothing but desperation in her voice. A calm desperation, though. Mabey was not one to panic – another reason he felt she was going to be okay. Mitch started to slide the Blackberry into a back pocket, then changed his mind. He didn't want to carry two phones, so he put Mabey's phone in the Jeep's center console. If Michelle wanted him, she knew to call his phone. Mitch started to cross the street when Jasper pulled up and parked next to him.

"Hell, Wilde, I figured you'd already be inside talking with Jack and figuring out how to teleport across the universe and find that damn pretty wife of yours. You okay?"

"I'm fine, Jasper. Still getting my feet under me, but, yes, I actually feel much better. And, shit, you're right. I completely forgot about that damn teleport thing. I hope I can do it."

Mitch looked across the street and then broke into a light jog, weaving his way in and out of a bunch of men from the town. Some he recognized; most he did not. He entered the Coffee Shack to the familiar cling-cling-cling and let the door close behind him.

There in the middle of the Shack were Jack, Junior, Debbi,

Cindi, Cindi's friend – Mitch couldn't remember her name – and another woman whom Mitch didn't recognize.

Mitch walked up to the group.

"Oh, Mitch, am I glad to see you!"

Debbi spoke first and gave him a hug.

Jack slapped Mitch on the back.

"How you feeling, you log-floating, son of a bitch?"

Jack had a devious smile on his face, and Mitch cringed.

He hoped Jack wouldn't tell everyone how much his manhood shrank while he was tied up in Crater Lake. Not because he felt inadequate, he just didn't have the energy for senseless male banter right now.

"I feel great, now that I have a little silver Alien juice flowing through my veins. Just like you, my brotha. Want to wrestle?"

Mitch smiled and gave Jack a fist bump.

"No shit, Mitch?"

Junior dropped his arm from around Cindi and approached Mitch for a hug.

"Do tell."

"Yes Mitch, do tell."

Both Jack and Cindi said the same thing in near unison.

Cling cling cling signaled another entrant to the Shack. Jasper strode in, planted himself right next to Mitch and joined the group.

"Everyone, this is my neighbor Jasper: the brains behind the group, clearly not the brawn."

Mitch smiled and got a smile back from Jasper. Mitch felt good about the relationship he'd developed with his neighbor. It was nice having an older father figure around. He'd missed his dad ever since he lost him to a heart attack the summer before he left for Portland State University for his freshman year of college. The loss devastated him. He turned down his athletic scholarship and quit football. He had no drive nor determination and mourned for months. Not until he met Mabey halfway through the year did he finally start to get over the loss.

"Jasper, this is Debbi and her daughter Cindi. They have been good friends of Mabey's and mine since Cindi was just a tiny little thing." Mitch at the last second thought he remembered Cindi's friend's name.

"This is Cindi's best friend, Shontey, I believe."

Cindi smiled, happy Mitch remembered and for the feeling she knew it would give Shontey in an inclusive way. Her friend needed support right now.

Jasper reached out and shook Debbi's hand and nodded at both the girls.

"And I'm sorry, but I don't know your name."

Mitch looked over at Delores, a little apprehensively. He didn't feel very trusting right now, but knew if Debbi included her, she was probably okay.

"Oh, everyone, forgive me. This is Delores. She helped Cindi and me with the ladies when they were still here. Then she had sense enough to figure out something was up and get us safely in the back while all the others were taken."

"You're Indian, aren't you, young lady?"

Jasper blurted out the words Mitch wished he could stuff back down his throat. The group tensed at Jasper's vernacular as well as the tone.

Delores stiffened, more for show than anything else and looked Jasper directly in the eye.

"Yes, as a matter of fact, I am. Is there a problem?"

The air stopped moving, and the rotation of the earth slowed ever so slightly in response to the silence.

Mitch piped in quickly.

"It's Native American, I believe, Jasper, not Indian."

"I didn't mean anything by it. I thought she was Indian and said so. I was going to call her Sacajawea, but I was afraid she wouldn't get the humor in it. Getting to where a person can't say anything anymore without consulting Google for the proper language."

Delores reached out and warmly shook Jasper's hand.

"I knew you weren't being offensive, old man; I was just messing with you. But it is better to say Native American these days. Just ask Google."

Everyone laughed. Mitch appreciated Delores handling of the situation and realized she was becoming part of the group. At least on the periphery. Full inclusion would take a little more time. She was off to a good start, though.

Jasper chuckled, gave Delores a big bear hug, and immediately felt a connection. He wasn't used to anyone looking him in the eye and calling him on his mouth, let alone a woman.

Mitch licked his lips realizing they were dry.

"Debbi, I don't suppose a guy could get some water and a bit of iced coffee? This is a damn coffee shop, after all, isn't it? At least it used to be."

"Cindi and Shontey, get everyone some drinks, please." Mitch smiled, winked at Cindi, and then put his arm on Jack's shoulder.

"My brotha and I have some Alien juice coursing through our veins, so if you all don't mind, I'm going to go to one of the booths in back with him and figure out what I have to do to find my wife. You are all welcome to join if you want."

"Finally the love fest is over, and we can get down to some business. I was starting to think, Wilde, that you forgot Mabey was gone."

Mitch tensed, spun and got in Jasper's face. Not as close as he had a day or two earlier with Sheriff Gunther, but close enough to stress his point emphatically.

"Jasper, don't ever say that again! Do you understand me?"

Mitch walked to the back of the Coffee Shack to find a booth.

A new tension filled the air, and Jasper swallowed hard knowing he'd crossed a line. He felt bad.

Jack patted Jasper on the back.

"Don't worry about it, Jasper. Mitch forgives and forgets very quickly. Just come back there with us and help us figure out how to get his wife back."

Jack walked away, and the rest of the group followed. Jasper gathered his pride and spoke to Cindi behind the counter.

"Could I just have a good hot cup of the darkest coffee you have, young lady?"

Cindi came back with what Jasper would later tell everyone was a brilliant response.

"If it will help you swallow a little crow, sir, then yes, you can."

Jasper laughed out loud. He was starting to like this group more and more.

Chapter 32

Robert Myron Gunther

Part 1

Sheriff Robert Myron Gunther pulled his squad car into the crushed cinder driveway and eased it into the carport. His tears of self-loathing had dried. He successfully shifted his focus from hatred of an Outlaw River German Shepherd who had deliberately peed on him back to Mitch Wilde. He felt Wilde and his better-than-everyone attitude had somehow brought on all the strange events plaguing this once quiet little town.

The river and mountains had always guarded Outlaw River and provided a level of isolation. Now that mystique, at least in his mind, had been shattered. The only thing he could think to at the moment was get rid of Wilde. It would make everything better somehow. He could once again enjoy a latte at the local coffee shop, walk through town without everyone snickering at him, and possibly get the Mayor's affection back. Shit, the Mayor was missing. His heart ached, and his stomach felt queasy. He loved the Mayor. Why did he have to get so mad at him and say such hurtful things? Gunther repeatedly slammed his palms with deliberate force on the steering wheel until they were bruised. He sat back and took a deep breath catching himself gag from the odor that permeated his once spotless cruiser. Not only was it banged up, but it smelled like a disgusting dog crate which hadn't been changed in weeks.

Gunther got out of his car and kicked off his shoes, knowing they would go into the trash. He walked with an unusual slow pace as if the dog's urine would somehow fall out of the cotton police slacks if he moved too quickly. He realized this made no sense as the stuff was all but dried, embedded in the strands of fabric. Looking around for neighbors who might be gawking at him, he couldn't see anyone. One thing he liked with everything going on was there was virtually no one in the streets. Perhaps he'd have to rethink wanting things back the way they were. There had been no snickers in over a day. Kind of nice.

Gunther walked stiff-legged toward the back door of his house, stopping short before entering. He unbuckled his holster and hung it from a large hook near the back door, then slid his pants off dropping them near the steps. Next his socks joined the pants in a stomach-turning pile on the concrete slab. Outlaw River's less than finest. He thought briefly about removing his Spiderman boxers, but they hadn't received the damn dog's lemonade so they were worth saving. He opened the door, grabbed the holster off the hook and headed to the shower.

He had to come up with a plan to get rid of Wilde once and for all. Everything going on around the town right now was providing him the perfect opportunity for an 'accident' without raising too many questions. As Gunther stood in the shower, a thought occurred to him. He needed to offer to help Wilde find Mabey. It was the right thing to do under the circumstances. Plus, finding Mabey could lead them to other missing Outlaw River citizens. And it would get him alone with Wilde out in nature where all kinds of crazy things can happen. Robert Myron Gunther smiled and grabbed the soap. It slipped out of his hands, and as he reached down to pick it up, he slipped.

Chapter 33

There is Another Way

Mitch frowned at Jasper when he approached the booth where everyone was gathered. Then he let Jasper's hurtful comments go. He figured the point was made and there was no sense in dwelling on a poorly chosen comment. Hell, he should know, since he was the master of foot-in-mouth disease.

"Jack, Jasper reminded me when we pulled up to the Shack about teleporting. Is that what you call it?"

"Yeah, Mitch, that's what the Native Americans call it. Although I did hear place-jumping as well. Near as I can tell, if you can visualize a place, you can teleport there. You'll feel like shit for a few minutes, but it wears off pretty quickly. The first couple of times I did it, I got pretty queasy, like motion sickness. I don't feel it anymore."

"So teleporting is how you got to Crater Lake and saved me?"

Jasper pulled up a chair and nudged in closer, listening intently.

"Yes, Mitch, correct. For example, if I want to go to the Santa Monica Pier near Los Angeles, I won't be able to. I've seen pictures of it plenty of times, but I've never been there, so no go."

"Well, shit, how much is teleporting going to help then, really? I jabbed myself with an Alien arrow so I can go sightseeing to places I've already been? Shit!"

Mitch lightly pounded his fist on the table. Coffee cups shook.

Debbi reached across the table and put her hand on Mitch's, trying to calm him.

Jack and Jasper stared at each other avoiding eye contact with Mitch. Neither knew what to say. Both realized throwing out some feel-good statement would be a mistake. Junior was sitting next to Mitch, and he began to fidget. Cindi arrived with Shontey from the bar and handed out some drinks and pastries.

"What's wrong, Mom?"

"Nothing, dear, we're just trying to figure out how to locate Mabey."

"What's wrong, Cindi, is your Uncle Mitch jammed an alien arrow into his shoulder so he could teleport himself to his favorite places without taking a plane or boat."

Cindi was sorry she asked. She'd never seen Mitch angry before. It frightened her.

Junior reached out and squeezed her hand, calming her immediately.

Cindi expressed her youthful exuberance.

"We'll find her, Mitch. If I know Mabey, she's probably giving somebody hell right now for messing with her, or she's escaped and is on the run. Mom always said you were the only one who could tame her."

"Cindi, be quiet. Now is not the time."

"Mom, I was just trying to…"

"It's okay, Debbi. She's right, and I can feel it. And thanks, Cindi."

Mitch gave Cindi a big smile. The tension had left the room. Mitch grabbed one of the cups of coffee and made quick work of a chocolate croissant.

"Does anyone have any kind of clue where these Alien fuckers are taking the people? Has anyone talked with Parsons or the men outside to see if they have seen anything? How about the Native Americans, Jack, what can they tell us? They must have shared something with you."

Mitch realized he was rattling on. He grabbed his cup with both hands, steadied it to his mouth, and took a big drink. He probably didn't need the caffeine right now, but he needed to do something.

"Fortunately for you, Mitch, I knew you were at Crater Lake with Jasper on a photo shoot, and I've been there a number of times, so the teleport was easy. You're right, though, we need to figure out where all the people could be and then figure out how to get there. I talked to Parsons, Mitch, while I was waiting for you, and I don't think anyone here has really seen anything. One minute all the ladies were in the coffee shop, and the next, they weren't."

"What did you learn in the pow-wow events you had at your house, Jack."

Mitch looked at the new addition to the group, Delores, and commented.

"My apology if pow-wow is offensive, but I'm not sure what else to call the meetings at Jack's house. Meeting alone doesn't cut it. Pow-wow, at least in my head, paints a different and appropriate picture."

"No offense taken, Mitch." Delores smiled and nodded her head in appreciation for Mitch's acknowledging her potential feelings. She wasn't used to it.

"Mitch, I'm afraid the pow-wows won't be a lot of help. I couldn't understand most of what was being said."

"Why not?"

"They were speaking in a weird language. I don't think it was Native American. I heard one of them make reference to the language of the "star people," whatever the hell star people language is."

"Well, shit, this just gets better and better. So frustrating. Anyone have any ideas?"

Silence. Then Jasper spoke after waiting, listening, and gathering his thoughts.

"Let's find some of the Native Americans and start asking questions, Mitch. Clearly they want to help, so lay it on the line; let them know we have two Alien blood sons-a-bitches in our midst, and we're ready to get to work."

"Jasper, haven't you been listening at all? Jack said all he and I can do is to travel to places we've already been. What good is teleporting if Mabey and the others aren't in any of those places? Besides, even if they were, which place? Are Jack and I supposed to start bouncing around from place to place in hopes of finding them?"

Jasper could hear the frustration in Mitch's voice, but he pressed on.

"I heard everything, Mitch. But sitting here isn't getting anything accomplished."

"That's for sure. I'm willing to walk the streets or drive around, Mitch, whatever it takes."

"Shontey and I will go with you, Mom. After all, her parents are missing as well. Please don't forget."

Everyone nodded in agreement.

Mitch repeated out loud, more of a way of thinking and reflecting than making a statement of something everyone already knew, as if throwing it out would somehow produce a plan he not only agreed with but could support.

"I can travel only to a place I have been before."

Silence filled the space around the table. The Coffee Shack was silent. Jasper shook his head slowly in frustration.

After a solid minute of no one knowing what to say or do,

Delores spoke, producing looks of contemplation and curiosity.

"It's not true, Mitch. And begging your pardon, Jack, but you aren't limited to going to places you have been before. There's another way."

Chapter 34

Robert Myron Gunther

Part II

Gunther grabbed his head feeling where he had hit it on the edge of the tub when he fell. He stared at the blood on his hand, not a lot, just enough to make him queasy. Nice, he thought; not only did his head hurt like hell, but now he felt he was going to vomit. Gunther gathered himself, got to his knees, and turned off the water. It was running luke-warm, almost cold, so he must have been knocked out. He stood and steadied himself against the shower wall.

Moments later he stepped onto the bathroom floor trying to avoid the curtain he had torn off the shower rod. Gunther grabbed his towel and dried off, used a wash cloth to clean the blood smear from around his scalp, then applied hydrogen peroxide. Not too bad, all things considered. He toweled off his hair and decided to forgo the blow dryer today and let it air dry. His dad would have approved.

"How in the hell did I have a faggot for a son? Robert Myron Gunther, you make me sick. You can't even beat out that fucking Wilde kid for quarterback. You're a goddamn embarrassment for me down at the mill." The phrases sounded as if his dad were standing in the hall right outside the door. *"Harold, leave him alone. It's just a hair dryer for God's sake."* The *typical response from his mother returned until she became so numb from the alcohol that all the fight left in her was in the bottom of a bottle.*

Gunther pushed the painful memories aside. He headed to the bedroom for a fresh t-shirt and pressed uniform.

"Shit!"

He had only two clean uniforms left. He'd need to get down to the cleaners to pick up a couple. He had made a mental note to order another one after the car accident and the damn German shepherd encounter.

Gunther dressed and laced up his black patent-leather police shoes. He returned to the bathroom and looked in the mirror. He liked what he saw; nothing like a uniform to make the man. Picking up the shower curtain and holding it at arms' distance over the tub to let the water drip off, he folded it as best he could before going to the kitchen. He put the curtain in a plastic grocery bag and dropped it by the front door.

Gunther directed his attention to the refrigerator. He opened the door and examined the contents, then grabbed a double vanilla protein shake. He chugged the drink and tossed the container into the recycle bin. After taking his vitamins, he surveyed the kitchen. Satisfied with its clean appearance, he grabbed the plastic bag with the shower curtain and headed out the door.

Gunther tossed the bag into the recycle bin, then picked up the dirty uniform, cursed under his breath at the German shepherd, and deposited his expensive uniform inside the trash bin.

"Fuck!"

Gunther lifted the lid on the bin, fished out his filthy sheriff's shirt, and removed his badge. He blew it off, examining it for any spots, and placed it on his clean shirt. He'd make sure it was perfect later. Walking to the cruiser, he decided he would swap it out for one of the deputy's cars. First things first, though. Gunther slid into the driver's seat and grabbed the mic on the police two-way.

"Dispatch, this is Sheriff Gunther. Over."

He waited a couple of seconds and repeated.

"Dispatch, Sheriff Gunther. Come in."

Still nothing but silence. He couldn't remember who was on duty today: Wendy or Sam.

"Wendy, this is Sheriff Gunther. Come in."

Silence.

"Sam, Sheriff Gunther here. You on duty this morning?"

Gunther set the handset beside him on the seat and started the car. He'd go to the office and see what in the hell was going on. He backed the cruiser out of the driveway, checking his rear-view; he saw nothing but the familiar static sights of his neighborhood, strange for the time of day. There were usually a bunch of damn kids roaming around. Gunther put the vehicle in Drive and eased up to the stop sign. He'd stop in the office quickly, see where the hell the staff was, switch out his cruiser, and then head into town to see about helping Outlaw's finest citizen locate his wife. After all, this was what a decent sheriff was supposed to do: help the town citizens.

Chapter 35

Jesus, Joseph, and Mary

"Okay, lass, you can't throw a statement like that around and not follow it up with an explanation." Jasper set down his empty cup. He fixated with deliberate and obvious intent on Delores.

Jack piped in, "I was told by one of the Indians, excuse me, Native Americans, the only way to guarantee a successful passage between dimensions was to go someplace I was very familiar with."

Delores looked over her shoulder toward the front door. Gazing with purpose at each individual around the table, those standing and sitting, she laid out circumstances.

"I think we all understand by now our predicament here, so what I'm about to share with you…" She paused in mid-sentence contemplating how to finish.

"What I'm going to tell you is not heard by anyone outside of Native American circles, hardly ever. With the extenuating circumstances right now, I feel my elders would agree with me in what I'm about to tell you."

"Could you please get to the point, no offense intended, but my wife is missing, this young lady's parents are gone, and the whole FUCKING town is in a shambles."

Mitch's raised voice caught everyone off guard, except for Jasper. He was feeling the same way and was damn glad someone else, in particular Mitch, spoke up.

"I understand your frustration, Mr. Wilde. I very much do. My people, despite the way we have been treated by the U.S. Government over the years, care very much for the residents of this land. I am a star traveler. I was born a star traveler. My grandfather passed on the ability to me. This is a learned skill, like riding a horse or hitting a golf ball. With a lot of practice, it can be mastered."

"Ten thousand hours, Ms. Gladwell?" Jasper threw in the Malcolm Gladwell reference: one, because it fit with what Delores was saying, and two, because he was hoping to impress a few people around the table. Seventy-five years old, and he was still looking for approval.

"Nice reference, old man. Gladwell is one of my favorites." Mitch put his fist out to Jasper for a bump, who smiled big and returned the gesture. Mitch couldn't believe the old guy just fist-bumped him.

"No, not ten thousand hours, more like a lifetime to perfect. However, if you can calm your mind and enter a peaceful transitive state, you can walk back and forth between dimensions with ease. This doesn't mean it will be any easier to locate loved ones, though, I must warn you. It simply means you can travel to more places than just stored memories."

"Then what do we gain, Delores?" Mitch was frustrated, and his voice showed it. He had hoped for a little more than what she shared.

"You gain the peace of mind that you can return from where you came without risk of ending up stuck in another dimension. How would you like to live the rest of your life somewhere else while you watched everything your wife did but had no way to be with her?"

Junior didn't want to sound stupid, but he had to know. He was in safe company, so he let it fly.

"Excuse me, Ma'am, but you said 'star traveler,' right? So you aren't just talking about traveling around earth and different dimensions, are you?"

Nearly everyone sat up or stood straighter at Junior's question.

"Nice, Junior, I wasn't paying close enough attention. All I can think about right now is Mabey and the fact I have no idea what to do."

Silence held the air around the table for only a second.

"Good to know at least one of you is listening." Delores smiled making it clear to the group she was relieved rather than being a critical voice.

"You are correct, young man. I've been traveling among the stars since I was ten years old. My first spiritual journey was with my grandfather to visit my parents who had been taken from me a year earlier."

Jack jumped in with a smile on his face, proud of his son.

"Okay, Star Traveler. At this point I would believe just about anything you told me. So how does this information help us in any way find Mabey and the young lady's parents?"

"In and of itself, this knowledge won't help you find them at all if they are no longer on this planet. However, if they are on earth, in this dimension or the next, you'll be able to locate them more easily. Not easily, mind you, but more easily."

"Jesus, Joseph, and Mary! Am I the only one who wants to gently hit her on the back so she'll spit it all out? I feel like a one-year-old being spoon-fed a meal. Hell with it, I am going down to the Cottage Café for a bite to eat. You can call me when you decide on a plan of action. That is, if you decide."

Jasper rose from his chair. The action forced those standing behind him to move. Mitch agreed with Jasper and was glad his old friend said something.

Cling, cling, cling.

Mitch looked up and sighed when he saw Outlaw River's finest, with a big smile on his face, walk into the coffee shop.

Chapter 36

Unrelenting Force

Part I

The Mayor lifted his head from the creek. Mabey dropped next to him and started gulping water as fast as she could.

"What was that, Mabey?"

The Mayor looked around and stayed close to the ground near Mabey as she continued to drink.

He knew he heard something, and Mabey had too. She was drinking as fast as she could. The Mayor noticed for the first time as he looked down at Mabey's hands that her fingers were bleeding. Not heavy, but enough to turn every one of her fingers a light red. The Mayor started to put a hand down on her shoulder to comfort her when he noticed his fingers were red as well.

Who the fuck shaved their heads and ripped off all their fingernails? And why?

Mabey lifted her head, wiped her mouth, and held a finger to her lips warning the Mayor to be quiet.

Larry nodded.

"BOOM, CRACK, WISP, CRACK, BOOM."

"Come on, Larry; we need to get moving, and now."

Mabey jumped over the creek where her foot found a sharp rock. She grimaced in pain but did not slow. She had no time for inspection as she darted through the woods. The Mayor was going to have to go all out in an effort to stay with her. Mabey fled in a desperate attempt to escape. Larry tried to keep up.

A bright light found its way toward them, and the Mayor felt heat on his back. Damn! Mabey was fast, he thought as he saw a glance backwards from her, almost as if she could somehow will the Mayor to stay with her. Larry pushed on and worked his legs as hard as possible, but it was no use. He tripped; his brain wanted his legs to move faster, but they were incapable. He fell and hit his head hard. Silence and darkness enveloped him.

The light moved over him without pause and focused its beam on Mabey. She desperately pushed forward through the woods thinking of Mitch and how much she loved him. Her feet hurt; her hands felt as though they were appendages she was dragging, useless and withered. A clearing ahead. Perhaps if she could get there and hide in the tall grass, she could lose the light. It seemed to be moving without effort through the tall pines, almost burning her neck, the one part of her body that didn't hurt, until now.

Something pulled at Mabey with unrelenting force. She stopped and turned. In her mind she screamed and ran. Her body stayed still. With her arms thrust upwards, her legs dangled, and blood dripped from the soles of her feet. Her chest pressed forward with a retching motion that bore no sickness. The light began to soothe her mind and comfort her. She surrendered. Thoughts of her Mitch pressed forward from memory one more time as she succumbed to the light.

Chapter 37

All Talk, No Action

Sheriff Gunther stood in front of the coffee shop door and looked over his shoulder. The stillness in the small town was eerie. The well-lit night clouds hanging over Outlaw River seemed to be hiding something. Gunther knew he should be going to the office, calling other local agencies, and checking in on his staff, but first things first. When he saw Wilde's Jeep out in front of the Coffee Shack, he had to stop. This opportunity might not present itself again. Gunther straightened his belt, checked his gig line, and took a deep breath before stepping inside. He walked in with care, closed the door behind him and walked straight back towards Mitch's group with the confidence of someone who would be welcomed.

Jasper noticed the Sheriff enter and rose in preparation for an altercation. Mitch braced himself, fully expecting the sheriff to draw down on him and demand he exit the booth so he could slap handcuffs on him. That was the Sheriff's usual style. All the shit going on in Outlaw River right now, and the Sheriff would have some singular focus on making sure Mitch paid for all of the wrong that life had brought down on him.

"Howdy, all. Glad to see a few of you are left. I hear Mabey Wilde, among others, is missing, and I want to know what I can do to help. You have a plan?"

The entire group looked directly at the Sheriff and stared with mouths agape and heads shaking in disbelief. Jasper looked at Mitch and smiled, trying to get him to take the lead and say something.

Mitch cleared his throat.

"Well, Sheriff, I very much appreciate the offer. I think we're good, though. I'm certain you have more pressing plans since your town is under siege."

The group paused in anticipation of Gunther's reaction.

Mitch saw Gunther's lower lip twitch a little after his polite response. He also saw him take a deliberate controlled breath. He assumed the Sheriff was not happy and was working hard to hide it. In typical Gunther fashion, it was all about appearance, only appearing to care when in fact Wilde knew damn good and well there was an ulterior motive in play.

"Of course, I do need to get over to the station. I'll check on my staff and see if I can figure out what's going on around the region, but this isn't just about Mabey. The Mayor is gone too and plenty of other Outlaw River citizens.

"My parents were taken, Sheriff."

Shontey said the words, but she wasn't sure if they could be heard.

"See, Wilde. This young lady's folks have been taken as well. And since you're all just sitting around drinking coffee and eating pastries, I figured you'd appreciate someone in authority helping out and coming up with a plan."

"Oh shit," Jasper quietly said. He later admitted to Wilde that he agreed with Gunther's statement, but he'd also say it wasn't the proper way to say it.

Mitch stood as best he could in the cramped booth. Debbi was sitting alongside him, the only thing keeping him from going after the Sheriff.

Jack, across from Mitch, stood as soon as he heard Gunther's comment and put his right hand out, pressing it firmly against Mitch's chest.

147

"Save your energy for Mabey, Mitch. It isn't worth it right now."

"I could deck him and then teleport out of here, Jack. Come on, just one good pop to the face. I'm sure no one in this group would back him up in court."

Debbi, feeling Mitch's energy increase, reached across her body with her right hand and put it on Mitch's shoulder.

"Back down, big guy. You aren't going to be any help to Mabey if you're locked up in a cell."

Gunther, sensing a new and unexpected opportunity, jumped in with full force.

"Wilde, you may have gotten away with a sucker punch on me in school, but there's no way I would ever let it happen again. You're all talk with no action and have everyone in this town fooled. A real shame Mabey made the mistake of marrying your prima-donna ass. Look where it got her. Missing and probably alone and afraid, wishing like hell she had someone who actually cared enough about her to look for her instead of drinking coffee with friends. I just don't get you…."

Mitch pushed Jack's arm down with focused intensity. He leapt across the table toward the Sheriff. Jasper, knowing what was coming, took a step back clearing the path towards Gunther for Wilde. The rest of the group moved back a couple of steps in reaction to the surprise.

Mitch slipped on the edge of the table as empty coffee cups and crumb-filled plates crashed to the floor. Gunther took a step back. He couldn't decide if he was happy with what he said, or if he was going to regret it. He braced for the worse.

Jack tried to push Junior out of the way and get out of the booth himself, but Junior resisted, holding his dad back. J.J. wanted Mitch to cut loose on the Sheriff. All he could think about was his mother; if anyone talked that way about her in front of his dad, he would do the same thing.

Mitch scrambled to his feet. Gunther's step back was a mistake – another serious one for the sheriff during the last couple of days. Mitch used his left to come up hard into the sheriff's stomach. The Sheriff's memory flashed back to high school and the football field. He knew what was next and was helpless to do anything about it.

Mitch cocked his right arm and unloaded across the sheriff's jaw. Jasper thought he heard bone crack. The force of the punch stood Gunther upright for a split second after being crouched from the gut punch. Mitch cocked his right again, but Jack managed to get out from behind Junior and grabbed Mitch around the chest.

Sheriff Gunther's eyes fluttered back in his head. His knees buckled, and he fell face down on the hardwood floor. He remained conscious somehow, but his recent tangle with his shower, along with Wilde's brief melee made him unable to move. He tried to get up, but his body couldn't respond. Out of the corner of his eye he saw Wilde standing over him.

"If I ever hear you say another derogatory thing about me or Mabey, Sheriff Gunther, I won't stop at two punches. Stay down if you understand."

Jasper smiled, Jack relaxed, Junior beamed, and Cindi and Shontey clapped.

Mitch turned with slow deliberation and eyed each of the group.

"Did any of you see anything here? It appears the Sheriff has fallen and hit his head on one of the chairs. I hope he's going to be okay."

Junior piped up first.

"It was like he tripped or something, Mitch, lost his balance as he was walking in."

Cindi smiled and joined in.

"I noticed he had some dried blood on his forehead. Probably from the little fender bender he had earlier. Should we get him to the doc's office?"

Jasper knelt down and rolled the Sheriff over. He looked into his eyes and saw they were still responsive. The Sheriff made an effort to sit up but collapsed on the floor. Blood trickled from the corner of his mouth. A small tear pushed its way out of the corner of an eye.

"He'll be fine. He's going to be sore for a while, but he'll be fine."

Delores, amazed at everything going on, dropped next to Jasper and the Sheriff.

"I have some EMT experience. Let me look at him."

Delores checked his eyes, and put her head down next to his chest to listen.

"His heart is racing, but that's from the adrenaline rush."

She grabbed his wrist and felt for his pulse.

"His heart rate's coming back down. Could someone get me a rag and some water, please?"

Debbi hurried back to the kitchen and returned with both, handing them to Delores.

Mitch sighed with relief. His anger had gotten the better of him, which under the circumstances he felt was warranted. As much as he despised the Sheriff's antics and attitude, he didn't wish harm on the man, at least not healthwise.

"Thanks, Jack, for stepping in. And thank you, Junior, for not." Mitch looked at Junior, and they both smiled.

"And, Jasper, thank you for clearing the path. I would have hated to have gone through you to do what I needed to do."

"Don't mention it, Mohammed Ali. Nice to see you get some fire in your belly at last. I was starting to get more than a little worried about you."

Mitch walked toward the front door.

"I'm going to find Mabey."

Chapter 38

Unrelenting Force

Part II

Larry gathered himself and rose to his feet with methodical deliberation and intense pain. The moonlight bathed the side of his face. He felt his head and found blood, dirt, and dried tears. He dropped, fell flat on his back, and stared skyward into the billowing darkness which was unable to hide the towering pines. He felt his chest and extremities: all appeared to be normal albeit sore as hell.

Larry called out, "Mabey! Mabey! Are you there? Mabey!"

He knew the weak attempt would illicit no response. He tried anyway with a small flicker of hope. Perhaps his fucking head was not aware of everything going on around him. One flashing memory after another carried the same result: Mabey had been pulled into a light while he lay helpless on a bed of pine needles.

The Mayor rose to his knees. He stayed there while his ears and eyes surveyed their surroundings. Water noise, running in the distance, pushed through his mind with the memory of tranquility. He rose to his feet and saw he was still in the dense woods. A thick woods generously offering up her protection.

He mumbled to himself. "What the hell is going on?" Larry knew he was on borrowed time. He needed to get help, but where was help, and who exactly could help?

He trudged back toward the creek where earlier he and Mabey had drank and deliberated about their next move. Mabey told him they needed to follow the creek downstream as Mitch had always encouraged her if she ever got lost. He always said, "Good things happen when you go downstream."

Larry didn't know shit about the outdoors except that the constituents of his little po-dunk town thrived on it. Hell, he was scared of the woods. Nothing good in there, only spiders, bears, and nasty, disgusting bad men. Out of habit he checked his wrist for his watch. Nothing but a beat up and raw wrist. His feet hurt like hell, and his fingertips were starting to regain feeling as if a thousand needles stabbed each one at the same time. If Mitch Wilde said a person should always "go downstream," then so be it. He would head downstream.

Something about the air pushing through the pines emitted a sense of calm. The night's moon provided the perfect amount of light so he could see where he was heading. He made his way back to the creek, dropped to his torn up knees, and drank as much as he could. The Mayor wiped his chin, looked upstream, and then down. He heard a chipmunk chirp, but his eyes couldn't find it. He turned and moved with heavy feet further downstream. A bird of prey screeched overhead, and the wind moved with effortless grace through the trees. The Mayor knew he needed to find help, Mitch Wilde preferably, and fast, if Mabey was going to be rescued. He had no idea how long ago she'd been taken, but it had to be hours at the very least.

With considerable pain and effort, the Mayor continued walking. He stopped and shook his legs one at a time. He tried to remove as many pine needles as possible before he began to jog down the deer path next to the creek; sore and bloody feet be damned. Mabey Wilde had helped him condition his body and trained it for endurance. He was not going to let her down.

Chapter 39

Your Little Sensation

Mitch exited the Coffee Shack and took a deep breath of fresh Oregon air. He strolled toward his Jeep deciding on the next move. No one knew where anyone had been taken. He was guessing, and felt confident about it, that a large number of people being transported against their will would have to be covert. This meant back roads and not the Interstate. The back roads led up to the mountains and, in a very long roundabout way, could lead to Crater Lake, the most likely avenue for transport and escape.

The problem was the near infinite options all those back highways, fire roads, and dirt roads provided. There were miles and miles of trails as well, although Mitch figured they wouldn't make as much sense with the large number of people taken.

Mitch stopped at the back of Black Steel and put his right foot up on the rear wheel. He tilted his head back and sighed, searching for an idea of some kind. At the sound of a familiar voice, Mitch dropped his foot and turned to see Jasper walking up with Jack.

Mitch spoke as the two approached.

"Is he coming around?"

"Yes, panty-waist, he is, and not to worry, your dear friend will be fine. He'll hate you more than ever now and probably invent a reason to lock up your ass, but not for a while. The young Indian lady is taking care of him now."

Jack smiled, stopped next to Mitch, and put his hand on his friend's shoulder.

"Any ideas? If not, I think we should start working our way up the back roads out of town and into the mountains. I have a feeling the Aliens will avoid the freeway at all costs. Much easier to hide in the hills than rolling down the freeway."

"You think so, Jack? I was just thinking the same thing. I don't have my normal intuition going on. I sense Mabey is okay, but where she is, I have no fucking clue."

Jasper looked at the two and spoke with deliberation. Mitch could tell the old guy was taking great care with his words.

"Look, you two. I don't have all the answers here, and I think you're both correct about the direction they would have taken. What we need to figure out is what the hell to do about your warp travel, or whatever the hell it is. Jack, you had some meetings with the Native Americans at your house. What the hell was going on?"

Mitch jumped in. "Shit, that's right, Jack. What the hell? I can't believe I forgot."

"Don't get too excited, Mitch. I don't know shit about what was going on."

"Nothing?" Old man Jasper asked with some hesitation in his voice.

"No, guys. Not a damn thing. Believe me, I wish I did. All I remember is some Native Americans showing up at my door and telling me something about my home having great magnetic properties and they would be needing it for a gathering. Then I was asked to take some fucking pill that would calm me and allow me to see the strange events that were going to take place."

Jasper leaned back against his Jeep and crossed his arms before he spoke.

"Strange events. Like when you had the Alien pow-wow in your living room?"

Mitch laughed. Jack and Jasper both stared at him.

"Sorry, guys, but I can't believe this shit. We're actually standing here talking about Aliens and Native Americans. I couldn't make up this shit if someone put a gun to my head."

The three heard a cling noise and looked up to see the entourage coming out of the Coffee Shack and crossing the street towards them.

Mitch spoke first.

"Where's Gunther? Is he okay?"

Jasper was a little moved. He could tell Mitch genuinely cared about the Sheriff. He could hear it in his voice, see it in his body language and eyes.

Debbi, leading the group, responded.

"He's going to be fine, Mitch. I think he also had a shot to his head from the car accident. Delores here says he has bruising on his scalp and a re-opened cut that you didn't cause."

Delores jumped in.

"Clearly something happened to him in the car wreck. He hit his head pretty hard. He's up and conscious. He doesn't remember anything though. He kept mumbling something about the Mayor and his tub."

Mitch's mind wandered with the last statement to a place he wished it hadn't. He looked at Jasper, and both men smiled. Mitch responded.

"Okay, everyone. The Sheriff, the Mayor, and a bathtub. Not a mental picture I wish to have in my head."

The group laughed and turned in unison as Sheriff Gunther walked out of the Coffee Shack. He crossed the street and headed for the group. Mitch stood straighter, and Jasper got up from his leaning stance against his Jeep. Jack moved a little, putting himself between Mitch and the approaching Sheriff.

"What's so funny, everyone? Why're you all standing out here?"

Mitch felt the Sheriff was acting as if nothing had happened.

Junior responded first. "Nothing really, Sheriff. Jasper and Mitch were calling each other names, and I think we're a bit slap happy from all the stress."

"Okay. Listen, everyone. Oh, and thanks for the aspirin, iced coffee and Danish, Debbi. I appreciate it. I can't remember the last time I ate. Other than my head being sore, I think I feel a bit better. What were we all doing in there anyway?"

"Strategizing, Gunther. Trying to figure out what the hell to do next." Mitch relaxed his posture and kept a calm voice.

"Since you asked, Gunther, do you have any idea where the people have been taken? Any chatter on your police radio?"

The Sheriff, standing next to Debbi, responded after putting a hand up to his forehead, feeling for what Mitch could only assume was blood.

"You know something else to mark down as weird? I'm not hearing anything on the radio. I need to get over to the office and see what's going on. I can't get hold of any of my deputies. What are all of you going to do?"

Mitch stepped forward.

"Jack, Jasper, and I are going to Jasper's place to come up with a strategy. Delores, I would like you to come with us. Debbi, I think you, the girls and Junior should go to the Wilde's house and stay put. You guys will be safe there. I would recommend everyone stay indoors."

Mitch looked around, not expecting anyone to argue, but he was prepared for dissent.

"Damn good plan, Wilde. How does everyone get there? I can take a few in my Jeep if necessary," Jasper said.

Jack looked at Junior and handed him some keys. "Ace, you take the women in my truck. Debbi, why don't you ride with him too? There's enough room for all of you."

What about my car, Dad? I don't want to leave it down here."

"Oh, right."

Debbi chimed in. "I have my car here as well, but I don't mind leaving it. It should be okay at the Shack."

"Okay, Ace. Take your car then. I'm going to move my truck to the side of the building next to your car, Debbi. I think it might be a good idea to have a vehicle or two in town in case we need them." Jack jogged down the block toward his Ford pickup.

"I'll be right back, Mitch. Don't leave without me."

Sheriff Gunther spoke up. "Okay, you all sound as if you have this under control. I'm going to my office to see if I can figure out some things on my end."

With that, the Sheriff walked toward his cruiser, repeatedly putting his hand to his forehead.

Mitch sighed with relief at the Sheriff's departure.

"All right, I'll stay here and wait with Jack. Delores, if you don't mind, could you ride with Jasper, and we'll meet at his place. Junior, like your dad said, you take the women to my place in your car. Maybe's sister Michelle is there, and she knows all of you. I'm sure she'll appreciate the company. You all make yourselves at home. Whatever you need, help yourselves."

Debbi gave Mitch a hug and thanked him. "Keep us posted as best you can, okay? We're worried about Mabey too.

Shontey stepped forward. "Mr. Wilde, can you find my parents too? Their names are Kala and Aaron."

"Absolutely. I think it's pretty safe to assume they're probably in the same place. I'll make sure we find as many people as possible and keep them safe. Your parents are top on my list with my wife, okay?" Mitch, sensing Shontey's intense worry, grabbed her, gave her a hug and whispered in her ear.

"Don't you fret. I'll move mountains to find my wife, and I'm sure they're all together."

Shontey teared up, and Mitch let her go.

"Thank you, Mr. Wilde."

"Okay, Debbi. You and the group get out of here and to the house. My recommendation for now, Debbi, is not to let anyone in the house unless you know them and feel it's okay. Any doubts at all, just don't answer the door. Michelle knows where my extra guns are in the safe upstairs and in the shed in back, should you need them."

Debbi said, "Got it, Mitch, and thanks." She then looked at Junior. "I'm going to get my purse from the Shack and lock up. I'll meet you and the girls at the car in a minute."

"Okay, Mrs. Howard, sounds good. C'mon, Shontey and Cindi." Junior grabbed Cindi's hand, and the three of them headed toward his car.

Jasper nodded to Delores. "Looks like you're stuck with me, young lady. This is my ride here. Hop in, and tell me why it isn't okay to say Indians anymore, will you please?"

Delores smiled, moved around the front of Jasper's Jeep, and climbed in on the passenger's side.

Mitch cringed and shook his head. "Jasper, you're worse than I am."

"What, Wilde, I'm genuinely curious. And who better to ask than a real live Native American?"

Mitch watched as Jasper got in and drove toward his home. He looked down the empty street. Then he looked across the street as he saw Jack pull in and park next to Debbi's car. He watched Junior and the girls get in the Mustang. Debbi exited a second later from the Coffee Shack, locked the door and walked toward the kids, waving at Mitch.

Mitch got in his Jeep and felt an odd sensation in his head. He looked in the rear-view mirror as if seeing himself would provide some answers. He couldn't believe how disheveled and filthy his hair was. He couldn't even remember the last time he bathed. His head swirled again, as if his brain were on a merry-go-round. The passenger door opened, and Jack stepped into Black Steel and buckled up.

"What's wrong, Mitch? You look as if you just got laid for the first time."

"I am not sure, Jack. Some strange feelings in my head, like my brain is twisting; I can't explain it."

"Shit, Mitch. Not good. Get out of here. Now! Your little sensation means they're near us."

Jack looked through the windows and crouched, trying to gain more visibility of the night sky. Mitch turned the key, started the Jeep, chirped the tires, and headed for Jasper's.

Chapter 40

Don't Bother

Mabey rolled over, opening her eyes to clear sky and tasting a mouthful of dirt. She gathered what little strength she had and raised herself to her hands and knees. She focused on breathing and worked at clearing the dizziness from her head. She spit out the dirt and started retching. Nothing came out. She could not remember the last time she ate. The little bit of water she got from the creek had already been absorbed into her body. She didn't think she was near dehydration, but she was very thirsty.

Mabey heard a voice and felt a comforting hand on her back. She shook her head with caution. She allowed her eyes to focus on the surroundings: she saw a bunch of bare feet, all filthy, and clothes the same as hers. None of the feet had any toenails, and most of them were cut up and bleeding.

"My name is Kala Williams. You're going to be okay in a minute. Check that, you will feel a bit better in a minute. None of us are okay."

Mabey, with Kala's assistance, rose to her feet. She looked more closely at her surroundings, and she could see there were approximately a hundred people in a tight circle of sorts. They were in a clearing surrounded by dense pines. There didn't appear to be any walls, but the people, young and old and nearly all female, huddled in the center of the area. Mabey was on the edge of the group. Kala held her by the elbow and continued to keep a hand on her back.

Mabey's feet hurt with a deep pain that made it difficult to stand. She remained upright out of sheer force of will.

"Why is everyone standing around in a circle? Why don't we get out of here?"

Kala looked around, motioned to a man to come over, and asked him to help her hold Mabey up.

"This is my husband Aaron. We can't walk away because there is some type of force field keeping us in. If you try to walk out, you get zapped, like one of those bug zappers, and it stuns you. Several have tried. Fortunately, everyone recovers, but no one has been able to get out."

"Hi, Aaron, my name is Mabey, Mabey Wilde. Thank you two for helping me. I'm starting to feel a little better. I think you can let go of my arm now."

Kala dropped her left hand from Mabey's elbow but kept her right hand on her back for a few more seconds just to be sure.

Mabey put her hands on her waist and concentrated on her breaths, similar to her actions after running a marathon. She couldn't believe she was taken again. She was so disappointed in herself. She wanted to find Mitch and tell her story of escape. She knew he would be impressed and proud.

"Mabey Wilde, huh? Do you know someone named Cindi Howard?"

"Yes, I do," Mabey replied to Kala.

"She's my daughter's best friend, and I've heard her talk about someone named Mabey. I figured it must be you since it's an uncommon name, and Outlaw River is so small."

A loud pop and thwack rang out, and Mabey saw a blue flash. Someone had tried to throw a rock through the barrier to no avail. It bounced back and landed with a thud.

"Cindi's mom, Debbi, and I've been friends for a long time. Cindi's like a daughter to me and my husband Mitch. It's nice to meet you both, and thanks again for being so kind. Where's Shontey?"

Aaron took his focus away from the rock, which was unable to penetrate the force field, and looked at Mabey.

"We told her to hide at home when we were being taken. We can only assume they didn't find her and she's okay."

Kala jumped in.

"She's okay, Aaron; I can feel it."

"I'm glad you say that, Kala. You've always been so in tune with her."

"So you two were taken right out of your home? Did you see who took you?"

"No, we heard something outside when some sort of gas started filling our house. Shontey was downstairs, so I yelled at her to hide. Next thing I know, Kala and I are on some bus driven by a human vegetable. Neither of us has any hair or nails, and we're in these gray jumpsuits, which by the way are creeping up my ass."

Mabey laughed a little laugh.

"Aaron, must you always joke? Now is not the time. And you never had any hair anyway, so what do you care?"

"I thought it was funny, Kala, and laughter helps. I feel for you, though, because my Mitch is a smart-ass and never knows when to quit. But I must admit, more often than not, his humor helps me. So, Aaron, please don't stop trying to be funny. It will help us keep our wits about us so we don't panic."

Mabey walked to the edge of the circle. She could see the grass pressed down. She assumed this was the edge of the barrier. She picked up a small rock up and flipped it underhand at the air. It snapped and bounced back towards her.

"You won't get a rock through there, Mabey." Aaron sounded more than a little frustrated.

"I'm sorry; I don't mean to sound rude, but we've all tried. Nothing gets through there. The guy over there, the big one on the ground, tried to run through. He's just now starting to recover.

Mabey paced back and forth listening to Aaron speaking. She

heard him, but she wasn't paying close attention. She was focused on solving a problem right now. Looking around the meadow, she saw what appeared to be a dozen or so similar pens. All looked to be filled with the same number of people as the one she was currently trapped in.

"Like I said, we've tried everything, and we can't get through."

Mabey picked up another rock and flipped it upwards from the palm of her hand. She watched with intensity as gravity pulled it back down. She repeated the effort while she thought of Junior Jenson. She wondered if he were here, could he throw the rock hard enough to penetrate the barrier? She guessed not.

"Don't bother throwing the rock, Mabey; it won't get through."

"Aaron, quit bugging her. She knows already."

"Well, I don't want to see the thing bounce back and peg her in the head as it did me. The damn thing hurt."

Mabey flipped the rock one more time and caught it. She took a step back and threw it as high as she could in an arc. Kala and Aaron, plus a number of others in the group who'd started paying attention to Mabey's pacing, watched as the rock flew up, out, and over the invisible barrier hitting the dirt outside their prison. No cracking, no popping, and no sizzle. The rock made it out without incident.

Mabey turned and forced a painful smile.

"It appears, Aaron, you all didn't try everything."

Chapter 41

A Magnificent Rider

Mitch pulled up to Jasper's home and hopped out. He noticed Jasper hadn't put his own Jeep away behind the gate, something he always did. This inaction reinforced in Mitch's mind just how strange things had become. He looked into the sky and felt the glowing moon was hiding something. He trusted almost nothing right now. Mitch crouched to the ground on one knee and straightened the shoe tongue on his left hiking boot and pulled the laces tight. Then he switched to the other knee and repeated the previous action. He stood and adjusted his belt in an effort to straighten his pants. The Levi's were starting to look filthy, but he didn't care. He wondered why in the hell he was thinking about dirty pants and a sneaky moon while his wife was missing.

Jack noticed the wondering look in his friend's eyes.

"Mitch. What the hell? You feel the swirling again?"

"No, Jack, just thinking. Would you mind going over to my house and making sure everyone's okay over there before joining us inside? Just knock on the side door when you get back."

"Good idea, bro. I'll be back in five minutes. Don't start without me, okay?"

"We won't. Knowing Jasper, he has a bunch of theories he's

running by Delores right now, grilling her and showing her all his amazing finds from the last ten years. Hurry up, though. I want to get going before we run out of time."

Mitch moved his neck from side to side, trying to pop it. The swirling in his head was gone for the moment. He watched Jack cross the street, then turned to enter Jasper's lair. He had just reached the door when he heard a familiar sound, the same one from a couple of days ago at the annual summer cookout. He wondered briefly if he had heard anything at all. He reached for the doorknob when he heard the damn noise again. This time, much louder and distinct. When Mitch turned with trepidation, he wasn't at all surprised to see the striking Native American in full regalia sitting atop the massive white horse reminding Mitch, yet again, of Gandalf's horse, Shadowfax. Mitch walked directly to the visitor and stopped a few feet from the magnificent pair.

The visitor spoke in a deep melodic voice.

"Mitch Wilde. You need to come with me now."

Chapter 42

Smarty-Pants

Aaron stood with his mouth open. Kala chuckled, gave Mabey a high five, and said, "You go, girl! That's what I'm talking about."

Mabey forced a smile and realized Kala exaggerated her language from excitement and hope.

"I couldn't just stand around and wait for the men to do something. A woman has to take the lead sometimes. Right? The world wouldn't be in such a mess if we worried less about the damn male ego and started running things the right way."

Kala laughed, and Aaron got a big smile on his face before talking.

"Okay, so now what, smarty pants? Are you able to jump like Hulk and get us out of here?"

"She figured out something none of the rest of us did, Aaron. Why don't you figure out what to do about it now? Do we women have to do everything?"

Mabey kicked at the dirt. She looked around to see if her rock-throwing stunt had attracted any attention.

"Aaron or Kala, have any of you seen anyone outside?"

Aaron spoke up. "Not one. Once in a while, though, a small craft or drone shows up and drops someone off as it did with you, but we haven't seen anybody – human being, Alien, whatever."

Mabey paced, looking at the ground. She started mentally

counting bodies figuring there were sixty or seventy people in their outdoor cell.

Mabey stopped and directed her words to Kala and Aaron knowing the others would here as well

"I think we should do something drastic and see if we can get one of us out of here."

Mabey bent over and started picking up rocks while talking.

"Let's all grab some rocks and see if we can figure out how high this barrier is. I have an idea."

Chapter 43

No Shit, Einstein

Jack knocked on Old Man Jasper's door at the side of the garage. He chuckled, thinking about Mitch's always calling it the Old Man's Sci-Fi lair. The door flew open. Jack saw Jasper standing inside with a remote of some kind.

"Come in. Glad to see you could make it. Where the hell is Wilde? Across the street at his house checking on everyone?"

"What are you talking about, Jasper? I just came from there doing that very thing. Mitch asked me to and said he would meet me inside your place."

Jack stepped inside. Jasper closed the door behind him and locked it. In an instant Jack saw what Mitch had been referring to when he described Jasper's place. There were computers and monitors all over the place. Every monitor was lit up, and they all appeared to be showing something different. There were large maps on the walls and some on tables with highlighter markings covering them. Jack noticed no actual garage door even though from the outside one was visible. There were no windows.

Delores was sitting at one of the computers staring at a video of what looked, on first glance, to be a volcano erupting. She nodded, acknowledging his presence.

Jasper turned from locking the door and planted himself directly in front of Jack.

"You say Mitch was coming in here while you went over to check on the kids?"

"That's what I said."

"He never came in. Delores and I have been here the whole time."

"I was gone only about five minutes, and he didn't come over to his house. What the hell?"

Jack unlocked the door and stepped outside. He called out Mitch's name, instinctively knowing he would get no response. He walked around to the front and called his friend's name again and again.

Jasper watched from the side door as Jack jogged across the street to Mitch's house. Jack entered the house leaving the door open. Seconds later, Jack returned, closed the door behind him, and jogged back across the street to Jasper.

"No one over there has seen him. What the hell, Jasper? It isn't like Mitch to take off without saying something."

"Do you think, pretty boy, your buddy black-hole jumped somewhere?"

"I suppose, but I'm not sure he really knows how to do it."

"Didn't you say if he was thinking of someplace strongly enough, it could happen?"

Jack hesitated before responding.

"Well, yes, but again, it's not like Mitch just to take off. Shit!"

"Don't get your panties in a bunch, Jack-be-nimble. Get in here."

Jasper guided him back into his house, closed the door, and again locked it.

"Come over here with me. Let's check my video footage."

Jasper went to a computer next to Delores and sat down. He pulled up some software and changed windows on his screen. Now they were all looking at the two Jeeps in front of Jasper's place.

"Shit, Jasper, he couldn't have gone far. His Jeep is still here. Seeing it out front didn't even cross my mind until now."

Jasper gave Jack a look of surprise, disappointed in himself for not realizing this fact on his own.

"That's right, Jack. Let's rewind and see if we can see anything."

Jasper clicked the rewind icon, and the screen blurred. Jasper stopped when he felt the time was right. The three of them – Delores now looked over their shoulders – stared hard and saw Jasper and Delores climb out of Jasper's Jeep and come inside. Jasper fast forwarded and stopped again. The monitor showed Jack and Mitch pull up in Mitch's Jeep and park.

"Hey, that's us, Jasper. Stop right there."

Jasper gave Jack a 'no shit, Einstein' look and turned back to the monitor. Jasper forwarded the video until he saw Jack take off across the street to Mitch's house. He clicked on the play icon, going back to regular mode.

All three watched as Mitch headed to the side of the garage. Jasper changed to the camera angle over the door where Mitch stopped for several seconds.

Jack spoke first.

"Look, Mitch froze as if he saw something."

Jasper nodded and continued watching the monitor. Mitch reached again for the door before reversing and walking back toward the street. Jasper changed to a different camera angle again, and Delores said, "shit", under her breath.

"Oh, my God! Do you guys see what I see?"

"Yes, young lady, of course we do."

Jasper wanted to let out another smart-ass comment but held his tongue for once. He knew her statement was more of a reflexive expression than a deliberate thought. He was more concerned about her quietly saying, 'shit'.

All three watched as the magnificent horse stood with its

Kachina-clad rider who spoke with Mitch. The looming figure reached down and grabbed Mitch's hand. With what appeared to be no effort, Mitch was flung upwards to sit behind the Native American rider. The horse raised its head and, at the pat of a hand from its commander, disappeared.

Chapter 44

No Pharaoh's Pyramid

Mabey, Kala, Aaron and a few others stood next to each other in their temporary holding cell.

Mabey rubbed her bald head and took a breath. Standing in front of the group, she directed traffic and barked out orders.

"Okay, Kala, you throw first. Everyone pick a landmark, like a tree, something stationary and large if possible. When Kala starts throwing the rocks, let's see if we can figure out the height of the barrier. If we can get a good estimate, I have an idea for how we can get over it."

Mabey stepped aside and Kala threw her first rock. Zap! She threw the next one a little harder and exacted the same effect as it hit the force field. She reared back again and fired another one as hard as she could. This one cleared the shield. She threw her last two as hard as she could, and they landed on the other side.

"Sorry, Mabey."

"Why? That was great!"

Mabey turned to the group.

"Okay, everyone, starting with you, Aaron, how high do you think the barrier is?"

Aaron pointed to the marker he had chosen: a tall pine tree well outside their circle.

"If I had to guess Mabey, and I suppose I do, I would say it's about thirty feet."

"Thanks Aaron. Okay, group, let's all use the spot Aaron picked and watch again as he throws."

Mabey turned towards Aaron and looked into his eyes.

"Aaron, throw as high as you can and work downwards decreasing the effort so we can try to better gauge the height, okay?"

"Got it, Mabey. Step aside, please."

Aaron thought back to his Little League baseball days and wondered, as he always did when baseball was mentioned, if he'd had a better childhood and more supportive parents, could he have played ball in college and then the pros?

He gripped the first rock and threw it, easily clearing the barrier. He took a little off the next throw and still cleared it. He took a bit more off the next one and cleared it still. On the next attempt, he got the familiar zap sound they all recognized.

"I'm out of rocks, Mabey."

Mabey handed him one of her few remaining stones.

"Aaron, let loose again. Try to throw this one higher than last time."

Aaron took the rock, reared back, and fired with increased effort over his previous throw. The rock cleared the force field.

Mabey looked at the group.

"Okay, did you all get a good idea of how high this damn thing is?"

The group discussed the matter, and Aaron did some calculations based on the tree marker he'd selected. The conclusion was the barrier was roughly 20- to 25-feet high.

Kala stepped forward and brushed her hands against each other to get some of the dirt off.

"Okay, now what, Mabey? We have an idea of the height, but how do we get over it?"

173

Mabey was counting the number of people in their holding cell. She got to 45 and stopped. More than enough, she figured. The entire collective was now standing around the group and looked to Mabey for direction.

Mabey raised her chin and with a strong, clear voice said, "okay, people, we need to hurry. Let's build a pyramid."

Chapter 45

What Did I Miss?

Jasper and Jack watched the video over and over. Jasper paid close attention to see if he could gain any information from it. Nothing jumped out at him or lurked in the periphery of the action. Jack just stared, mesmerized by the horse.

"Damn, Jasper. I never teleported like that. On the back of a horse. God, what a beautiful animal! You see how big that thing is? Made Mitch look like a child. Looked as if it could fit another two men up there."

Jasper peeled his eyes from the monitor and looked over his shoulder at Jack. They locked eyes, and Jasper lowered his chin. His eyes stayed upwards with a sarcastic stare pleading with Jack.

"Dang, motor-mouth. Take a seat and relax. Mitch is gone, yes, but from the looks of this video, not against his will. The good news: Mitch is probably closer to figuring out where Mabey is now. The bad news: what the hell can we do without him?"

Jasper sat back in his chair after his last statement and put both hands on his forehead. He crossed his calloused fingers in a locking position.

"And should we do anything?" Jasper asked.

Jack started pacing.

"I don't think waiting and playing it safe is the answer, Jack.

What if the Aliens are waiting to make another sweep or two through town and come for us? I for one don't want to be sittin' here with my dick in my hand hoping for the best. Excuse me, young lady, for the reference to my rather large…"

"Geezus, Jasper, really?" Jack cut him off before the old guy could finish the sentence. They all knew how it was going to end anyway.

Delores, who had been studying Jasper's maps, charts, photographs, and everything else she could get her hands on, burst out laughing.

Jasper smiled. "I love when a woman has a sense of humor. So, young lady, what do you think about my rather large…"

"…. amount of information you have on display here, Jasper?" Delores finished the sentence and smiled at Jasper. She appreciated the flirting even if it was from someone so not her type.

Jasper had a large grin on his face while replying.

"Exactly. I have been compiling it for at least half of my lifetime."

"Jasper, where's your restroom?" Jack had been pacing for a while, and he could wait no longer.

"Go through the door and down the hall, first door on the left."

"I'll be right back."

"So, Jasper, from what I can gather and what I know already, you have a good handle on what's going on, and I'd be willing to make a small wager you know what's going on in your little town. How close am I to guessing?" Delores locked her eyes on Jasper: a direct stare straight into his eyes. Not the kind where you look at someone and then stare at their nose or forehead, too timid to make direct eye contact.

Jasper paused a moment and looked into Delores's eyes. He sized her up and realized how much he liked this woman. She was tough, direct, and no doubt could handle herself. He sensed she was loyal as well. Not one to run off with another man looking for a way to escape her own self-doubt and fear. His cheating, heart-breaking wife popped into his memory, just for a second. He shoved the memory away and focused on the task at hand.

"I haven't been able to piece everything together, young lady, but I have many suspicions, several of which have proven to be correct lately."

Jack walked back in and pulled up a chair next to Delores.

"So what'd I miss, you two?"

"Not much, Jack. Jasper was just about to tell me he knows the Aliens really aren't Aliens. At least not in the sense we all think."

"They're not? What in the hell are you talking about?" Jack fidgeted in his chair. From the back of his mind, thoughts surfaced fast. He knew where this was going, but he was reluctant to admit it, and it bothered him he was nervous about saying it out loud.

Delores stood and took a step towards Jasper. Jack couldn't see Delores's face, but he could see Jasper's. Jasper's eyes glistened with clarity and with fear. Jack was startled to see Jasper's shaken state and waited for Delores to speak.

Jasper took a step back from Delores. He was fearful for the first time since his days logging. Jack felt sweat trying to burst from his skin. He focused on calm, controlled breathing and worked to steady his heart rate and relax his mind.

Delores smiled a thin smile. Her voice reflected confidence as she stared at Jasper. She noticed the old man's eyes had relaxed. Her experience with eyes were their inability to hide fear. She had respect for the old guy. His eyes didn't give away much.

Delores's eyes shifted from a dark brown, almost black, to green. For those who knew, the eye-change showed a relaxed state. Jasper stiffened his back. He pushed the words out with deliberation.

"Perhaps they aren't Aliens, per se, Jack. They are us – from a parallel universe or a parallel world."

Chapter 46

Difficult Decisions

Mitch held tightly to Wise One as the horse carried them forward. They were surrounded by darkness with intense bursts of blurred light flashing by, reminding Mitch of a dance floor with bright strobe lights. There was a chill in the air, and the speed made Mitch nauseated. He wasn't sure it would work, but he closed his eyes hoping the stillness in them would soothe his stomach. He relented – vomit be damned; he wasn't going to miss this, so he kept his eyes open.

The horse was running, Mitch looked down to be sure, but there didn't appear to be any ground under them. He held tight wondering where the hell they were going. He hoped it wasn't so mundane and simple as hell. Hell would be a disappointment, and Mitch couldn't imagine going there on a horse with a Native American guide.

In a calm voice, the handler of the magnificent beast on which Mitch rode seemed to sense Mitch's doubt and spoke.

"We are almost there. The sickness will not last long."

Mitch was startled when the Native American spoke, but he wasn't sure why he was startled. Shit, nothing should surprise him anymore. He noticed the softness of the horse's hair and felt the power of the animal beneath him. The motion seemed to be slowing. Ahead he could see the darkness and wash of lights slowly turning into more familiar landscape. It was as if someone were turning the lights on with a dimmer switch, rotating the switch so the light came up a little at a time. The horse slowed with no effort and transitioned from a full gallop to a trot, then to a walk. Mitch looked around, waiting for his brain to catch up with his eyes. He squinted, blinked and focused. It appeared they were in a cave, warm and damp. The horse turned a corner, and Mitch saw hundreds of other people. At a glance or two, they all appeared to be Native Americans. Shadowfax stopped, and Mitch, recognizing a cue from the handler, jumped down. His Native American handler stayed on the horse.

The cave was filled with silence, and Mitch thought everyone had turned to look at him. He flushed and then relaxed as he saw the people weren't looking at him. They were looking at the man on the back of Shadowfax.

"What am I doing here? Is my wife here? What do I call you?"

"You, Mitch Wilde, may call me Wise One."

Mitch was impressed with the way he spoke: confident and proud with great clarity and deliberation. Like a macho Mr. Rogers.

"No, your wife is not here. She has been taken, as you know. And here? You are in a cave, as you see. A cave which possesses great spiritual power. It is not far from Outlaw River. It is a protected place in the mountains that my people have used for centuries to hide from your people and from the star people when they come."

"Why did you bring me here? I need to find my wife."

"You were brought here because of your Native American heritage and because I like you, Mitch Wilde."

"You like me? Um, okay, I am flattered, I guess, but again, I need to find my wife. If you can't help me find her, or won't, then please let me go. I don't care if the mountain comes down around me as long as I'm with her."

A Native American man assisted Wise One down from Shadowfax. They spoke in what Mitch assumed was their native language. Mitch understood every word with great clarity. He laughed to himself wondering what next? Now he could understand a Native American's tongue. Fantastic and surreal.

The new arrival asked Wise One if he needed anything. He said there was nothing new to report. They had located the camp where many of the illegal aliens were being held, and did he have any instructions?

"Whoa, excuse me, Wise One, sir, but did I understand your friend to say they have located a camp with a bunch of illegal aliens? I have to assume 'illegal aliens' means us European bastards who came over and systematically took over America. Am I far off?"

Wise One put a hand on Mitch's shoulder and signaled the other one to leave them. He didn't respond to Mitch's probing question.

"Walk with me, Mitch Wilde."

The two walked away from the crowd.

"I love the fire in your belly, Mitch Wilde, and I respect the deep love you have for your wife. I too once loved a woman as you do. It is a gift from the gods to share that kind of connection with another."

Mitch felt strength emanating from the man. The energy from the hand on his shoulder was evident; it both warmed and calmed Mitch.

"Yes, Wise One. I love her very much. She would do the same for me if I had been taken. I owe it to her."

Wise One stopped and removed his hand from Mitch's shoulder. He stepped in front of Mitch and looked down at him with calm eyes.

"You have some difficult decisions to make, Mitch Wilde."

In an instant, Mitch felt nervous and afraid. He wondered if he should just run. If he didn't hear what was about to be said, then it may not be true, right? SHIT!

"What do you mean difficult decisions?"

"We can find your wife, and we can rescue her, Mitch Wilde, but we cannot rescue them all. We simply don't have the numbers necessary."

"Okay, that's easy then; if you can't rescue them all, then let's at least rescue Mabey. I can live with this decision."

"Yes, but can you live with all of my brothers and sisters down there," Wise One pointed toward the other end of the cave, "being killed rescuing one person? Another thing to consider: if we try and help all who are captured in the meadow, the star people will resist and return back to your towns and take more people. I am certain you have many close friends in town."

Mitch's heart sank. He felt his knees start to buckle. What's the fucking point then? he thought. He was just going to have to do this on his own.

"No, Wise One, I couldn't live with myself if either of those things were to happen. I'm afraid we need to part ways then. Point me in the right direction, and I'll try on my own. I would rather fail trying than stand around and hope. Hope is such a passive word. Nothing is ever accomplished with hope."

Mitch kicked at the ground in an effort to control his frustration. He thought about the journal entry he would write about the current scene and discussion once he rescued Mabey. He made a deliberate series of stretching motions from his toes and knees as a way to warm up. He stopped and addressed Wise One.

"No, I won't ask you to risk all you love to help me find the one I love."

"Not so hasty, Mitch Wilde. I think the Universe is testing your patience. Perhaps your loved one doesn't need rescuing."

Chapter 47

The Fragrance of the Pines

Mabey turned towards Kala and Aaron.

"All of us aren't going to be able to get over this wall and out. I'm not even sure I'll be able to get out, but I have to try."

Aaron looked at Kala, then back at Mabey.

"What's your plan? You said a pyramid?"

"Yes, build a basic pyramid with bodies; I climb up to the top when it's high enough. I'll jump over the wall, hopefully, and land on the other side. If we do it correctly, I think I can jump over to that oak tree just outside the wall. Not sure if I can grab a branch, but the plan is the tree will slow my descent. We aren't talking about a big drop, anyway, so I should be fine. My biggest concern is twisting my ankle."

"What about Aaron and me, Mabey? And all the others? We'll still be stuck here."

"You're right. I'd like to say I can bring back help, but I have no idea how far we are from help, and who could help, really? The military? I have a feeling they're preoccupied with more than residents of Outlaw River right now."

"I wonder if the rest of the country is under attack. I couldn't get much information on TV or radio except that lakes around here were being hit with unknown objects. Then all hell started breaking loose in Outlaw River," Aaron said as he looked around expecting something else to happen.

"Kala, I think you should climb up after me and follow me out. Then you, Aaron."

"Hey, what about the rest of us? Why should just you three go?" A woman about Mabey's age spoke up. Mabey didn't know her.

"As many as possible should follow. At some point I think we'll be noticed, and they'll try to stop us."

An older man stepped forward and spoke to Mabey.

"So, who goes, and who stays?"

Mabey started directing people, putting larger, sturdier individuals on the bottom row.

"Not for me to decide. Since this is my idea, I'll go first. I think Kala and Aaron should follow based on their strength and fitness, and being separated from their daughter. After them, my recommendation would be for those most fit who are able to jump. This could all be over quickly. I may not even be able to get out."

People started arguing about who would go and who would stay. The man who asked the first question spoke loudly.

"Listen, everyone; we all can't go. The pyramid will start to shrink. Some of us aren't fit enough to climb the pyramid, let alone make the jump. You know it, and so do I. As much as I would like to, I can't make it. Our best shot is to get some of you out of here to go looking for help."

He took Mabey's arm with care. Mabey, startled, spoke to him.

"What can I do for you, sir?"

"Tell me where you want me. I can help anchor this pyramid. We'll get some of you out of here."

"Thank you, sir. Why don't you get in the middle? It's the most important place."

Mabey led him over to where she thought the pyramid should start. She guided others as they stepped forward, trying to pick the biggest and the strongest. Most took their places without complaint. A

183

few knew exactly what to do and started dropping on all fours. The others followed. There were enough people, so Mabey guided others to make two rows facing each other for the base. The next rows took longer to form, but Mabey knew she couldn't hurry this as much as she wanted. It had to be stable, or no one would get out. People were sore and climbing on top of strangers wasn't easy. After what seemed like an eternity to her, and when she thought it was high enough, she asked those who remained to stand around the pyramid and brace it as best they could.

Kala stood next to Mabey, and in a low voice spoke.

"I like the way you did that, Mabey."

Mabey thought she knew what Kala meant but said, "What?"

"Leaving people out of the pyramid who can probably escape after us."

Mabey smiled. She reached down, grabbed a few small rocks, and held them in her left hand.

"Kala and Aaron, you guys follow me quickly. You don't have to wait until I jump. This thing has a good base and can take the weight, for two of us anyway."

"I think you should follow her, Kala. I want you out of here. If something should happen to the pyramid, I want to know you are out of here and free."

"What are the rocks for, Mabey?" Kala asked.

"To make sure I don't dive right into the wall."

"Oh, good thinking." Kala looked around on the ground and found a few for herself.

Mabey started climbing. Her bare feet were swollen, sore, and torn to shit. She ignored the pain and scaled the pyramid without any trouble. The thing felt sturdy. She wished it were a little closer to the trees, but they didn't have time to rebuild.

Once at the top, Mabey looked around the small valley and saw other groups staring at the cell she was in. She couldn't be sure, but it appeared there were six or seven other groups in cells like hers. Mabey unclasped her left hand, took a small rock and tossed it straight forward. It snapped and bounced back.

"Shit!"

She took another one and tossed it a little higher; this time it cleared as she'd hoped and landed outside the shield.

"Okay, here goes," she said out loud.

Mabey got in a crouching position and prepared to leap. She looked over her shoulder and saw Kala was scaling the pyramid with speed.

Mabey jumped and flew over the shield. She heard a crack right after she leapt. Her heart beat harder, and her adrenaline surged. She realized she had released the remaining rocks from her left hand as she jumped. They'd bounced off the shield causing the cracking noise. Mabey had guessed the distance pretty well, and the tree limb approached fast. She grabbed it with both hands. Her lower body swung like a pendulum, and before she got parallel, she let go hoping it would slow her enough to prevent a painful fall. She dropped about twenty-five feet and landed hard on both feet. Her knees flexed and absorbed the landing pretty well, and her body rolled through the grass. She lay flat and still, pausing a second. She looked around, afraid she might be shot or zapped. Nothing happened. She thought of Mitch and wondered what the hell he was up to and if he was okay.

She stood and looked up. Kala was at the top of the wall throwing some rocks forward.

"Here I come, Mabey."

Kala sprang forward and hit the side of the tree. Mabey braced herself and grabbed for Kala as she fell. The two crashed to the ground, arms and legs sprawled.

"You okay, Kala?"

Kala stood, relieved to be out.

"A bit sore, but I'm fine. How about you? I hit you pretty hard."

Mabey, stood, smiled and let out a nervous laugh. "I'm as good as I'm going to be for a while, I think. Nothing's broken."

Mabey turned toward the pyramid where Aaron had just reached the top and called out.

"Try to catch that big branch when you jump, Aaron. I'm not sure Kala and I can slow down your fall."

"Mabey, look!"

Kala pointed toward the other end of the meadow.

"Is that what I think it is?"

"Damn! Not now!" Mabey said.

She turned back towards Aaron. "Aaron, you need to jump!"

Aaron sprang forward and hit the tree hard. He grasped the branch and then slipped. His body crashed against the big oak. He fell fast toward the ground. Mabey tried to brace his fall but was of no help. He hit the ground hard with a loud thud.

Kala was still staring down the meadow.

"Those ships are hovering over the other groups and sucking them up, Mabey. My God! I can't believe this is happening! What are we going to do?"

Mabey grabbed Aaron. "Can you stand, Aaron? We need to get going."

Aaron got to his feet, grabbed his head and fell back down. He reached for his ankle and then with great effort, stood again while grunting.

He got an arm over Mabey's shoulder, and she helped him stand.

"Kala, get over here on the other side of your husband. Come on, snap out of it."

Kala was staring at the events taking place at the other end of the meadow, mesmerized by bodies flying upwards into large crafts which looked almost invisible. She could barely make out silhouettes of the ships and only briefly. When the bodies flew up, as soon as they entered the ships, they too disappeared.

"Oh, I'm sorry, Mabey." Kala moved over to her husband's side and got his arm around a shoulder.

Mabey turned to the group still stuck inside. "You need to hurry up if you're going to get out. It looks as if ships are coming to take us away. We're going into the woods. If you get out, scatter and run. Try to find water, and then head downstream."

"Kala, come on. Let's get over to the edge of the woods. We should have time unless more ships come. Hang on, Aaron, and help as much as you can."

Aaron could put very little weight on his right foot. He thought the ankle was broken but hoped it was nothing more than a bad sprain. "I'm trying, Mabey. It hurts like hell."

"Oh, suck it up, Aaron. You're always bragging to me about your athleticism. Show me what you're made of," Kala said.

Mabey smiled. Aaron smiled too and felt an adrenaline rush. The three hobbled, and within a minute they were at the edge of the woods with some cover. Mabey felt better but knew they had to clear this area and get some distance from their holding cell.

The two women let go of Aaron. He could put almost no weight on his right foot because of the pain.

Mabey stood at the edge of the woods, looking back. Something happened in the cell they had just left. The pyramid had fallen, and there was a pile of people on the ground. Several were running and slamming into the shield in a panic, trying desperately to get out. A ship hovered overhead and started sucking them up one by one.

"Oh, my God! This is so sad. I feel bad we got out and they didn't."

"Don't, Kala. We knew not everyone was going to get out. Think about your daughter. Focus on her. Nothing matters but surviving. Now, you two, we need to get farther into the woods. We aren't in the clear yet."

Aaron limped forward.

Kala stayed by his side. Mabey stopped and bent over to the

ground touching it with both palms. She stretched and tried to ascertain the condition of her body. She was thankful she was healthy and physically fit, but no amount of training had prepared her for this. She was damn near spent, but she focused on Mitch and her sister.

"Let's go, you two."

"I can't. You're going to have to go without me." Aaron said, words Kala didn't want to hear.

"Come on, Aaron, you can make it. I'm not leaving without you," Kala pleaded.

"Yes, you are. I'm going to be okay, but I'll slow you two down. One of us needs to get clear of here and back to Shontey. So go. This isn't open for discussion."

Mabey moved toward Aaron and bent down to look at his ankle. It was swelling quickly.

"Do you mind if I grab your ankle, Aaron?" Mabey said

"No, why?" Aaron replied.

"I want to see if it's broken."

Mabey, with the gentle deliberate care her profession as a physical therapist taught her, took hold of his ankle. She moved it back and forth. Aaron grunted and groaned but clenched his teeth to stay quiet.

Kala looked out into the meadow, worried they would be seen.

"He's right, Kala. We need to get out of here. His ankle is not broken, but it looks like a level-three sprain, the worst you can get."

Mabey looked up at Aaron and then stood.

"At least it isn't broken. But you have ligament damage, torn, to be precise. Aaron, my recommendation is to get as far from the edge of the meadow as you can. Then head south, and try to find water. Soak your ankle in the water as long as you can. Then go downstream. Avoid roads. You can walk without doing more damage, but it's going to be painful."

Mabey turned to Kala.

"If you're coming with me, let's go."

Mabey turned away and started a slow jog into the woods. She wanted to get back to Outlaw River and find Mitch. She wondered if Mitch would be there. She closed her eyes and lifted her chin upwards. Keeping her eyelids shut for a moment, Mabey inhaled through her nose as she moved into the cover of the trees. She felt the breeze against her face and bathed her senses in the fragrance of the pines.

Chapter 48

A Strange State

In what seemed, to Jasper, like an odd transition from what they were just talking about, Jack turned toward him and started talking.

"I can't believe she's gone. It's been a year now almost, and I miss her so much I get twisted inside. It feels as though the pain will never go away. I have days when I don't even want to get out of bed. If it weren't for Jack Junior, I would just give up and call it good. I'll never forget that morning, the phone call at work. I went in early. I was a day behind paying the bills for the sporting goods store. I hate being late. So I went in early to get them done. I stopped for coffee at the Shack. Black with some steamed milk. I hate lukewarm coffee. Either hot as hell or iced."

Jack paused and stared. Jasper let the empty air hang uninterrupted. Delores fidgeted but kept silent. She wasn't sure what the hell Jack was talking about, but the look on his face, the tone of his voice, and his body language told her enough. So she kept quiet. Her silence would make what she had to do easier for her.

Jack rolled his eyes and closed them for a second. When he opened them, he started speaking as if he were in a one-act play. The audience was hanging on every word.

"The coffee was so damn hot. The cheap lid popped off when I slid into the pickup and it spilled onto my pants. Not a lot, but enough where I would carry a stain for the day if I didn't go home and change. I also remembered I hadn't taken out the trash, and Ginny would be upset with me. I figured Junior would do it, so I didn't go back. I wanted a head start on the bills. I used a couple of napkins to dry the coffee spot and then pointed the dashboard vent directly on the spot and turned up the fan."

Jasper finally knew where this was going. He remembered the police stopping by and asking him if he had video tape of the incident. He did and shared it with them.

Jack continued.

"I got to the store, and one thing led to another as it so often does, and I didn't get the start I wanted on the bills. The next thing I know I'm getting a phone call from Sheriff Gunther that I needed to get home right away. Ginny had been hurt. He wouldn't say more. Just said to drive home and don't speed. I got home, trying to call anyone I could think of during the twenty-five-minute trip. I couldn't even get Mitch on the phone. I pulled up to the driveway, and there was an ambulance and a couple of police cars. Mitch came running out to me, grabbed me by both shoulders, looked straight into my eyes and said, 'Jack, Ginny is gone. The dump truck backed over her. She was pinned under the back of the truck. It isn't pretty, Jack, I'm warning you. Come on, I'll be right by you.' Mitch guided me around the end of the truck as Sheriff Gunther and his deputy backed away. Sure as hell, there was my wife crushed under the filthy garbage truck. She had blood coming out an eye and seeping from the corner of her mouth. Her eyes were vacant but in my head seemed to be begging me for help. I can't get the image out of my head. No matter how hard I try, I always see those eyes. Every time I take out the trash now, I see her eyes. Every time I drink coffee, I see her eyes. I can't escape them."

Jack paused again and wiped his eyes.

Jasper started to speak but didn't know what to say. He couldn't remember ever feeling so bad for someone. Hell, he felt worse right now than when he found out his wife had left him for a rodeo clown. He kept silent.

Jack dropped his chin and continued speaking.

"I had a chance to go home that morning after spilling coffee on my pants. Something told me it was for a reason, but I didn't listen. I pressed on to work for those meaningless bills. I didn't even get to them. One more day. What the hell would one more day have mattered?"

Jack looked up at Jasper and Delores. Neither answered. Jack stood up, closed his eyes and stretched both arms towards the ceiling. With deliberation he stretched his neck back and forth. He spoke with a new clarity, and the sad tremor in his voice was all but gone.

"I didn't go home when I knew I should. I didn't trust my own instincts."

Jack looked at the ground and then over his shoulders as if someone might walk through the door. He looked into Jasper's eyes, avoiding Delores for some reason.

"I do not want to face Mitch and tell him his wife is dead as he had to do with me, Jasper. We have to help Mitch find her."

Jack straightened, then rolled his head on his tense neck, a steady back-and-forth motion as he spoke.

"I have to help Mitch find her."

Jasper watched as Jack closed his eyes and appeared to start humming, at least to Jasper it sounded like humming. Perhaps it was mumbling. Jasper thought about a yoga class he stumbled into when he was younger where all the women, and one really buff-looking guy, were making noises in unison. Jasper stood, ready to speak to Jack. His desire was to snap him out of his strange state. But he waited too long.

Jack disappeared.

Chapter 49

Not Yet Ready

Mitch locked eyes with Wise One as he worked toward an understanding of his last statement.

"Perhaps she doesn't need rescuing? Is that what you said?"

Wise One spoke with great clarity. Mitch thought his voice sounded more clear and authoritative than any voice he had heard in his life. It almost didn't sound real. Mitch felt he was living in an analog world, and this ancient one's voice was digital.

"Follow me, please, Mitch Wilde. You need to sit a moment and relax. I want you to try something."

Mitch fought to overcome his impatience. He did not want to follow. He wanted to get on a horse or flying carpet and get to where the people were being held. He was sure Mabey would be there. She had to be.

Wise One walked away, and Mitch was drawn to follow. He fell into place a couple steps behind him as they wove their way through people and their stares. Mitch heard whispers throughout about his presence there. From what he could make out, he was not welcome, being called 'the outsider.' He didn't care. At the moment he felt he could take on the whole lot of them if need be. He focused on Mabey and continued to follow, wondering where he was being led. With clarity and an intensity he had not felt before, he focused on Mabey with flashes of their past together: many moments of great joy and a few of heartbreak and pain. Mitch looked down at his hands as he walked and watched as they became almost translucent, then solid and normal again. He didn't think much of it at first. He continued thinking of his Mabey as they walked. He saw a fire ahead and many Native Americans sitting around it. He thought for a second that he was going to smoke a peace pipe. He didn't have time right now as intrigued as he was with the whole scene. They were thirty to forty feet away Mitch guessed as he looked at his hands again. Translucent, what a cool word. He thought about Mabey and her love of flowers. How she had done such a wonderful job with their landscaping and how he could sit for hours and watch her work. She was grace in the soil. Mitch's boots and feet now appeared to go translucent as well. He started to feel as though he were fading somehow. Out of consciousness, perhaps? He thought about the night he and Mabey had recently gone to her flower show and how beautiful she looked. How upset she was when they left and how he felt bad for her with all the work she had put into the fundraiser. Mabey smelled really good after the flower show. Her scent filled his senses. Mitch felt like she was right next to him.

Mitch noticed Wise One was almost at the fire. The others stood in a show of respect. He was still behind Wise One who, along with the others, appeared to be fading from Mitch's view.

The fire was disappearing, as was Wise One and the others, when Mitch felt strong hands grab him around his shoulders and a booming voice spoke.

"No, Mitch Wilde. Come back. Come back to my voice. You are not yet ready to look for her."

Chapter 50

Pressed Against the Trees

Mabey looked at her bare, swollen, and tattered feet pressing against the earth. She contemplated kicking the ground, then dropped to her knees, and fought back her tears. Mentally she felt she had held up under the circumstances pretty well. She knew Mitch would be impressed with her. Her mind was starting to slip, though, and she could feel it. Her body was weakening. She got back on her feet and focused on moving forward. She could not remember the last time she'd eaten. Except for a bit of water in the stream earlier with the Mayor, she had not been able to put anything into her body. Mabey knew she could not last much longer without some food. Her body was strong but pushed to its physical and mental limits. She knew she was getting close to exhaustion. Looking around at the vegetation, Mabey wished she knew more about edible plants. She wondered if ferns were edible. There were certainly plenty of them. Pine needles as well, but they couldn't be edible. Could they? Pine nuts. How could she find those? She figured not so easily since they were so expensive in the grocery store. Someone had told her once they were actually buried deep inside the cones. How could she get them out if that were true? Could she eat them right away?

Mabey stopped and looked at her companion, ten feet behind and straining to keep up.

"Kala, how are you doing? Better than me, I hope."

Mabey watched as Kala forced a smile. She arrived within seconds, stopped and stood next to her.

"Okay, I suppose, Mabey. I'm worried about Aaron and Shontey. And I guess in a bigger sense I am wondering what in the name of all that is good in this world is going on?"

"I know, right?"

Mabey bent over and rested both palms on her knees. She focused on her breathing, one slow, steady breath at a time. Blood rushed to her head, and she felt light-headed. Damn, she needed to eat. She stood and addressed Kala.

"Aaron will be fine by staying under the cover of the woods away from the open spaces. Whatever it is that's taking us, I don't get the impression they will search through the woods for a single straggler. They'll suck up everyone from the cages and get the hell out of here. As for Shontey, I imagine she's with Cindi somewhere in town. She was hiding in the house when you and Aaron were taken, correct?"

The two women stared at each other in silence.

Kala responded, "thank you Mabey."

Mabey turned, Kala stepped next to her, and the women started trudging their way through the woods. Both looked over their shoulders with regularity.

"Yes, she was hiding. Knowing Shontey, I'm sure she waited until she thought it was absolutely clear and then took off to find Cindi."

Mabey noticed a thin smile on Kala's lips as she talked about her daughter.

"Those two are damn near joined at the hip. I never much liked the phrase, but it pertains to those two without a doubt."

"It must be nice as a parent for your daughter to have such a good friend and one who has it together like Cindi. My husband and I have known Cindi since she was a baby. We spent more than a few nights over the years babysitting her. She's a great kid."

"It is, Mabey, and Cindi is a great kid. I like her mother as well. At least as much as I know her, which isn't that much, I hate to admit. Small talk over the phone and 'Hi' every once in a while when I stop in her coffee shop. Lives get so busy. Aaron and I haven't taken the time to get to know people that well. I regret it now. I'm going to have to make it a point, once we get back to town and things settle, to spend some time with Debbi."

"She would like that, Kala."

Mabey clutched Kala's hand and squeezed trying to comfort her. The women froze and looked skyward through the towering trees.

Mabey lowered her voice and spoke carefully. She was impressed with how calm she was being. She couldn't wait to tell Mitch. He would be happy with her and tell her so.

"Stay next to me, Kala, and let's get over next to a tree. It'll be harder for us to be seen."

The air forced its way around the women who were now pressed up tight against a couple of towering pines. Neither wanted to look up but Mabey forced herself.

She saw a large ship of some kind. It looked like a kind of plane to her but was a different color, almost invisible or translucent. The darkness made visibility a challenge. The humming sound coming from it was not a noise she immediately recognized. With further thought, it sounded to her like her hybrid car when it was running in electric mode.

Mabey quit counting after five as the damn things passed overhead. Those were just the ones she saw.

As soon as they appeared, they were gone. It seemed like minutes, but Mabey knew it was merely seconds. Both she and Kala remained speechless, tight up against the trees.

Kala broke rank and slumped to the ground. Mabey got on the

ground next to her.

"You okay, Kala?"

"You don't have to keep asking me, Mabey. I appreciate it, but I am as good as I'm going to be for a while. I'm just relieved they're gone. And I'm wondering about Aaron. I'm sure you're correct; as long as he stays back from the meadow and out of sight, he'll be fine."

"Okay, then let's get going and find a stream. I'm thirsty and concerned about dehydration. We both need to get some water in us."

Mabey stood and reached for Kala's hand helping her to her feet. Their hands were clammy and torn from the past day. But the energy flowing between them was reassuring to Mabey. She knew no matter what was going on around them, human contact was important to her sanity right now. A rock pressed hard into Mabey's right foot. Mabey thought it probably should have hurt more than it did. Her swollen feet were pathetic to look at. Some spring water would feel good on them about now.

The two women moved forward in search of a stream.

Chapter 51

The Protected Area

Jasper stood, mouth agape, staring at the empty space Jack had occupied only moments before. He reached forward and waved his hand back and forth, a futile effort to see if he could feel Jack. His first thought: Jack had gone invisible and was still standing there staring at him. Jasper knew better but made the motion anyhow. He wasn't one to be startled, but Jack's disappearance, he admitted later, surprised the hell out of him.

Jasper's mind raced, a feeling unfamiliar to him since his youth. Hell, the only other time he remembered was the logging accident, the serious one when a tree fell on him and crushed his pelvis. He'd scrambled after hearing 'Timber!' and realized the tree wasn't falling the way it was supposed to. During the dash toward an escape, he was impressed how quick on his feet he was, agile like a running back dodging tacklers. The thought lasted for only a second or two as the falling tree found him and slammed him to the ground, breaking dozens of bones in his body.

Feeling his body temperature rising, Jasper wondered if he was going to be wiping sweat beads from his forehead. He thought of Spring Creek and the crystal clear water, always icy cold. The old logger focused on his breathing, preparing himself for more unexpected events. At this moment, they seemed to be flowing free.

Jasper turned and looked at Delores. Jasper later described her eyes to Mitch: "flat out screwy, strange, hell, there isn't a word that fits." They were glowing or shining, and perhaps both. They changed with regularity now. They certainly didn't look human even though the rest of her did. With trepidation disguised in confidence, Jasper spoke.

"Well, young lady, are you okay? Your eyes look as though they came out of some Hollywood special-effects shop. Not a pair of eyes I've ever seen anyway."

"They're fine, Jasper; why?"

"Because they are flipping around as if they aren't sure what state to be in. Hell, I've never seen anything like it. You look like a god-damned Alien. Not human. At least no human I've ever been around. You stay here, okay? I have to go use the men's room. I'll be right back."

Jasper had found genuine confidence in his voice again and projected his words. He liked the assurance he'd found after his logging accident, refined over the years. It made him feel strong and in control. He knew this was no time for going all pansy ass. Jack had left of his own volition so no worries about him. Mitch got up on the horse willingly as well, so nothing to worry about there. However, the *X-File*-like-Alien lass in his house was a different story. He needed an equalizer. Jasper scooted away. As Delores reached for him, he brushed her hand aside.

For an instant Jasper could have sworn he felt a significant difference in heat emanating from her outstretched hand. He was reluctant to look at her and address his atypical fear. He wanted out of the room for a minute or two to gather himself.

Jasper exited his research lair to go to the main portion of the house.

"Where are you going, Jasper?"

Shit! Even her voice sounded different now, Jasper thought. Only another second to get through the door and avoid this creature. His mind raced; the door seemed so far away, and yet it was right in front of him. How could mere inches seem an impossible chasm?

Jasper did not respond to her question. He knew he could close the door behind him and brace it. He'd practiced so many times. The reinforced steel brace would drop behind him quickly once he was through if he chose to release it.

His hand finally, thank the gods, found the knob. He watched his wrist, noticing the muscles flex as his hand opened the door. He pulled with force and speed. Jasper lifted his left foot to enter the expected protection of his inner sanctum.

Heat rushed through Jasper's right shoulder and flowed down through his body. He could no longer move as his brain commanded. Someone, or something, had hold of him and wasn't letting go. Jasper knew exactly who and now had a better understanding of what it was.

Chapter 52

The Bitter Residue

Sheriff Myron Gunther pulled his police cruiser into a parking spot in front of the Sheriff's office building just off Main Street. Gunther had a private spot in back, but he didn't want to take the extra minute to go there. He needed some answers, and some Tylenol, as soon as possible. His head was throbbing. The pain came and went and reminded him of the beatings he used to endure from his father. One way of keeping the memory at bay was no headache. Right now the pain was a constant reminder, and he needed to put it down.

Sheriff Gunther slid the cruiser into park and reached for the key. He turned off the ignition then slumped at the waist. His chin drooped and fell against his chest. His body fell over onto the seat.

Moments later, the Sheriff pushed himself upright behind the wheel; he saw the car keys on the floor under his loafer and figured he must have dropped them but couldn't remember. He grabbed his hat off the dash, took a deep breath, and opened the car door.

The Sheriff exited the car, stood next to the cruiser, and looked at the empty streets. The town had never been a bustling metropolis, but it rarely lacked movement and human noise. Until now, he hadn't noticed the sound of the river bordering the town. The lack of mechanical noise allowed him to hear the river from outside the office for possibly the first time. If not for the FUCKING pain in his head, he might enjoy it.

Sheriff Gunther closed the car door and headed for the front door of the Sheriff's Office. Losing his balance, pain shot through his head and he almost tripped on the steps as he grabbed for his head. He stopped, bent over, and focused on quiet. The pain seemed to be getting worse. He thought for a second about lying down on the ground and praying for calm, but he couldn't afford to appear weak. He gathered himself and pulled open the door into the office. He looked back and wondered how he had gotten here. He didn't understand why his head hurt so damn bad. He went straight for the first room to the right where the medicine cabinet hung on the break-room wall.

Gunther fumbled through the small cardboard boxes on the first shelf. He found the Acetaminophen packets, grabbed a handful, and stuffed all but two in the front pocket of his pants. Tearing them open, careful not to drop their healing power, he placed the four tablets in his mouth, tilted his head back, and swallowed. Then he grabbed a Styrofoam cup, filled it with water, and drank allowing the water to chase the pills.

Gunther laid his head on the table, closed his eyes, and tried to enjoy the absolute quiet, a rarity in the small building. He closed his eyes and smelled an odd smell on the palm of his hands. He didn't think Acetaminophen had a smell, but it must have. He knew it wasn't the Styrofoam. Gunther bounced his right heel up and down quickly in a nervous twitch. He took a deep breath. All he wanted right now in this moment was to remember how he got here and what he was supposed to be doing.

Chapter 53

Mother's Voice

Junior felt flustered. He liked all the women around him, one in particular, but his youth hadn't yet taught him how to deal with all the estrogen in the room. Cindi and Shontey were on the couch, and Cindi was doing her best to keep Shontey's mind off her missing parents, presumably taken by whatever things were wreaking havoc on Outlaw River. Mabey's sister, Michelle, was talking non-stop to Debbi, and he felt as though she might pass out at any time from lack of breath. He excused himself and went into the backyard.

He needed some time to think. The dogs, General and Delilah, came running over to greet him. They had not a care in the world. They had food, shelter if they needed it, and a protected backyard. Junior knew though, if the Aliens wanted the dogs for some reason, they could get back here and take them. He patted each of the dogs and headed to the back of the yard and the trail leading the short distance down to the riverbank. Junior closed the gate behind him leaving the dogs in the backyard to play; they didn't seem to mind since they had each other.

The riverbank had always been a soothing place for during his childhood. He could think of no place on earth he would rather be than on the banks of Outlaw River, by himself, sitting or lying down listening to the water splash over the rocks.

He'd downloaded the white noise app for his phone to help

with sleeping in all the nasty hotels while traveling with his baseball team. The sound was realistic, and he figured the app helped him some, but it wasn't the same as the real thing. It probably had something to do with the smells, the feel of the air around his body, and the touch of the ground under him.

Junior reached the moonlit bank, picked up half a dozen flat rocks, and skipped them across the water. He was careful not to throw too hard and damage what he hoped one day would be a multi-million-dollar arm. Unsatisfied with the skipping effort, Junior dropped to the ground and sat on a large rock. His feet were inches away from the water but would stay dry. He swung his right arm in a circular motion, one of his warm-up exercises for pitching, and wondered if he would ever pitch again. He wished he were with his dad right now. He didn't like the fact he was off on his own. He knew it would be different if his mother were still alive, but she wasn't. His father was all he really had, and he was worried; he couldn't bear the thought of not having his dad around.

Junior looked at the ground, jumped down from the rock and felt the earth under his palms. It was warm. He couldn't feel any moisture in the bank's grass. He plopped down and lay back looking into the sky. A brilliant blue sky with spotted clouds was the backdrop. River water pulsed stereo-like in his ears. He closed his eyes and thought about his mother and all those times she had walked with him along the banks of this very river, telling him about the plants, flowers, and trees, and how he needed to be responsible and treat the earth as if it were part of him.

"You treat nature the way you want others to treat you, Junior. It's a wonderful place, and we're lucky to be living with so many wonderful things – so many colors textures, smells and noises. It's almost as if we're in our very own movie. So be kind, Junior, because the cameras are always filming you." It wasn't until Junior turned 12 or 13 that he realized he wasn't actually being filmed. He understood what his mother was saying to him, though, and he loved her for it.

His mother was a true gentle soul. Tough as nails and wouldn't take crap from anyone, but at the same time she would give her last dime to a total stranger she felt was in genuine need.

Junior took deep controlled breaths. He felt the river air surge through his nose and fill his lungs. He heard the breeze pulsing its way across the water and over the riverbank. An occasional bird fluttered by singing. A fish slapped against the water as it returned from its skyward thrust. An airboat hummed in the sky.

Junior opened his eyes slowly. They took a minute to adjust as they searched for something his brain knew was in the sky. He lay still, afraid to twitch a single muscle. The sky above him flowed like a river in the air. Squinting and focusing, he could tell there was something, several somethings, moving over the river, and heading north. They looked large, hummed like electric car engines, and seemed as long as a 747 but much wider. It was impossible to tell since they were all but invisible and further cloaked by the darkness of night. He remembered what Mitch had described hovering over his house while his dad was inside. Junior couldn't tell for sure, but he thought he counted at least five of them. He waited a minute or two after he thought the last one passed. He started to rise when he heard something running at him and breathing heavy. He froze again and lay still. His first thought was the damn things saw him, had landed and were going to pick him up.

Seconds passed; then he got a face full of tongue. His heart stopped racing as he sat up, grabbed General around the neck, and gave him a big old hug.

"What are you doing out of the yard, you little stinker? Does Mitch know you can get out by yourself?"

Junior got to his feet and looked at the empty sky. He heard his mother's voice echoing through the clouds reminding him to trust nature and his own instincts.

Chapter 54

Falling Tree

Mitch regained full awareness as he felt strong hands lowering him to his knees. Without thinking, he crossed his legs and sat by the fire. The fire had to be hot, but he felt almost no heat, perhaps because of the vast expanse of the cave and the heat's dissipation. He wasn't sure but figured it wasn't worth further thought.

Wise One was on his right, and seven other very distinguished and well-seasoned Native Americans sat around the fire with them. No one spoke. They all stared at Mitch with caring eyes, eyes Mitch had never seen before. It was as if they were part of the earth's transcendent humanity. They belonged here at this time, and Mitch knew he was the outsider. It made him a little uneasy, but not unwelcome. For the first time since he had entered this cave, he felt he was supposed to be here.

Mitch spoke first, directing his words at the fire.

"I know Mabey is okay, and she does not need my help. I'm not sure how I know, but a voice has washed over me in reassurance. Something else is now tugging at my heart and mind, and I don't know what it is."

Wise One put his left hand on Mitch's right shoulder and smiled. Mitch could not help but be mesmerized by the glow of the fire in the man's eyes. They reflected the flames, but Mitch swore he could see much more in them than a fire. It was as if the pupils were earth-like – how Mitch imagined the earth must look to an astronaut; green, brown, and blue all encapsulated in a sphere.

Mitch took the pipe offered to him by Wise One. Another Native American sitting across from him spoke words to Mitch telling him to, "breathe the smoke in deep, hold it, and let it go. When it leaves you, watch the smoke with your eyes wide open. If you trust, you will see what needs to be done."

Mitch looked around the fire and felt as though he were in a movie. Looking at the intense eyes around the fire, he knew he needed to play the part and play it well. This was a serious moment, and his big mouth and desire for constant levity would not be appreciated. Hell, it wouldn't even be understood. Mitch looked at the pipe and put the end in his mouth. The wood was moist. He hoped like hell whoever was toking on it before him wasn't sick. He couldn't afford a cold right now. Mitch smiled thinking of Jack and Mabey. Neither of them would believe he didn't crack a joke. He breathed in deeply and felt the warm rush of smoke fill his lungs. He really didn't know what to do; he'd never smoked before in his life, but something took over. He could feel the smoke swirling in his lungs. It turned and burned as it built its story. Mitch removed the pipe from his mouth and held his lips together. When the moment was right, he opened his mouth, and the smoke flowed over his lips and moved toward the fire before stopping and spreading in front of him like a flat screen. Images appeared, and Mitch focused on what he was seeing. His head felt light, and even though he was sitting, his legs felt wobbly. Strong hands supported each shoulder and comforted him. As if on cue, Mitch watched one of the Native Americans close his eyes. Mitch followed his lead, closing his own eyes. The smoke image which hovered in front of his open eyes only moments ago, gained new clarity. Mitch saw a clown with Alien eyes, a falling tree, and an old man running for his life.

Chapter 55

Estrogen?

Junior grabbed the stick from General's mouth and tossed it into the water. General leapt in after it and returned. Delilah now came crashing down the trail with a recognizable voice not far behind.

"We wondered where you went, J.J. I'm glad I found you. Why didn't you tell someone where you were going?" Cindi's voice shook a little, and Junior felt bad. She was concerned, not nagging, and he thought this a good sign. No one liked being nagged.

"I'm so sorry, Cindi; I should have. I intended to just step out back and spend some time with the dogs to try to clear my head. The next thing I knew, I was going down the trail to the river and got sucked into my own little world. I used to spend a lot of time at the river with my mom when she was alive. It's soothing for me. I seem to do my best thinking when I'm down here. Is everything okay at the house?"

Cindi reached Junior and took his hand. They both turned and looked at the dogs playing together in the water. Neither spoke for a couple of minutes.

"Is everything okay at the house, Cindi?"

"Sorry, you asked that once already. I got caught up in the view and having some quiet time with you down here. I could get used to this myself. I can see why your mom liked it."

Junior squeezed her hand and smiled.

"The question, Cindi. You still haven't answered it."

Cindi giggled and sounded eighteen for the first time to Junior.

"Yes, everything's okay, at least as good as can be expected. Shontey is sleeping. Michelle gave her a sleeping pill with my mom's blessing, and she is lights out. I feel so bad for her. I can only imagine what it's like to have both your parents gone. One is enough."

"Amen," Junior added.

"None of us knows what to do, Junior. Mom wanted me to find you and bring you back to the house so you can brainstorm with us. She thinks you'll have some male wisdom or something to that effect. I told her I was just as smart as you are, perhaps even smarter."

"Perhaps? What you may have in intelligence, I have in experience and wisdom."

"Oh, yeah, by a whole three years, Mr. Big Shot."

Cindi reached out and tried tickling Junior in the stomach. He reacted and tickled her back. Junior wasn't sure tickling was appropriate under the serious circumstances they found themselves in, but he reciprocated and felt better. Cindi took off running toward the house, and Junior was hot on her trail. General and Delilah stopped playing in the water, looked at each other, and then chased after both of them, barking the entire way.

Junior backed off his sprinting to let Cindi stay in front of him, but only a little. She was fast. Her speed surprised him. Cindi slowed just before the gate and put the brakes on. At the last second, hoping she timed things right, she spun and faced Junior. His momentum carried him into her; she waited with open arms. She grabbed his face and planted a long wet kiss on him. Junior could feel his heart pound and blood surge through his entire body. He focused on staying cool and kissed Cindi back. He felt her face get warmer and relished the feel of her lips against his. Yes, he could definitely get used to this.

Cindi pulled back and smiled. Junior smiled back, and neither said a word. A moment passed, and both realized the dogs were hovering around their legs working at getting some attention of their own. The two petted them both.

Junior took Cindi by the hand, reached up with his opposite hand and opened the gate.

"Come on, Cindi. Let's go inside so I can explain to all the estrogen what I just saw at the river and what we need to do next."

"Estrogen?"

Tickling her in fun, Junior replied.

"That's right, estrogen; Google it."

Chapter 56

Clear-Headed Vigor

"So, Mitch Wilde, what did the smoke show you? Is your Mabey in trouble, or did you see something else?"

Mitch struggled against his light-headedness. Thoughts didn't seem to have the utmost clarity right now. He fought to remember what he'd seen about Mabey. Nothing. All he could remember was a damn clown chasing an old man from a falling tree. He wanted to stand, but he didn't think he could.

"Take a moment, Mitch Wilde."

Someone took the pipe from his hands. Mitch noticed the Native American on his left wiped off the mouthpiece on his shirt. Shit, Mitch thought, why didn't he wipe off the damn thing before he stuck it in his mouth? The man in a beautiful beaded leather shirt then placed the pipe in his mouth and took several big drags. Mitch could feel his own lungs respond as he watched the man inhale. The fire crackled and popped, as the smoke billowed upward and seemed to pause before lying flat against the cave's ceiling. Then it slid sideways and upward beyond Mitch's view. Mitch started to fall backwards from his sitting position, but Wise One grabbed him by the arm and steadied him.

"Count to 100, Mitch Wilde, and take your time. I know you have something to share with us."

Mitch obeyed without question and started counting to 100. He was so damn glad he didn't have to count backwards.

At about 75 Mitch started to feel more like himself. His lungs were no longer burning, and the light-headedness was dissipating. At 94 he stopped and turned to Wise One.

"I saw an old man running from a falling tree and a crazy Alien-eyed clown."

"Nothing about your Mabey, then?"

"No, Wise One, nothing about Mabey. What does this mean, if anything?"

"You tell me, and then I will tell you what I think, if you still want to know."

Mitch paused and looked at the other men around the fire who seemed no longer to be paying attention. They were in their own smoke-filled world at the moment.

"I suppose it means Mabey is fine, and there is something else I'm supposed to be focused on. An old man and a crazy-ass clown, I guess."

Mitch watched Wise One as he sat there and stared into his eyes. He said nothing, offered nothing, and looked poised to sit through eternity without another word if necessary. Mitch stared at the fire hoping the flames would create a mouth and speak to him. He closed his eyes for few seconds and concentrated on the smoke image emblazoned in his memory.

There was a faceless old man, quick on his feet. He had a look of fear on his face as he ran not only from the falling tree heading right for him, but from a clown that moved without effort around trees and bushes, almost toying with the old guy.

Mitch could not believe it had taken him so long to figure out the smoke's message. Everyone else who knew anything about this story had probably long ago come to the correct conclusion. Wise One smiled, and Mitch stood with newfound clear-headed vigor. He spoke aloud, bringing all the internal bustling of the cave to an end.

"I am so blind. Jasper is in trouble."

Chapter 57

Regret

Mabey and Kala pressed on. The meadow, and captivity, faded from their thoughts. Lack of food and water deprived them both of clear heads. One step after the other, staying in sight of each other, and out of sight of others consumed what little cerebral energy they had right now. Kala struggled with Shontey's status, her worry about her husband all but forgotten. She knew he would be fine. She hoped he was limping through the woods toward them, working his overweight body.

The afternoon air cooled as the sun lowered and found it harder to pierce its way through the tall pines.

"Kala, I think we aren't far from a creek. We can hydrate and soak these ugly feet of ours. As much as I wish I had a pair of shoes right now, there's no way they'd fit."

Kala chuckled. She didn't have the energy to laugh. Her brain was tired, and she wasn't registering anything accurately right now.

"My feet look like giant sausages stuffed in casing. At least they don't hurt anymore. I think they're so swollen my brain can't even register the pain. I mean, they have to be sore, right?"

"Oh, my God. Too funny, Kala! I suppose mine look like the

Michelin man. When I get back with my husband, he is going to have to rub them gently with some coconut oil and then my back and shoulders, and neck and…."

Kala worked at lifting one foot after the other. Hearing Mabey talk helped her press forward. She was sure of it.

"Why did you stop, Mabey? What comes after neck?"

"Um, we just met, Kala, too personal?"

Mabey smiled and hoped Kala understood she was just joking.

"Oh, I see how it is. Get a woman anxious for what comes next and then leave her hanging, leaving it all up to her own mind."

Mabey stopped, turned, and smiled at Kala who was about ten paces behind her. She hoped when this was all over she could stay in touch. She liked Kala's sense of humor and determination.

"Well, let me tell you, I think the next thing going to be rubbed with some coconut oil by that husband of yours is…."

Bam, thwack, crack! The sounds howled through the woods. Mabey, propelled by instinct, dropped flat to her stomach. She realized immediately that a threat was coming from behind. She scrambled to a crouching position and braced herself against a tree. She peered back over her shoulder and saw Kala was standing still: frozen. She was in plain sight. Her head was buried in her hands. Mabey worked at getting her attention. Her attempts were futile. Kala was panicked and unable to move.

"Kala! Drop to the ground and crawl. You'll be harder to see. Kala, look at me. Kala! Damn it, Kala, take your hands away from your face and look at me!"

Nothing. Kala was panicked, and nothing Mabey could do, short of running out there and wrestling her to the ground, was going to work. For a second, Mabey contemplated doing just that, but she knew giving up her position could be fatal. She desperately wanted not only to live, but to see Mitch again. She took some deep breaths and pressed her back firmly against the tree wishing she could merge with the bark and become invisible. The noise stopped. Mabey peeked around the tree. What she saw surprised her. Two men – she had been expecting other-world creatures – something about these two looked familiar. They were spinning around Kala and poking her. The disgusting excuses for human beings were taunting her. Mabey grew angry as she watched Kala start to cry.

Kala had dropped her hands, and Mabey thought her friend had found some inner strength.

"Hey, Brown Sugar, what're you doing out here all by yourself?"

"We like what you done with your hair. Oh, wait, you have no hair."

Mabey heard the redneck pig's laughter echo from pine tree to pine tree. Anger welled up inside her. She looked around trying to figure out what she could do. Two strange, dirty men were tormenting Kala. Mabey was convinced this was going to go somewhere bad and fast.

The two had left their truck. They were on foot and had all their attention planted securely on Kala who was now bathed in the abandoned truck's headlights. Mabey was channeling Mitch yet again.

"Take every opportunity you get, Mabey, and stay focused. Most people aren't attentive and fully aware of what is going on around them. When they get so zeroed in on what they are doing especially in stressful situations, they lose sight of the forest for the trees. Huey Lewis, Babe."

Mabey thought her Huey moment was presenting itself. She took off on a dead run, taking a wide angle around the Kala situation and focused on the two shit-heads' vehicle. Adrenaline kicked in and propelled her body. Sound stopped. Time started to slow. Her body melded with the earth. The darkness hid her and the trees protected her. Her feet felt the earth below her but only slightly. She liked the way the breeze felt against her hairless skull. In a matter of seconds, Mabey reached the worthless duo's truck. She dropped to the ground and tucked her body against the front wheel. No one was in the cab or the pickup bed. Good! She looked back at the trio and saw Kala was now on the ground flat on her back. Her hands again covered her face. Mabey thought she heard her cries of panic, but she wasn't sure.

No time for hesitation now. Mabey got to her feet, went around to the cab of the pickup, and jumped in. She pulled the door behind her ever so slowly, closing it as best she could. She didn't care if it latched or not. No noise was the most important advantage she had right now. She looked around the cab. There was a gun on the seat next to her. Looked to be a 9 mm, best guess. She pulled the action back, dropped the clip and saw it was full. She let out a sigh of relief and glared through the front windshield.

"Thank you, Mitch," She whispered.

At this point Mabey figured she had only seconds to make a decision and take action. She played out the scenario of her plan in her mind. She saw one of the men now lowering his body over Kala. The other stood by laughing. They had no idea Wilde-Hell was about to come down on them in the form of a shaved-headed, foot-swollen, body-bloated, water-deprived madwoman named Mabey. No maybe about it, the two pigs were about to learn the female meaning of the word regret.

Chapter 58

A Deep Hearty Laugh

Jasper woke and found himself sitting in his recliner. He was a bit foggy still but found himself coming around. Delores sat across from him on his sofa. She was drinking one of his beers and eating some chips.

"Help yourself to my beer, young lady? Can I call you young lady, or should I be calling you something else?"

"Well, I'm not young really. At least not by earth's standards. Where I have been time slows, skewing my actual earth age."

"And where exactly do you come from?"

"Not so much where, Jasper, but when."

Jasper thought about bull rushing her right now, taking the Guinness bottle and smacking her over the head, but he couldn't really move his legs. He could feel them and see them move a little, but that was it. He was powerless.

"Jasper, I can tell what you're thinking. Let me warn you. Coming after me would be a no-win situation. I am quicker and stronger, and I have tools at my disposal you don't even know. You are outmatched. So just relax. Can I get you a beer or make you a sandwich?"

"Fuck off!"

"Now, Jasper. Keep it civil. No need whatsoever to get angry.

As long as we work together, we can accomplish what is necessary and go on about our business."

Jasper moved his head a little and blinked his eyes. They were dry, and he tried to create some moisture in them. His ears needed popping as well. He opened his mouth wide and stretched his muscles trying to equalize the pressure. It worked on one side but not the other. He tried again, same result. He plopped his head back against the chair and sighed.

"After-effects of what I did to you, Jasper. Your body's reaction will wear off in another ten minutes or so, and, other than being somewhat groggy, you'll feel fine. You have some strength and fight in you for an old guy. I had to hang onto you longer than normal."

"Dispense with the small talk, if you don't mind, and tell me what it is you want."

Delores rose, walked from Jasper's living room, and into the kitchen. She yelled back.

"No recycle container, Jasper?"

"It's out back. Like you really care."

Jasper heard the back door open, then the familiar clank of the Guinness hitting other bottles in the can. Moments later, Jasper heard her lock the door behind her and walk back into his living room.

"Nice to see someone who recycles. It does make a difference for the planet, but you know, that's why you do it. Right?"

Jasper stared as Delores paced around the living room picking up a few photos, a coaster, and a book or two. She examined them half-heartedly and then set them down, all the while talking to Jasper.

"Not going to respond to anything I have to say, Jasper?"

"I don't feel a need. I don't like to chit chat with people I know, let alone strangers."

"Okay. Then let's get to the point."

"About damn time. I was about to wish you had killed me so I wouldn't have to listen to your drivel."

Delores chuckled and sat on the couch.

"Okay, Jasper, here's the deal. As you know, I think I told you, I was given up by my tribe a very long time ago to keep peace: a kind of exchange that would alleviate added pressure and more widespread abductions within my tribe. Anyway, I've grown bored of my place among the Star People, and I want to come back to earth."

"What in the hell are you talking about? You're on earth now."

"True, but only temporarily. You see, I've been allowed to come back on one condition: I've six months to find a replacement."

Jasper laughed out loud.

"And I'm your replacement?"

Now it was Delores's turn to laugh, a deep hearty laugh where her head went back and exposed her neck. Jasper wished he could dive and cut it open.

"No, Jasper, you are not my replacement."

"What gives then?"

Delores sat forward on the sofa, put her elbows on her knees and leaned closer to Jasper. She lowered her voice and spoke in a very deliberate, almost eerie, voice.

"No, in order for me to stay here permanently, I need to find a young female, someone with a lot of birthing years ahead of her. I know of a particular one across the street from this very house that will do nicely".

Jasper swallowed guessing what the next sentence would be. If it were indeed the case, he wished he were dead.

"Cindi is going to be a perfect replacement for me, Jasper, and you're going to help me get her."

Chapter 59

Here Here

Junior and Cindi entered the Wilde's home through the sliding door leaving the dogs outside. In the living room Debbi and Michelle had their feet up on the large maple coffee table Mabey's father had made for her and Mitch when they got married. It was distressed, rock solid, and called out to feet. The Wildes insisted their guests use it this way and make themselves at home, a promise Mabey's father insisted they both give him when he delivered it.

He said, "Now Mitch, and you too, Mabey – perhaps you the most, Mabey, now that I think about it – let people put their damn feet up on this thing. It's sturdy as hell and can take it; I distressed it on purpose. Nothing worse than a pretty coffee table everyone's afraid to touch."

Mabey told Mitch on more than one occasion stories about how her mother always nagged her father about setting cups, papers, and, God forbid, his feet on the coffee table in the living room.

Shontey, sprawled out on the couch, fell fast asleep. The sleeping pill Michelle had given her had done the trick. She was purring like a well-fed, belly-rubbed cat. Cindi was grateful and dreaded the moment when she woke up and remembered everything that had transpired the last twelve hours. Cindi didn't think Shontey's parents would show up anytime soon, so the issue of their being gone remained. She felt she didn't have anything left worth saying to Shontey. She would take her own mother's advice: "Be a friend who is supportive and present. You don't always have to say something"

"Ah, there you two are. Michelle and I figured you were floating on a raft away from all this mess."

"Mom, even if there were a raft at the river, it wouldn't occur to me to leave you."

"I agree, it seems to me right now more than ever, there's a need for all of us to stick together." Junior said.

Debbi took her feet off the coffee table, stood up, and stretched.

"Wow, you two are so serious. I was trying to bring a little levity into the room. It's so dang dark and depressing right now."

Michelle settled deeper into her chair and stretched her feet out on the coffee table.

"I think we're all going to get taken and ass probed, and there isn't a damn thing we can do about it. I just hope I'm unconscious when it happens. How's that for a little levity, Debbi?"

"Jesus. Don't say that in front of the kids. Hell, don't say it in front of me. You are impossible, Michelle. You don't actually believe that, do you?"

"All I know is my apartment was ransacked by something. I'm convinced whoever it was, occupied the same space and I couldn't see them. They could have done anything they wanted to me, and I would have been powerless. So do I really believe it? Yes, and I will channel Fox Mulder here: 'I do believe.' Why the hell else would they want us?"

Michelle took her feet off the coffee table and stood. She had newfound strength after her little rant. She wasn't sure why, perhaps getting her fear off her chest.

"I'm going to get a glass of wine. Does anybody want anything?"

Junior piped up immediately.

"Actually, I'm hungry. Mabey wouldn't mind if I helped myself to some food, would she?"

Debbi and Michelle responded at the same time with the exact same phrase.

"Of course not!"

Junior smiled, and Cindi grabbed him, squeezing his hand. She led him into the kitchen.

"Come on, J.J., follow me. I know where Aunt Mabey keeps all the good stuff. Let me make you something. I'm quite handy in the kitchen."

Junior couldn't help but blush, and he avoided looking back over his shoulder at Debbi who he figured at this point must be sweating. Her sweet little daughter, not even out of high school yet tugging on his arm and all but begging to cook for him.

"Perhaps Junior wants to cook something for himself," Debbi replied.

"Oh, Mom, let it go, and stop worrying. I am taking him to the kitchen not down the aisle. Relax." Cindi evidently also felt her mother's concern.

"And besides, not that a man can't cook, but how many men do you know, Mother, who don't want a woman to pamper them with a good meal?"

Michelle spoke from the kitchen loud enough for Debbi to hear.

"Your daughter is very wise, Debbi."

Cindi and Junior reached the kitchen as Michelle polished off some wine straight from the bottle.

"No sense pouring it in my glass, you two. There was just a little left. Now, time to open a new one. Care to join me?"

Junior responded first.

"A small glass sounds great. I might need it depending on how this meal goes."

He smiled and squeezed Cindi's hand.

"On second thought, Clayton Kershaw wanna-be, how about you cook your own meal then?"

Junior smiled, and then laughed a deep belly laugh that sounded much older than his twenty years.

"Just kidding, and you're right, Cindi. I can cook, but I'd much rather have a meal cooked by a beautiful woman. My mom used to cook for me every night. Man, she was a good cook."

Debbi entered the kitchen and joined the three. Cindi started digging through the cupboards and refrigerator while Junior took a glass of wine from Michelle.

Michelle raised her glass and offered a toast.

"To Mabey and Mitch: may they be safe, and may all the slimy Alien fucks die a grisly death at the hands of us humans."

In enthusiastic chorus from the little party, "Here, Here!"

Chapter 60

Calm and Warm

A loud sound rousted Gunther from his mouth-drooling position on the break-room table. He looked at the wet spot on his shirt sleeve where moments ago his mouth had been firmly planted. For a brief second he thought he should go to his locker and put on a new shirt. No one should see him like this. He wondered where everyone was and why it was so quiet; then, as if on cue, he heard noises coming from the front of the station.

Gunther went to the locker room, the opposite direction of the noise. He stepped in front of his locker and stood there staring at the tumbler on the lock. He grabbed the stainless lock and spun the dial. He had no idea what the first number was. At least he remembered the right locker. Hell, it had his name on it. At least it matched the name on his shirt. Gunther decided to forgo a clean shirt for now and check out the noise. It might be one of the dispatchers, a good thing; he could figure out what in the hell was going on. He tightened his belt a notch and straightened his shirt making sure his gig-line was perfect. Lifting his right foot, he rubbed the toe of his shoe against the back of his left leg. The loafers weren't shiny. He liked them shiny, didn't he? Gunther repeated the action with the left shoe. Looking down at his sleeve, he could see the drool was starting to dry.

More noise out front, sounded like wrestling. Gunther checked to see if his sidearm was in its holster. Relief flowed through him with its recognition. He kept his right hand on the gun and walked down the hall. The noise stopped. He called out to see if anyone was there. No response. He stopped in the hall and listened. Gunther looked back over his shoulder to the hall leading back into the break room. Nothing but empty space. He tucked his back tight against the wall and felt the bones in his shoulder blades press against the painted sheet rock. He took a breath, closed his eyes and concentrated on what he was supposed to do. Opening his eyes, he could see dusk was upon the once sleepy little town of Outlaw River. He wasn't used to seeing the trees and mountains at this time of the night from the Sheriff's station. At least he couldn't remember the view out the hallway window at this time. The wind pressed hard against the building, and the windows vibrated. Gunther drew his eye in on the glass, losing focus on the outside world. The glass was dirty, and the outside world didn't exist. More noises from inside, not the wind.

Gunther moved along the wall and approached the entrance to the front office, home to the dispatcher and waiting area for the public. The sheriff's desk doubled as dispatch since the town was so small, and the sheriff's office had limited service. Gunther figured some office staff must be out there because they should be, but a part of him warned caution, so he proceeded tentatively, expecting the worst.

There was a loud crash and then a thud. Gunther dropped to the ground, only a few feet from the door now. The rectangular glass insert in the door provided no view from a distance. He took a breath, gathered himself to his feet, and walked to the door in short, careful steps. He peered through the glass but could see nothing. No one was behind the counter, and no one was on the other side in the public area. He opened the door and poked his head out.

"Anyone out here? You'll show yourself if you are smart. I have my gun out of the holster and fully loaded. I've been waiting years to use it, so speak now, or die."

Gunther wasn't too happy with the last part of the statement. He replayed it in his head. 'Speak now, or die' – What the hell does that mean? Weak, he knew, but he wasn't really prepared to say anything. It should have been better, though.

"Hey! Anyone out here?"

Gunther slid out and let the door close behind him. He holstered his gun but kept his hand on the grip. The front door was blowing in from the heavy winds. But there was no way the wind and door had caused the noise he heard. He grabbed his head with his left hand and pressed his fingers against his temple. The pain was lessening, thank goodness, but it still hurt like hell.

"Myron."

"Myron, help."

Gunther spun and looked down the hall through the glass in the door. He saw nothing. He turned and looked down at the desk thinking the microphone for the dispatch radio had gone off. He grabbed the microphone. It was turned off.

"Gunther, help me, please."

A hand from the other side of the counter appeared on the top. Just some fingers, and they were badly bruised and bloody, apparently missing all the nails. After Gunther's feet stabilized on the linoleum again, his heart slowed. He moved towards the counter and peered over.

Lying on the ground was someone in a gray jump suit – head shaven, dirty as hell, with bleeding hands and bare feet.

Gunther walked around the desk and out the swinging knee door to the front of the counter. He secured his revolver in the holster and knelt down near the person he figured was a vagrant. Outlaw River had a few in the summer months, and this must be one of them. He grabbed the shoulders of the man lying face down and rolled him over. The face was swollen and bloody and covered in dirt; there was something familiar about this vagrant.

The Sheriff ran to the break room where he tore off half a

227

dozen paper towels and stuffed them in his pants' pocket. He stripped another handful and dampened them, then walked down the hall toward the intruder. Once through the main door, he stopped and grabbed the pump jar of hand sanitizer and put himself on the floor near the stranger.

Gunther took his time and carefully cleaned the man's face. He put some hand sanitizer on a dry towel and wiped the man's face being careful to keep the alcohol-based gel away from his eyes. His own eyes were starting to register more, and the strange face was losing its unfamiliarity. There was something so calm and warm about the eyes staring back at him. Gunther recognized them. He'd seen these eyes up close, oh, so many times. He took the man's head in his hands and held it close to his chest.

"Larry, I'm here. I'm here. You're going to be okay now."

Chapter 61

A Sad and Heavy Energy

Mitch looked at Wise One and started pacing away from the fire. He felt a new nervous energy boiling inside of him. Good, he thought, knowing he would need adrenaline to kick in and send away the cobwebs in his head.

"What do I do now, Wise One? How can I find Jasper and help him? He must need me, right?"

"Mitch Wilde, stop pacing, and stand still. Face me."

Mitch stopped on the dirt floor of the cave. He noticed paintings on the walls of the cave for the first time. They seemed very old and similar to the images he had seen in books and online over the years. He wondered if, when things got back to normal, he could spend some time here and photograph these images. He couldn't recall ever seeing anything in the literature about this cave. Documenting it would be fantastic; something so remarkable should be shared with the outside world. Mitch knew how much of Native American culture had been bastardized and lost over the years. The history books should see this.

Mitch drew his attention back to Wise One.

"What is it? Did I miss something? Is there something else?"

"Only you will know if you missed something, Mitch Wilde. I have another matter to talk with you about before I guide you on your way."

"Okay, what is it?"

Mitch and his companion turned in unison at the sounds of loud voices coming from the other end of the cave.

A young man ran up to Wise One.

"Wise One, you need to come with me, please. I have been asked to get you. There is someone you need to see. An intruder."

Wise One smiled at Mitch.

Mitch felt strange. The look, only a glance, held so much information, and Mitch could feel it seeping into his own consciousness, one piece at a time.... Jack?

Wise One put a hand on the messenger's shoulder.

"Take us to this someone."

The young man turned, and Wise One followed.

"Walk with us, Mitch Wilde. I think you know who is here."

"It's Jack, isn't it? I'm not sure how I know, but I can sense it."

"Be careful, Mitch Wilde, you are getting in tune with nature. Once you journey down the path, everything will change for you."

Mitch placed himself a pace behind Wise One and several steps behind the eager messenger. In moments they were at the other end of the cave; the gathering of Native Americans separated to make an opening. Mitch followed Wise One into the inner circle.

There were two strong-looking Native Americans, one on each side of the intruder. They held his arms and were not letting go. Wise One stopped in front of them, raised his hands, and touched each one's shoulder. Without a word, they released their grips.

Wise one spoke.

"Welcome. I think you have come to the place you imagined. Well done. What you are looking for is here."

Wise One stepped to the side and revealed Mitch.

Mitch smiled.

"And what brings you to this neck of the woods, friend?"

Jack looked around, and his face began to relax. His furrowed brow loosened, and his distrusting eyes started to lighten.

"I'm trying to find you, dumb ass. I thought you were in trouble. But it would appear that you are anything but in trouble. Why are you hiding here? Why aren't you looking for Mabey?"

Mitch moved forward and gave Jack a big old Wilde hug. He couldn't remember the last time he had hugged Jack. Theirs was more of a hand-shake, pat-on-the-back type of man love.

"Shit, Jack you're shaking. What the hell is wrong?"

Mitch backed off and looked his friend in the eyes.

Most of the Native Americans, including the two huge warriors who had Jack under control, went back about their business. Wise One hovered and stayed near the two Anglos.

"Let's see, Wilde. I go place-jumping looking for you and get light-headed and woozy. Anyway, I'm worried about you and end up here surrounded by a bunch of Native Americans who don't look welcoming at all, and they have me pinned down. They looked at me as if I had just shit in their Wheaties. How would you be doing?"

Mitch laughed and put his arm around Jack's shoulder. He rotated him so they both faced Wise One.

"Wise One, this is my best friend, Jack, since the age of fifteen. We'd have been friends sooner, but we didn't live near each other until then. Jack, this is Wise One. He gathered me in front of Jasper's and brought me here. He is large and in charge, if you know what I mean."

Jack reached out his hand to Wise One

"Nice to meet you, sir. Thanks for grabbing Mitch, I guess. He seems okay."

"You are welcome here, Mr. Jack. I believe we accidentally shot you with an arrow days ago. I apologize. The arrow was meant for Mitch. What is it that brings you here besides your friend?"

Mitch looked at Jack and smiled. They were both thinking about the "meant for Mitch" statement. They smiled at each other but didn't feel the need to reference the comment.

"I don't know really. Just a gut feeling I had all of a sudden about Mitch needing to be rescued again, similar to the time I rescued him from the cold water of Crater Lake."

"You'll never let your rescuing be forgotten, will you, Jack? Don't make me regret being saved."

Jack smiled and noticed the smoky atmosphere of the cave for the first time. His body was calming, and his senses were coming back into focus.

"Why are you here, Mitch? Do you know anything about Mabey?"

"I'm here because I was about to go and do a few rash things. Wise One gathered me and brought me here to shed some light on the situation. I had a vision, kind of like your gut-feeling, I suppose. Anyway, Mabey is fine, but I think Jasper's in trouble."

"What makes you think that? I just left him with Delores, and he's fine. We were going over events in his old-man conspiracy garage when I got a feather up my butt about you. I'm not sure why now. I guess my fear is you'll get yourself in danger again like at Crater Lake."

Jack smiled, knowing Mitch registered the jab.

Mitch started to respond but knew Jack was waiting for a retort. So, he left the jab unsaid.

Wise One stepped forward.

"I am most certain you came here for a reason, Jack. Mitch was just about to go on a chase for his beloved when he sat with us at the fire and waited for his vision. You sensed him in his time of frustration before the quest when he was able to relax. So you find yourself here for a reason. The gods want the two of you together for a final journey. I don't know what is in store, but I know it has something to do with your town, the people of the town and the ones you call family. Blood and no blood. Your place-jumping travel is about over, Jack, since you have no Native American blood in you, or very little. You may or may not have been told, but the energy flowing through you from the arrow has limited effect on those who don't share the blood of the earth."

"Blood of the earth?" Jack questioned out of curiosity.

"Yes, he means you're a mere mortal and don't share any Native American blood like your brother and good friend." Mitch smiled and puffed out his chest. He could counteract Jack's Crater Lake rescue jabs.

"Well, Wilde, it didn't seem to help you much while you were tied to a floating tree and about to die in Crater Lake."

"I knew you were going to bring that up again, Jack. Who says I needed rescuing? Did you ever think I was one with the earth and on a quest of my own? I had a bird keeping me company, a tree I was connected with, and the water was washing away all the impurities of my soul and its fleshy vessel."

Jack burst out laughing. "Oh, man, you're full of so much shit, Wilde. I can't believe you're going to go down this path. I shouldn't be surprised, though."

Wise One watched and listened. He liked their bond, but his heart was growing heavy. He sensed something off with Jack. He directed his words at Jack.

Walk with me, you two.

Mitch and Jack fell into step with Wise One, moving toward the fire pit.

"Jack, can you tell me more about this Delores who is with the Jasper you speak of? I am sensing a strange energy right now, and I believe it is coming from you. There is something odd about her I am picking up. I feel a sad and heavy energy."

Chapter 62

Try Me Again

Mabey took a breath, looked in the rear-view mirror, then twisted around to look directly into the back of the pickup bed. It was empty except for a couple duffle bags. She wasn't sure what was in them, but based on the gun in the seat next to her, the shotgun in the gun rack behind her and the look of the two men surrounding Kala, she could make an educated guess. The steering wheel felt slick under the torn skin of her nail-less hands. She was nervous and afraid. Both Kala and her lives hinged on the outcome of the action she was about to attempt.

Flashing in her brain was her recognition of these two jug heads towering over Kala. She now remembered where she'd seen them before. She was certain they were the two who had blasted the alien hovercraft from the sky when she and Mayor Jenkins were on the run and hiding. She shifted her thoughts to Mayor Larry, wondering if he was okay.

A loud scream brought Mabey back to what was transpiring in front of her with the *Deliverance* wannabes. Mabey turned the key, started the pickup, grabbed the shift knob, and felt the muscles under her skin flex with rage and purpose. Putting the truck in gear, she floored the accelerator. The pickup bounced over the rough terrain closing the distance between the target and herself in an instant. Mabey kept her eyes intent on the two men and Kala as the seconds passed. Right before she got to them, she hit the brakes. She hadn't planned perfectly: the sudden force of the stop threw the gun to the floorboard. Mabey remembered the recent event when she slammed her brakes on and her phone flew to the floor in much the same way. This was different. It was a gun. Fortunately, it didn't go off. This time she had a friend who was about to be tortured or raped. Their very lives were hanging in the balance.

Mabey slammed the pickup into park, and in one fluid motion, threw the door open, jumped out, found and then grabbed the gun off the floor. It seemed like minutes but only seconds had passed. Mabey moved from behind the door, a mere twenty feet away, close enough to rain some fear down on these assholes, but far enough to get away if she needed to. She aimed the gun at the strangers.

Mabey remembered Mitch again: *"You can be scared, Mabey. Fear provides adrenaline and courage if you channel it. Embrace the fear and stay calm. Think. Surprise is a great equalizer; use it to your advantage."*

Mabey focused on the task-at-hand. Yelling, she directed her fear at the two next to Kala.

"Get away from her right now! Back up slowly, or I'm going to blow you away!"

The two were startled. Mabey could see it in their bodies and facial expressions. The one who was on the ground about to rape Kala stood. Their expressions changed to condescension and arrogance.

"Well, what do we have here? We each have one now."

"Yep, no need to share."

Mabey flashed back to the woods where these two podunks shot the hovercraft. She remembered they had shouted their names through the woods, proud of their accomplishment. Another opportunity to surprise.

Mabey took a confident two-steps closer to the men. She released the safety on the gun, then slid the action back in a slow and deliberate fashion making sure while doing so there was a round in the chamber. She wanted no doubt of her familiarity with the weapon. She leveled the gun again, got in a proper shooter's stance, and put one of the shitheads in the crosshairs.

"Don't make me say it again. Back away from her. Kala, get up. Get up right now! Get in the passenger side of the pickup."

Kala didn't move causing Mabey some frustration.

"DO IT NOW, KALA!"

Kala gathered herself and jogged to the pickup while the two men stood motionless. An embarrassing lesson in control, front and center at the hands of a woman no less. They were used to being the aggressors. When Mabey heard the passenger door slam, she took two steps back toward the pickup, keeping the gun leveled on the two. One of them started to make a break straight at Mabey. The other stood frozen.

Mabey fired a shot over the charging man's head. Close, but an intended miss.

"STOP!" Mabey shouted.

"You both listen and listen well. Turn around and start walking away. If either of you makes a move this way again, I will drop both of you."

Mabey took a step closer to the man who had just charged. He was only ten feet away now, too close for comfort, but Mabey had the gun, and she was in no mood for idle threats. If challenged, she would do what needed to be done and lose no sleep.

"Turn around and start walking. NOW!"

The man farther back and in the safer position started to speak.

"She can't get both…"

Mabey yelled one final time at both of them.

"Try me again, Dusty. Or is it Billy?"

Chapter 63

Black Obsidian

Jasper felt strength flowing back into his legs. His mind had stayed sharp throughout, but his body simply would not respond. Whatever Delores had done to him was effective. It seemed related entirely to the physique, no drugs or chemicals of any kind. Jasper would have to do some research. He thought the Vulcan neck squeeze was made-for-TV bullshit.

"So, Jasper, you must be about to get the feeling back in those legs of yours. You about ready to help me with my little need?"

"Your little need? Is that what you call it? You saw that sweet little lady, not even out of high school yet. Her father left her when she was young, and all she and her mother have is each other. And you want to take that away from them?"

Delores stood and paced the room. Jasper fidgeted in his position when she wasn't looking. When she was looking, he remained motionless except for his head.

"It happened to me, when I was only six, being taken, that is. I don't remember my mother at all, and my father is a distant memory at best." Delores stopped in front of the family room window and stared into Jasper's backyard lined with an apple tree, various oaks, and backed with giant tall pines. Delores tried to remember her father. All she could capture was a name.

Jasper wiggled his toes inside his shoes: tingly but fully functional. The backs of his knees ached but carried muscular response to his brain. He was sure his body was a full go. What the hell could he do, though? He had a gun in his bedroom. He could make a break for the room, close the door behind him giving him valuable seconds to get the gun and blast the bitch when she broke through the door. Option two, less favored but still giving him a chance, was a gun he had placed in a holster under a table behind the couch. If she got far enough away, he could make a break for it and hope he got the gun out in time to get the drop on her. Another option: do nothing, string her along as long as possible, and give her a good whack on the head with a lamp. This was his least favorite option, but it still gave him a chance.

He knew of course, there was one more option: do nothing: go along with the evil bitch, and play it out. See what happened. Jasper wasn't one to let things just happen though. The last time he gave up control, a rodeo clown had stolen his wife. This was quite different though, he admitted to himself, while he sat in a chair and feigned paralysis.

"Jasper, I imagine you are sitting there trying to figure out any number of ways to stop me."

Delores turned from the window and approached Jasper. She stopped in front of him and stood between his legs. Jasper wanted to jump now and go for her throat and head. He was so unsure of his strength, though, he knew it would be a fool's mission. Instead, he stared straight into the eyes of change. Jasper thought of Delores as a child being given away by her father, how painful it must have been for the father, and how demoralizing and heartbreaking for a little girl to know her father gave her away. She was too young to understand that her father had had no real choice and that he'd saved countless lives because of his sacrifice. No little girl should have to understand.

Jasper set aside fleeting compassion for the woman standing in front of him. She could break the cycle and leave another young lady to her normal life. She chose to be selfish. Jasper had to figure out a way to stop her. Where the hell was Mitch?

Delores glared down at Jasper. "Are you ready, old man?"

"I can't move yet, so I'm not sure what kind of help I can be to you."

Delores smiled, bent over at the waist, and put her hands carefully on Jasper's thighs. Her face was inches from his.

Jasper thought Delores's eyes were amazing. One second they were bluer than the depths of Crater Lake; the next they were as dark as the richest black obsidian.

Delores spoke directly into Jasper's face. She worked at being sultry, demur, and sexual, thinking the effect would tug at the male in Jasper.

"Jasper, c'mon. Don't play me for a fool. I'm fully aware of what you can and cannot do. I applaud you for your delay tactics, but we both know these legs of yours are just fine. You will take me across the street now, sit them all down, and explain exactly what is going to happen and why. Cindi, you, and I will get into one of the cars, and we'll drive to a location where I will place her in a cell to be picked up. Once done, you'll be free to go, and I'll be free to live out the rest of my life on this Alien-forsaken planet. Do you understand?"

"What I understand is my legs don't fully work yet, and I don't know what you think I can do for you. I don't know those people very well. I could walk in there like Tom Hanks and not be able to get them to buy the bullshit you're selling."

Jasper watched as Delores removed her hands from his legs and stood up. She swiveled her head and moved her neck around. Jasper contemplated taking action now, but he was in no position of strength. She had him right now, and they both knew it.

"Okay, Jasper, let's go."

Jasper watched as Delores raised both her hands over her shoulders. She made fists, and her hands came down hard on Jasper's legs; he screamed in pain.

Chapter 64

Georgia Roots

Mabey watched as Billy and Dusty walked away from her.

"Keep walking until I say you can stop."

She fired a shot above their heads. One jumped, and one ducked. Both of them were frightened.

"Geezus, lady, okay. Ya know, payback is a bitch. We won't forget this, and you will pay. You should get rid of both of us now."

"Shut the hell up, Dusty, you idiot. She'll do it."

"No, she won't. She's all talk."

Mabey watched as the two idiots bickered but kept walking. She jumped into the pickup's cab and set the gun on the seat between her and Kala. Maneuvering the pickup back to where it came from and checking the rear-view mirror, she expected Dusty and Billy to be running toward them. She chuckled as the mirror revealed the two rolling on the ground fighting.

"Hopefully, those two morons will kill each other."

Mabey took her eyes away from the mirror. "Are you okay, Kala?"

"I am now. A bit shaken. I'm mad more than anything. I can't believe I froze, Mabey."

"Kala, we're beat to shit, weak, and in a lot of pain. You had no energy to fight back."

Kala responded without hesitation.

"You did."

"I had a pickup and a gun. Those were the reasons I was successful."

"It was more than a gun and a truck, Mabey. It was your attitude. I'm not so sure you even needed a gun. You had me scared. Where'd you learn to act so damn good? And, hell, woman, you know your way around a gun. What in the world do you do with your free time?"

"My husband Mitch has some survivalist in him. He's not the type to build a bomb shelter or dig a cellar in the backyard; he's more the type of guy who imagines himself duking it out in an apocalyptic setting. So he taught me to use a gun and shoot a bow; he constantly talks with me about what to do in situations. I kind of enjoy it, and I'm so damn glad he did. I've been able to survive the last day because of it."

"Can I sign up for a couple of classes once this is done? I have no clue what to do, and neither does Aaron. We should start a club."

Mabey smiled, Kala smiled, and then they both laughed, releasing pent-up fear and tension.

Mabey wiped a few tears from her eyes with her dirty shirt sleeve while Kala rolled down her window to let in some air. Dusk had turned to night, so Mabey turned on the pickup's lights. She wasn't sure where to go and wondered if they were headed towards a road. In escaping, she pointed the pickup in the opposite direction from which it was facing. Now she noticed a few broken shrubs and small trees, which at a glance appeared snapped off by something other than nature.

"Kala, help me look for broken trees and tracks from the pickup's going through the bushes. Those two idiots probably came from the road and not some deep woods hideout. I hope we aren't driving right back into a trap."

"Oh hell! Don't say that."

"If that were to happen, Kala, are you with me in that I'd rather die than be taken alive."

"Hell, yes. Driving this damn pickup into a river ravine would be a better ending than being on my back with those two standing over me again."

"Good. Can you look out the back window and see if they're back there anywhere? I have to slow down; looks like a large dip up ahead, and I don't want to get high-centered."

"Sure."

Kala turned and looked back over the pickup bed. All she could see in the deepening darkness was the red glow from the taillights splashing off the tree bark. Mabey slowed the pickup to a crawl taking her foot off the accelerator and feathering the brake. She decided to keep her right foot hovering over the accelerator in case Kala saw something, and they needed to get going fast. She noticed her hands on the wheel, the crusted blood where her nails had once been. Her fingers were swollen as were her feet. However, neither had let her down in a time of desperate need. She couldn't wait to soak in a bath run by the lord of her manor. Mabey thought of Mitch and wondered if he still had his hair and nails.

Kala yelped, and Mabey's blood surged.

"What, Kala?"

"Oh, thank God. I'm sorry, Mabey. It's nothing. It was just a deer, I think."

Mabey broke out in laughter as the pickup crested the dip and pointed downhill. There were fewer downed trees and rocks, and a smoother surface.

"Kala, turn around and look."

Kala turned and sighed. She put her hands on her face and took a deep breath.

"Thank God, Mabey, and thank you again. Do you and Mitch like soul food?"

"Mitch and I like everything, Kala. Why?"

"Because I make some great soul food – my Georgia roots and a mother's passion for the kitchen. Anyway, a meal isn't enough, but when we get through this, I want to have you and Mitch over for dinner. Okay?"

"Absolutely, I look forward to it."

Mabey guided the redneck sled onto the hard-packed gravel surface of a road. Her hands and feet felt a little better as her mind massaged them with the security of the road and the distance from evil's dynamic duo. She sighed and reached over, putting a comforting hand on Kala's leg.

"Now c'mon, Kala. Let's go get that husband of yours."

Chapter 65

Forget About Mitch

Gunther carried Mayor Jenkins to the couch He'd bathed his face, hands, and feet as best he could with the supplies he could find. The first-aid kit came in handy, and the towels from the small locker room were sufficient. The Mayor was finally drinking a little water. Gunther wasn't sure, but it appeared his dear friend had been near dehydration. He had no fingernails, no toenails, and a shaven head. Gunther didn't ask, but he surmised that all the hair from his entire body had been removed.

Seeing his friend and one-time lover lying on the ground, and wiping away the dirt, blood, and grime from his face helped Gunther's cloudy memory. The last couple of days rushed back into his memory banks like wheels spinning from the force of river water. He needed explanations, but right now he needed to attend to the Mayor.

"How're you feeling, Larry, any better at all?"

"Much better, thanks. My feet and hands hurt the worst, and I can't seem to drink enough water."

"You should stop drinking for a few minutes, I think. Let your body start to absorb all you've put into it these last few minutes. You're safe now. The Tylenol should kick in soon. Can you tell me what happened?"

"When?"

"Well, for starters, do you remember who did this to you?"

"No, I don't. I remember driving in my car, going home for lunch when my car stopped, just shut down."

Mayor Jenkins took another sip of water and sat up. Sheriff Gunther placed a towel under the Mayor's tattered and torn feet for a softer platform. The Mayor wasn't surprised at Myron's actions; he could be so sweet and caring at times.

"Then what happened?"

"Well, I coasted it over to the side of the road as best I could before it stopped. I grabbed my cell phone to call the office and get a tow truck, but it was dead too. I got out and looked under the hood. I figured the battery just gave out since all the electronics were gone. I was standing there, and the surrounding woods and road were so quiet; the lack of noise was obvious. Kind of eerie. I fiddled with the battery, tugged on some wires, got exasperated and decided to start walking when I heard a humming noise overhead. I looked up and saw the air fold and move, like waves in the ocean."

"Waves in the ocean?" Sheriff Gunther was puzzled, and he was sure his face showed it.

"I'm not sure how to explain exactly. It was as if something was there, but it wasn't. The air moved around it."

"You said there was a humming noise?"

"Yes, it sounded like an electric car. Quiet but definitely not natural."

"The next thing I know; I'm waking up on a bus with a bunch of other people like me. All of us had our heads shaved and all finger- and toenails removed. We were in these grey jumpsuits."

Sheriff Gunther stood and started pacing. He was going into investigator mode. His headache was diminishing, and he was gaining energy and new purpose.

"There were other people on the bus with you? How many?"

"A lot. I don't know, thirty or forty probably, and there were a half a dozen or so buses besides ours."

"Who was driving?"

"Someone like us. I don't know who it was, but he also wore a grey jumpsuit."

"When you say like us, you mean shaved?"

"Yes, exactly."

Mayor Jenkins took a small drink of water. His feet hurt like hell. He looked at his swollen hands wondering if his nails would grow back. He figured they would and wondered if it would hurt.

"How was the guy driving?"

"He appeared to be in some kind of trance like Mabey, me and the others."

"Mabey Wilde?" Gunther stopped his pacing and spun to face the Mayor. This could be an interesting twist.

"Yes, Mabey Wilde. She saved my ass."

"Was Mitch on the bus with you?"

The Mayor lifted his resting head from the back of the couch.

"No, Myron. Mitch was not on the bus with us. I'm afraid to ask why, but go ahead and tell me why you want to know."

"No reason, just curious more than anything."

Sheriff Gunther lied. He felt a flood of emotions when the Wilde name was mentioned. Anger boiled up inside him. It was comforting in a way, feeding his emotions, stabilizing him. Calming was what it was. Anger and hate made him feel normal. He remembered the taillight, the coffee shop treatment, the football field incident so many years ago, and how he hated Mitch Wilde. If he, not Mitch Wilde, had been high-school quarterback, so much would be different.

"Myron, you need to forget about Mitch right now. We have to figure out what is going on in this town and do something, if we can. If not, we need to hide somewhere until all this shit blows over. And it will blow over. Whatever took me and had us on that bus must have been

Alien. Why would humans do something like this to one another? Besides, we don't have stealth technology and the ability to shut down electrical systems in cars like happened to me. At least I don't think we do."

Gunther heard only a few of the Mayor's words. He was in his own little Wilde world right now with one thing on his mind – making Mitch pay. Hell, he wanted to kill him if possible. With everything going on right now, he had the perfect opportunity. He could get away with some serious shit right now: murder and the ability to blame it on the other-world shit storm going on around them.

"What direction did you come from, Mayor? Do you know?"

"I'm pretty sure the bus was taking us up East Evens Creek Road. I think we were going north. All I could think about was what was going to happen to all of us on those buses. I feel sure we were being taken somewhere for transport. North toward the mountains, there are plenty of remote places up there where buses could be hidden, and spaceships could get in and out without a lot of gazers."

"I'll bet you're right, Mayor. Everyone is probably going to be taken somewhere and tested or probed. Not so sure about spaceships, but, hell, what do I know? It could just be the government taking advantage and rounding up people to exterminate. It's happened before although some Indians in town were rumbling about 'Star People'."

"What are Star People, Myron?"
"Hell if I know, but they must be Aliens. So, did Mabey walk back with you? Where is she now?"

"No, she was captured again. I managed to go unnoticed somehow. Whoever had us on the bus got her back. I hid and then took off running toward town. And here I am now."

"East Evens Creek, huh?"

"Yes, had to be."

"Listen, Mayor, you'll be okay here for a while. There's coffee and food in the break room. Help yourself to whatever you can find. If you want, you can take a shower in the locker room. I have something I have to do."

Sheriff Gunther exited the building while the last word left his mouth. He was in hurry-up mode as he headed for his cruiser. He needed to find Mabey Wilde. Wherever she was, Mitch was sure to be close.

As Gunther exited, Mayor Jenkins sat on the couch, watching as the front door swung closed and rattled in the wind. The pain in his body momentarily forgotten; he wondered when he would see the Sheriff again.

Chapter 66

Maria de los Dolores

Sorrows

Part I

Mitch picked up a stick and poked at the fire. A few sparks danced upwards; Mitch watched as they kissed the top of the cave and disappeared.

Wise One, seated next to Jack, spoke first.

"What can you tell me about this Delores?"

"Not much really. Mitch might know more than I do about her. She was with us at the coffee shop and then went with us back to Jasper's place. She listened as Jasper and I stepped through different scenarios waiting for Mitch to show up."

Wise one wasn't satisfied.

"What about you, Mitch Wilde?"

Jack wondered why Wise One always called Mitch by his first and last name. He knew now was not a good time to ask, but he was curious.

Mitch, hearing his name, stopped playing in the fire where he hoped to see more smoke and images showing him exactly what to do.

"Um, let's see. Oh, yeah, she claimed to be a star traveler. She also said something about being taken from her parents or grandfather at a really young age. I think she claimed to be about six years old. She said her parents were missing, or had been taken, and her grandfather trained her in the ways of the force."

Jack laughed. Mitch smiled, and Wise One sat there perplexed.

"Sorry, a little levity. She went on to talk about the ability to travel around with some basic training and reiterated we weren't tied to places we'd been. It sounded as if we could travel to a place we were able concentrate on, whether or not we'd had any real experiences with those locations. She doesn't like being called an Indian, prefers Native American, but she isn't condescending about it. Very confident and well-spoken. What did an ex V.P. say once? 'Clean and articulate'. "

Jack laughed again. Mitch was on a roll.

"What does she look like?"

"She's about 5' 4" or so. Beautiful long black – jet-black – hair, high cheek bones, perfect skin with a reddish brown hue. Quite gorgeous, I must say."

"Is that all?" Wise One questioned.

Jack jumped in.

"I didn't notice while we were at the coffee shop, or outside, but once we got to Jasper's house, her eyes seemed to glow, as if they were liquid: mesmerizing. So much so, I didn't want to look at them very long."

Mitch poked at the fire some more. Jack turned his attention to the fire himself as he felt intimidated and uncomfortable staring at Wise One for any length of time.

Mitch watched as Wise One closed his eyes and hummed.

Jack looked at Mitch and shrugged.

Mitch shook his head and waved his hand, making it clear Jack should sit and wait.

Wise One raised his head, lifted his hands upwards, and spoke.

"I am certain this Delores you speak of --- beep ?a gew gatba."

Mitch dropped the stick, felt his blood pressure slow as his stomach dropped. He looked at Jack and spoke.

"Wise One just told us his granddaughter has arrived."

Chapter 67

With Any Luck at All

Sheriff Gunther stopped at the driver's door of his cruiser. He looked around town and the empty streets. The darkness of night had set in, and he was used to seeing a more bustling town with everyone home from work and preparing for the next day at the gas station, diner, and supermarket. There were no pumps running at the station today. The local food mart parking lot, normally filled as people poured into the store in search of items for dinner and tomorrow's breakfasts, was near empty. There were two cars in the lot, both parked hastily and one with a door wide open. He'd never seen the town look this way. Police training, handbooks, seminars, and casual conversations among lawmen hadn't prepared him for this. Riots, robberies, kidnapping, hell, even terrorist actions, were all part of his sheriff's repertoire, but Alien abductions and invasion – there isn't even a paragraph on them.

Gunther took the keys from his front pocket and slid inside his cruiser. He checked the rearview mirror and made a minor adjustment. He slid his key into the ignition and held his hand steady deciding what to do. Looking out his front window at the sheriff's station, he contemplated going back inside to sit with the Mayor and wait until morning. Perhaps things would return to normal, and the Alien intruders would be gone. Then the two of them could start cleaning up

Outlaw River and get it back to some semblance of normalcy. Hell, he wasn't sure if normal was possible anymore. Everything had changed. He thought about TV shows and the books he saw displayed at the supermarket: dead people walking – as if that made any sense at all. This was something he could deal with. At least there were chapters in police books on how to handle mass viral attacks and flesh-eating freaks whacked out on bath salts.

Again, Gunther looked in the rearview mirror and at the same time, he turned on the car. He thought of Mitch Wilde and how he fed the anger inside him: it was building and made him feel alive. It also made him feel ashamed, but the shame always came later. He could deal with it then. Right now, he wanted and needed to feel the anger. The only way he was going to go through with this was to feed his hate and let it lead him to rage.

He drove through the streets, picking his way through the abandoned cars, until he reached the main road. The pain from so many years of unresolved anger caused tears to stream down his reddened face; his chest was pounding with a purpose, and his headache was all but gone. He knew he would be at Evens Creek Road within minutes, and with any luck at all, within an hour or two he would find his prey and put an end to all the pain and agony he had endured for years. Gunther floored the accelerator to eighty miles an hour; then he backed off and maintained a fast but controllable speed, slowing only for corners. He rolled down his window to smell the river air and feel the cool breeze on his face. Sheriff Myron Gunther smiled, deep in thought. Tonight, Mitch Wilde was going to die.

Chapter 68

Maria de los Dolores

Sorrows

Part II

Wise One held out his hand to Mitch. Mitch started to take it when something in him realized the gesture wasn't about him but the stick. Mitch picked up his fire-poking stick and handed it to the Native American. Wise One took the stick and poked the base of the fire. Mitch could see he was in deep thought. Hell, the guy seemed always to be in deep thought. Mitch gave Jack a pat on the shoulder, and the two sat in silence, waiting.

Wise one scooted himself back a little; Mitch figured the heat must be getting to him, perhaps not, though, as the fire had died down significantly, and it wasn't as if the cave were blistering hot. He watched as Wise One now started to draw with the stick in the dirt between himself and the fire. Mitch gave Jack a look of bewilderment and frustration, thinking it was a hell of a time to be making cave drawings.

"I am not wasting time, Mitch Wilde. I am thinking. Decisions will have to be made: difficult decisions which will affect the three of us seated at this fire."

"Could you be a little more specific, Grandpa? I'm not sure I follow."

Jack smiled at his friend. He loved the way Mitch could so easily become comfortable with folks. He called Wise One 'Grandpa' already, and it didn't seem to piss off the chief.

"Delores is my granddaughter. I gave her to the Star People many years ago as a token of friendship and trust so they would leave my people alone. Every day I think of her and wonder why the gods asked me to do what I did."

Mitch felt Wise One's pain and struggle.

"I can't imagine how hard it must have been to do that. In your position, you had to take into account the welfare of everyone involved, and you had the courage to do what needed to be done. I couldn't have done it, and this inability would have cost dearly. On the upside, so many years have gone, and now you have the chance to reunite, true?"

"It isn't so simple, I fear, Mitch Wilde. What is revealed to me is that she is here to make a trade in order to be released from her burden."

Jack jumped in. "What exactly is her burden, Wise One?"

Wise One replied without hesitation. "Giving birth to humans so the Star People would have laborers, among other things."

Mitch, not wanting to miss an opportunity to learn from Wise One, asked right away.

"Other things?"

"Probably experimentation, Mitch Wilde. The Star People say they created life on our planet. They watch us constantly. The planet is like their, how do you say, dollhouse."

Mitch nodded yes. Wise One continued.

"You have both heard of cow mutilations, crop circles, Alien abductions, random catastrophic weather events and more, I presume."

Mitch said "Yes," and Jack nodded. Both were intent on catching every word.

"Many long years ago, they sat with me and explained who they are and why they do the things they do. I did not pretend to understand.

I listened and asked questions. Much has faded from my mind, but I remember some things. One thing I do remember is they can do whatever they want to the planet."

Mitch looked at Jack but spoke to Wise One

"So we are their ants."

Mitch couldn't help but think of Jasper. The old guy was dead on.

Wise One stood and put a hand out to Jack who grabbed it and stood with him. He then reached for Mitch, but he'd already jumped up.

"The three of us need to go, and I must make another very hard choice."

Mitch brushed off the seat of his pants, wondering how dirty the back of his jeans were. He turned to Wise One and, with impatient confidence, spoke:

"Okay, get the horse, and let's get out of here."

Chapter 69

Frightened Silence

"Do you think Aaron will still be there, Mabey?"

Mabey rolled up her window to avoid the dust kicked up by the oversized tires. The air in the Redneck Sled further dried out her arid throat. She knew they needed some water, but Aaron might need medical attention. Now that they had a vehicle, their priority list changed.

"Definitely, Kala. He might not be in the exact position where we left him, but he'll be near there. His ankle was in pretty bad shape."

"It was?"

"Yes, nothing to worry about long-term; it will heal. He'll need to rest and to stay off it for quite a while. So yes, my guess is he waited until he thought he could move without detection and then tried to distance himself from what was going on. Once he realized he couldn't stand the pain, making more noise than it was worth and attracting unwanted attention, he probably found a tree and made himself as comfortable as possible for a long cold night."

"I'm going to warm him up when I see him. Do you think we have enough gas to get him and then make it back down to Outlaw River?"

"Shit, I haven't even looked at the gas gauge, Kala."

Mabey took the opportunity to peer at the needle in the gauge console of the pickup truck.

"Whew, we have three quarters of a tank so we should be fine. Hard to tell with these pickups, but even if it gets horrible mileage, we should be okay. Worst case scenario, we can coast part of the way back since it's downhill. We'll make it. First things first."

The two sat in silence for a couple minutes, both feeling pain. Mabey couldn't remember ever feeling this sore, both mentally and physically, even during the peak of her training when she'd pushed her body to its limits, and every muscle in her body was tender and sore. That was nothing. This was pain. She focused on the good. They'd escaped Aliens and rednecks; they had a pickup, and they were on their way to get Kala's husband.

"You haven't even mentioned your husband, Mabey. Do you know where he is and if he's okay?"

Mabey laughed --- a combination of nervousness, fear and anxiety. She didn't know; she could theorize, but she didn't really know.

"Let me tell you something about my husband, Kala. He is either the most blessed or luckiest man on the planet. His father used to tell him he could shit gold if he wanted to."

Kala chuckled and held her smile, distracted from the pain, and noticed when she smiled, she felt better.

Mabey continued after a moment of reflection.

"He is a great man to be married to. He has his thick-headed asshole moments like all men, but at the end of each and every day, I know he loves me and would do anything for me. Plus he's fun as hell to hang out with."

"Where is he right now?"

Mabey felt nervous. She'd been so focused on Kala and their survival, she hadn't spent much time worrying about Mitch. Mitch permeated her mind. She couldn't even remember the last time she saw him. The night before he left for Crater Lake? WTF, how could she not remember? She needed some water and food.

"I don't know, Kala. The last time I saw him was yesterday I think. He had to get up really early to go to Crater Lake and take photos of the sunrise. He's a freelance outdoor photographer and has won a bunch of awards for his Oregon nature photos over the years. I don't usually say anything to people, especially in front of him, but he's really good. If you look at the *Oregon Sentinel* on a regular basis and the outdoor section, in particular, you've most likely seen a photo or two of his."

"Oh, I love Crater Lake. It's one of Aaron and my favorite places. We stay in the lodge every summer. We have since we moved out here from Chicago. Both of us agree it has to be one of the most beautiful places on the planet."

Mabey slowed for a sharp corner. Her bare feet could barely feel the brake and accelerator. They were so tattered and torn it would take some time before she could wear her shoes. She wondered how long it would be before she could run again. Not long. If she had to buy different shoes while her feet healed, she would. The corner subsided, and she accelerated.

"Crater Lake is amazing, isn't it? Mitch and I were married there. They don't allow any sanctioned events, being a National Park and all, but we found a place; actually Mitch found it taking photos. Anyway, we had a rushed ceremony and honeymooned at the lodge. It was fantastic beyond belief. So I'm with you, Kala. One of the best places on the planet."

"Mabey, it just occurred to me. How do you know where to go?"

"I hate to admit it, Kala, but it's all instinct right now. I don't know with complete certainty. Just a gut feel and a hunch based on the bus I was on, the direction you and I escaped the meadow on foot, and my time spent hiking in the area with Mitch. I could be going the opposite direction of where we need to be for all I know."

In a nervous reaction, Kala threw her head back and laughed. A small tear formed in the edge of her right eye. She wiped it and then placed a finger in her mouth in search of the moisture. She started to retch when she realized she was willing to suck on a tear in search of moisture. However, her body had nothing to give up.

"Remind me not to ask you any more serious questions, Mabey, okay?

Mabey smiled and turned off the headlights. There were bright lights filling the sky and making night into day just ahead. She guided the redneck sled to the side of the road and cut the engine. She and Kala stared at each other in frightened silence.

Chapter 70

Let's Go Save The World

Mitch grabbed Jack by the arm and pulled him close so he wouldn't have to shout. The noise in the cave was loud.

"The horse is awesome. When you're on it, you don't even hold on. It's as if the horse is holding onto you. I'm not sure how to explain the feeling and make sense. You'll just have to see."

"We will not be using the horse, Mitch Wilde. It isn't necessary. We can go where we want with meaningful thought. No horse needed."

"Damn, too bad. I liked the horse, and I wanted Jack to see what it was like riding him. You sure we don't need him, Wise One?"

Mitch's eyes pleaded like a little kid at the carnival hoping his father will turn right back around and get in line for the same ride.

Wise One smiled, not something he did often, but something about Mitch Wilde made him feel at ease. He was a white man who seemed to be comfortable in his skin and proud to be part of Mother Earth.

"Mitch Wilde, since you have been open with me, looking for solutions rather than divisiveness, I will grant your desire."

Mitch got a big smile on his face and popped his eyes at Jack as if he were a big deal. Jack grinned back and shook his head at Mitch in disbelief over his ability to get his way in even the strangest of circumstances.

Wise One whistled, and the massive white horse appeared from nowhere. Mitch and Jack looked at each other in disbelief and laughed. The white beast knelt down, and a Native American got on all fours to provide a stepping platform for Wise One to get on his steed. He stayed in place, and Mitch pushed Jack to go next.

"I'm not going to get sandwiched between two males, bro. Not how I roll."

Mitch laughed. Jack grudgingly stepped on the man stool and got on the beast behind Wise One. Mitch looked around the cave, raised his hands in the air and said,

"That's all, everyone. Mitch Wilde is about to leave the building."

He got on the horse and let his arms hang at his side knowing he didn't need to hold onto Jack. He spoke to Jack, who was white-knuckled in his effort to latch onto Wise One and keep on the horse:

"Damn, Jack, I haven't seen you hang onto something so tight since your fishing pole at the pond. You really like him, huh?"

"Fuck you, Wilde."

Mitch laughed aloud. Jack did as well, but Mitch could not see his reaction as the horse rose to four legs, shook its head, and whinnied. Jack tensed in his legs, and Mitch turned and waved to everyone as if he were in a parade acknowledging the crowd with the understanding they wished they were in his position.

Mitch blurted out, "Okay, Wise One, let's go save the world."

Chapter 71

Dull Brass Objects

"You fucking evil squaw!" Jasper yelled out in pain. He had regained plenty of strength in his surgically repaired legs over the years. In particular since he was told long ago he would never walk again, but certain areas, like his hips and thigh-bones hurt more than the average body. Delores seemed to have an innate sense of knowing which parts of his body to attack. His eyes started to water. He fought back tears and focused on anger right now. The pain lessened, but he knew it would not go away for hours as it reverberated from his thigh bones through his hips. His stomach recoiled, and he willed away a growing nausea.

"Since we have established you can move now, let's get up and go across the street. I'm on a time table here. The rendezvous time is in about ninety minutes, and by my calculation we have forty-five minutes of travel. I figure you'll need about fifteen minutes to help me convince the group this is what's best for everyone involved. So we'll have about thirty minutes of fudge time."

Jasper stood and winced, but he didn't let her see his face. He paced, trying to walk off the pain.

Incredulous, Jasper responded.

"It's the best for everyone? You really think so?"

Delores furrowed her brow, paused and replied.

"Okay, perhaps not for everyone, but, hey, life isn't always fair, and we don't always get what we want. She'll be treated like royalty and given the best of everything. She'll just be expected to pop out a kid every thirty-six months or so. Between times it isn't so bad. There are other humans there, so she can fall in love and do many other human-type things."

"Do they have baseball there, bitch?"

"I'm sensing a lot of hostility from you right now, Jasper. You shouldn't be angry with me. I'm merely the messenger."

Jasper rolled his eyes and started to move away from her.

"I'm going to the kitchen to grab an aspirin or three and a glass of water. Follow if you want."

Jasper moved more slowly than normal to the kitchen. Delores followed. Just as well, Jasper thought, since he didn't have the strength right now to make a break for his bedroom and a weapon. Perhaps in a minute or two. She was too close to the table in the living room so the gun taped on the underside was also out of the question for now. He grabbed a clean glass, a large bottle of aspirin and swallowed four tablets with a full glass of water.

Delores, who'd moved over to the door near the back of the kitchen, stared out the window. She spoke while watching Jasper's reflection in the glass. The full moon lit up the back yard.

"What's a place like this cost, Jasper?" She paused and let the words hang in silence before continuing.

"I won't be able to buy in Outlaw River; heck, I wouldn't even want to after the last couple of days, but I could see myself settling somewhere in the Pacific Northwest. I love the mountains and all the water. Is it green like this most of the year? How much snow do you get here, or do you not get any at all?"

Jasper set his glass in the sink and, out of habit, grabbed the scrub brush to do a quick clean-up of the stainless sink. He set the brush in its holder and thought about what he should do, or could do. His legs hurt almost as badly as his hips right now. They weren't damaged, so any effort he made right now to overpower Delores would be a simple calculation and management of pain.

"Jasper, I'm not a bad person really. I realize this must be hard to comprehend considering what I'm asking, but I've done my part, and I want an opportunity to have some type of a normal life myself."

Jasper broke for his bedroom. His first step was a great one he thought. He sensed he caught her by surprise. His quick burst towards potential protection surprised even him. It was sure and clean. As he ran, he felt as though it was similar to a hurdler getting away from the starting block with perfection, or his mad dash away from a falling tree oh so many years ago. He hoped this result would be better.

Jasper reached his bedroom door and headed straight for the walk-in closet. He thought about diving in there, but he didn't sense Delores on his heels, so he stayed on his feet. Not looking back and risk wasting potential precious time, he slid out a wooden box from the lower shelf meant for shoes. He knew inside was one of his Smith & Wesson .38 revolvers; loaded and ready to go. He lifted the lid, and there she lay. He grabbed the gun and spun, ready to do what needed to be done. He would kill her if necessary. Under the circumstances, people would believe him, he thought.

Jasper walked out of the walk-in, and there standing in the doorway was Delores. She leaned against the door jam and had a sincere look of disappointment on her face. Jasper felt perplexed. Shouldn't she have some semblance of fear at this moment? He leveled the gun at her chest. Aim small, miss small, right?

Delores didn't move, hell, didn't even flinch. Jasper's first thought was how calm and confident this woman was. His second thought: is she confident, or does she just not care? Either way, he had the upper hand now, and he wouldn't make another mistake with this lass. He held his draw on her and spoke.

"Looks as though you either underestimated me, young lady, or you have some type of bulletproof skin I'm unaware of."

"There's always another option, Jasper. There almost always is. One that someone like you never considers until it's too late."

Jasper stood positioned like a rock, steadfast in his decision to drop this selfish bitch if he had to. His hand stayed steady with arm extended. He rotated through his options trying to isolate what she said. What could he have missed? Something felt odd in the moment, beyond his being held against his will and expected to help abduct a young lady. He couldn't quite figure out what it was.

Delores reached in her front pants pocket and dug. Jasper watched as she gathered whatever it was she was searching for. She pulled her hand out of her pocket and tossed her find through the air. Before he fully recognized what items she tossed, the nausea returned to his stomach, and the bile in the back of his throat reactivated. He now knew what the additional option was she spoke of. In his moment of relief in making it to his walk-in and grabbing the .38, he'd blocked out something the muscles in his arm reflexively knew. The gun wasn't as heavy as it should be.

Jasper lowered his arm, and the .38 hung by his side. Landing on his queen-sized bed with its off-white comforter were six dull brass objects; objects that should be in his gun.

Chapter 72

Jane Tunuda Returns

Debbi opened the refrigerator out of boredom to see what Mabey had. She wasn't hungry. Whatever Cindi was cooking smelled good, but it still didn't whet Debbi's appetite.

Junior was hovering out of the way, sipping on a small glass of red wine, chatting with Cindi while she cooked.

Michelle was taking big drinks of her wine and refilling her glass as often as needed. She was in the middle of tuning the Elite Stormtracker survival radio and TV Mitch kept in the garage. She'd brought it inside and set it on the kitchen counter. She couldn't get any television but heard some radio chatter. Everything she could find was nonsensical rubbish from people spouting ideas about the end of the world, zombies on the loose, the doom of everyone, and the internet-driven phrase of the day.

"J.J., will you go check on Shontey and see how she's doing?" Cindi asked while lifting the lid of her dinner creation to examine the contents.

"Sure, be right back."

Junior exited the kitchen after setting his wine glass on the counter near Cindi. He was next to Shontey in seconds. She was out cold and snoring a little. Like a kitten, Junior thought. He grabbed the afghan off the back of the couch and covered her. He thought about sliding her shoes off so she would be more comfortable, but he was concerned that might be a little too familiar. He didn't know her well enough.

"What are you making, Cindi? Your wonderful rice and tuna dish?"

"How the heck did you know what I was making, Mom, the smell?"

"No, I know it's easy to make, and you're always happy with the way it turns out. I suppose the smell did come into play though. It smells good as usual."

"Thanks, Mom. Cook what you know, right? Hopefully J.J. likes rice and tuna. I didn't even think to ask; I was so excited just to cook for him."

"Don't worry, honey. Even if he doesn't like it, you'll never know. This will be one of his favorite meals the rest of his life, no matter what happens with the two of you."

Cindi blushed and was swept up in her own dream.

"Honey, did you make enough for everyone by chance? I'm starting to get hungry myself."

Cindi closed the door to the refrigerator and looked over her mother's shoulder.

"Yes, Mom, I doubled up on everything because I figured J.J. would eat a lot, and whatever we don't eat, will keep."

"Good, and you're right. If there are any leftovers, Mitch will most likely devour them as soon as he gets back home."

Cindi bent over and checked the stove's gas flame. She lowered it to simmer, then stirred the rice dish, and returned the lid.

"Do you think Aunt Mabey and Uncle Mitch are okay, Mom?"

"Knowing those two, I'm sure they're fine and making the best out of whatever situation they may be in."

Debbi wasn't one hundred percent confident in her response, but under the circumstances, as a parent, her job right now was to project assuredness and confidence, not speculate on what she didn't know. She had read enough single-parenting self-help books to know this.

"Those two always seem to come out on top, Honey. I'm like you, though; I'd like to know for certain. Perhaps after supper you and Junior can walk across the street to Jasper's and see if Jasper or Junior's dad has heard anything."

"Sure, Mom. I would go anywhere with J.J. He makes me feels safe."

"Dear God, girl, take a breath." Michelle spoke up for the first time since her toast. Cindi laughed in agreement. The radio crackled, and a voice, recognizable to Southern Oregon residents came over the airwaves. Michelle wrestled with the knob and locked in on the announcement.

This is Jane Tunuda coming to you live from a bunker in City Hall, Medford, OR. If you can hear this message, stay indoors and lock your doors. Keep the lights out, and stay together in groups if you can. Do your best to hide. No one is sure at this point with exact certainty what is going on. It appears the objects spotted crashing into so many of our lakes and reservoirs have Alien entities inside them, and they are rounding up hundreds of humans and taking them. No one, as of yet, knows where they are taking them, only that large numbers of people are being taken. The chaos resulting from so many people afraid for their lives and their loved ones' lives is stretching the police, fire, and emergency services across the board to the brink of complete collapse. This is why I have been asked to broadcast the need for people to stay off the streets. Martial law has been put into effect across all communities in the Pacific Northwest and maybe in the nation. Anyone testing the limits of the law with looting, disorderly conduct, or general malfeasance runs the risk of being shot on the spot. The Aliens appear to be able to take the shape or appearance of you or your neighbor, so right now, stepping outside is risky at best. I repeat: stay in your homes, lock the doors and gather in groups if possible. Turn off your lights, and stay tuned to this radio station for periodic updates.

This is Jane Tunuda, KAJO.

Michelle spoke first. "My God! Am I lucky! I knew one of those damn things was in my apartment."

"We had one in our house too," Cindi added without hesitation.

Junior had returned after checking on Shontey and realized from the facial expressions of the kitchen's occupants he'd missed something. "What's going on? What'd I miss?"

Michelle raised up from leaning on the counter and working with the radio. She turned, grabbed the wine bottle off the kitchen Island, and topped off her glass. She set the bottle down and looked at Junior.

"What you missed was Southern Oregon's very own Jane Tunuda letting us all know that we are summarily screwed. She told us to turn off all the lights, huddle in the corner of the house, and fear for our lives."

Debbi was concerned about Michelle with her attitude and drinking, but she didn't know her well enough to say anything yet. She was Mabey's sister, and they were in Mabey's house after all. Instead she focused on Junior.

"Junior, why don't you let the dogs in? Let's make sure they're okay."

"Good idea, Mom. I'd love to have them in here with us."

"Sure thing, ma'am."

Junior set his wine glass on the counter. He was determined to get a drink, but it would have to wait another minute. He exited the kitchen and opened the siding door. Both dogs were lying on the deck and so glad to see someone. They greeted him, and General burst into the house. Junior turned and gave the ever-so-polite Delilah permission to enter.

"C'mon, Girl. It's okay; come keep us company."

Delilah was all too happy to oblige and was soon on her brother's trail. Junior looked skyward and saw the moon peeking at him over the crest of the trees. He slid the door shut behind him and hoped things could get back to normal soon as he headed back to the kitchen and a drink of wine.

"Thanks, Junior, and please don't call me ma'am. It makes me feel so old. Call me Debbi; I insist."

"I'm sorry, Debbi. You've asked me before, but it's a habit my dad drilled into my head."

"You are old, Mom."

Debbi scowled and rolled her eyes. Junior laughed and took a drink of wine. Michelle grabbed a plate from the cupboard, a fork for herself, and sat on one of the stools at the kitchen bar waiting for Cindi to complete her cooking. Cindi thought she looked drunk.

"Shoot, I forgot. J.J. How's Shontey?"

"She seems fine. She's snoring like a cat. I think she's in a deep sleep. I covered her with the blanket on the back of the couch so she wouldn't get cold."

Debbi thought how sweet this young man was.

Cindi smiled and felt just a little bit jealous. She focused her efforts back on the food, concentrating on making J.J.'s belly happy.

"Okay, everyone, this is ready. Grab a plate out of the cupboard and fork out of the drawer. I'll scoop it out for everyone to make it easy. Mom, will you see if there's soy sauce and hot sauce in the fridge?"

"Sure thing, honey. I'm going to go grab a couple of Mabey's candles and light them in here so we can turn off the lights. We don't want to make things any easier than we have to."

Michelle handed her plate across the kitchen island and got first dibs on the food. Cindi wanted to serve J.J. first, but she ignored Michelle's rudeness and got her out of the way. She piled on a helping for J.J. next and smiled at him. Cindi was thinking how fun this was and wondered why her father would leave. J.J. made her feel so safe; she hoped he would never leave her and that the feeling would never end.

Debbi returned with three candles, set them on the countertop, and lit them all. She noticed her daughter staring dreamy-eyed at Junior. It comforted her as a mother to know that right now her daughter basked in the glow of infatuation, a feeling she herself had longed for. After she lit the candles, she turned off the lights.

"This is good, Cindi, really good. I love tuna."

Cindi beamed as Debbi returned from the switch and took a plate, turned off the burner under the pan and dished out a small portion of her daughter's specialty for herself.

"Hey, listen, as soon as the two of you are finished eating, I want you to go across the street to Jasper's, okay? You can take the dogs with you. Hurry, please. I have a bad feeling."

Chapter 73

The Crest of the Pines

Sheriff Gunther's headache was gone, at least the deep pain. There were occasional remnants of pressure, but he chalked those up to his fast driving and the slight elevation change. He'd slowed once the road reached the switchbacks in the mountains, and no matter how much he wanted to end the pain created by Mitch Wilde, he had to arrive in one piece. He wasn't sure what he'd do if he couldn't find his nemesis. Perhaps put a bullet in his own head. The thought crossed his mind daily, but he was a fighter. At least that's what he told himself. He'd seen several suicides over the years while in the sheriff's department, and he could never get over the feeling how final it was and how selfish, at least for those who had loved ones left behind. He had none of those, so selfishness wasn't an issue for him the way he saw things.

He pounded the steering wheel and screamed aloud.

"Ahhhhhhhh!"

Around the next corner Gunther spied a pickup on the side of the road. He slowed and peered inside the cab as he drove past. He didn't see anyone. The license plate said RDNKSLD, so he knew it was Dusty Johnson's truck. He and his brother were probably out hunting illegally again. No time tonight to investigate. He'd talk with Dusty later.

He feathered the accelerator and noticed intense lights ahead, probably less than two miles away. He dimmed his lights and kept his speed under thirty. There was no reason for lights like this up here. No active mines and no movie filming right now. If Gunther's memory served right, the next film project was slated to start in early August. He had read somewhere, the local newspaper rag he thought, the film was going to be a Tim Krooze project about a transgendered logger. Gunther laughed out loud and mumbled under his breath, "like that will ever make money."

The lights grew in intensity the closer he got. He couldn't quite tell, but it looked as though the sky above the lights rippled like water receiving a diver. He thought of the one day on the banks of the Outlaw River when he remembered having fun with his father.

He was only seven or eight. There was a planned day with his mom and dad to do some fishing, pan for gold, and hike, but his mom got sick at the last minute. Thinking back, Gunther thought she was probably drunk. No matter, his dad went ahead and took him out by himself. Gunther welled up thinking about his father's teaching him how to fish; how to tie a knot with the hook, how to thread the worm on without tearing it all up, and how to cast. His father was so patient and kind that magical, sunny, and warm-winded day. It was one of the greatest days of his life. What the hell happened? His was a lifetime with an emotionally abusive and absent father who'd died from cancer: a lifetime with only one pleasant memory. How is this even possible?

"God damn Mitch Wilde."

Gunther slammed on the brakes. He killed the headlights and eased the car to the side of the road. He sat in dark stillness for a second, hoping he hadn't been seen. Hovering over a meadow were aircraft of some kind. He'd never seen anything like them before. They hung suspended in the air, and most of the time they were damned near impossible to see. If he stared long enough with intense focus, he could make out the sky being displaced. It seemed his vision was being partially blocked from seeing the stars in the background.

Gunther reached up adjusted the rear view and stared at his pathetic and recently tear-filled eyes. He climbed out of the car and closed the door without latching it. He didn't want to make a sound. About a hundred yards separated the road he was on and thick woods. Under the lights ahead was an apparent opening. Must be a meadow or small lake he guessed. He looked up and down the road to see if anyone else was coming. He saw nothing, so he worked his way with caution toward the lights. He was still consumed by Mitch Wilde, wondering if the pretty boy was around here somewhere. Perhaps he wouldn't have to kill him. With any luck his nemesis was already dead or taken.

Suddenly, his feet slipped out from underneath him, and his body slammed to the ground with a thud, stomach first, knocking the wind out of him. He stayed motionless wondering if he'd made enough noise to attract attention. He kept his head down and caught his breath for at least a minute. Gunther lifted his chin and stared forward, expecting to see some evil Alien being standing over him with a fancy laser gun. Nothing but ferns and pine bark, backed by bright lights. He got back on his feet and brushed off his chest and crotch without looking. The sheriff, reflexively, lifted the leather holster latch off his gun and put his right hand on the stock in preparation for the worst. A few more yards and he would be at the edge of woods able to see into the meadow.

Gunther looked behind him. He then looked skyward, straight above his current location. He saw nothing but woods and a star-bathed sky. He closed the gap between himself and the meadow's edge without incident. With his hand on his gun, he crowded next to a massive pine that hid him from the lights and meadow. He dropped to his stomach, turned over, and lying flat on his back, took several deep breaths and mentally counted to ten.

"One, two, three, four, five, six, seven, eight, nine, ten..."

Gunther rolled onto his belly outside the limited protection of the tree. His gun was out and leveled forward in anticipation of shooting. The light was intense, but after a second or two of eye adjustment, he was able to look without pain. Gunther concentrated on holding his bladder as he watched in disbelief. Hundreds of people were being sucked skyward, disappearing into the night sky. He felt giddy, hoping a certain someone was among them.

Chapter 74

Far Too Long

"Cindi, this was the best rice stir fry I've ever had. Where'd you learn to make it?"

Cindi blushed and shared her beaming smile with everyone.

"My mom, believe it or not."

"Hey, what's that supposed to mean, young lady? Are you taking a shot at my cooking?"

Junior chuckled, noticing the easy relationship Cindi had with her mother. It was nice to see parents who got along with their children, and the children's respect for their parents. With most of his high school and young adult acquaintances, this wasn't the case. It made him appreciate his own mother and father even more.

"No, Mom, I didn't mean it like that; sorry."

"It's okay, honey. I didn't take it wrong. I admit your rice is better than mine."

Debbi turned her attention to Junior.

"My precious daughter, the one I brought into this world, won't tell me what she does differently, Junior. Can you believe it?"

Michelle knocked over her empty wine glass reaching for the wine bottle.

"Ooops, hee hee. I can't believe you're all sitting here giggling and laughing as if nothing is going on outside. Don't you even care about Mitch and Mabey?"

Silence spread like wind-driven sand. Debbi made quick eye contact with Cindi and Junior, whose faces had instantly changed. Damn little bitch, Debbi thought.

"Michelle, we all have our own way of coping. You get drunk and act like a fool; we laugh and think about good times."

Michelle scowled, picked up her fork and plate, pushed her chair back, and stumbled over to the sink. She dropped both the plate and utensil in the sink and left the kitchen. Debbi watched as she headed up the stairs, figuring she was going to lie down. She hoped so anyway.

Junior rolled his eyes over Michelle's actions and turned his attention to Cindi. "Cindi, again, thanks. I was hungry, and your food took care of my rumbling stomach. Shall we go check on the crew across the street?"

"Don't worry about her, you two. No doubt she's having a difficult time with Mabey missing."

"I'm good, Mom, but thanks. She's always been nice to me before, and I know Aunt Mabey likes her."

"Same here, ma'am --- I mean, Debbi."

"Ah, see? Much better, Junior, thank you. Yes, you two get out of here. Why don't you take Delilah with you and let General stay here with me?"

"How about we help your mom clean up first, Cindi?"

"No, you two, get. I want to know what's going on over there. I'll take care of this."

"Should we put the leftovers in a plastic container and take it with us? Perhaps they're hungry."

"Good idea, Cindi, I'll do that. Junior, stack the plates in the sink for me while I put the rest of this food in a container. You can take it with you. Your dad's probably really hungry."

"I'm going to go use the restroom, J.J. I'll be right back."

Cindi walked over and gave Junior a big kiss on the cheek, then glided out of the kitchen.

Debbi smiled at Junior.

"I haven't ever seen her take to someone like you, Junior. She's dated plenty as you can imagine. She's so attractive and independent, but I don't think she has gone out with any one boy more than once or twice."

Junior held back a blush and responded.

"She is sweet, and we seem to click. It's soon though, and we've been thrust into a lot of crazy stuff, so I wonder if the feelings are more emotionally need driven right now than anything."

"How old are you, Junior?"

"Almost 21, why?"

"Because you sound like a fifty-year-old man, wise beyond his years."

"Really? Thanks, nice compliment."

"I mean it, Junior. But I think your concerns are unfounded. I can tell. The only other man I've seen her care so much about is Mitch."

Debbi finished scraping all the food from the pan into the container. She popped on the lid and handed it to Junior.

"Here, the crew as you called them should enjoy this across the street."

"Thanks, Debbi. I'll put in a good word with my dad about you."

It was Debbi's turn to blush.

Cindi returned from her brief absence and sidled right up to Junior.

"Why are you blushing, Mom?"

"What are you talking about? I'm not blushing."

"You sure are. I know because I can't remember if I've ever seen you blush before."

"I told your mom I'd put in a good word for her with my dad."

"Ah, ha! It's true. I was picking up a little something from you, Mom, when you were around him at the coffee shop earlier today."

"Oh, you did, huh? You're a crazy girl. Now you two get the hell out of here. Take Delilah with you."

Cindi laughed and grabbed Junior's hand.

"Come on, J.J. Let's get out of here and leave Mom to her fantasies."

Debbi kept her back to the kids and busied herself at the sink with the dishes.

"Should we take Delilah with us, Cindi?"

"Yes, c'mon, Delilah. General, you stay."

General barked his disappointment. Debbi called to him and knelt, grabbing him around his neck. Junior handed Cindi the food container, and with his free hand, carefully took Delilah by her collar.

"Two hot females, one on each side, how lucky am I?"

Cindi gave him a gentle elbow to the ribs.

"Very lucky."

"Would you two lovebirds get the hell out of here already and see what's going on? I can't hold General all night."

"Sure thing, Mom."

The two 'lovebirds' headed to the front door. Cindi spoke over her shoulder toward her mother as her and JJ continued towards the front door.

"Hey, Mom, J.J. and I are going to talk wedding plans on the way over to Jasper's. How about we have a double wedding?"

Cindi smiled at Junior, and he knew she was joking. They closed the door behind them and embraced the crisp night air with a slight shiver at the sudden temperature change.

Inside Debbi stood, releasing General who ran straight for the front door barking in displeasure at being left behind. Debbi felt blood rush through her body and hit all the right places as she thought about a double wedding. Far too soon for Cindi, but she was more than ready. It had been far too long.

Chapter 75

A Soft Kiss

Cindi stared at the night sky admiring the stars. She looked across the street at Jasper's house and wished it were further away. The fresh night air, although a bit on the cool side, called out for a moonlit walk. She held the hand of a pro baseball player she was crazy about, and her dog Delilah paced ahead making sure the path was safe. What more could a girl want?

"What do you think is going on, J.J? Any ideas?"

"I have some theories, but that's about it. When Mitch and I found my dad at the library a couple of days ago... or was it yesterday? Man, the last few days are a blur. Anyway, he had a stack of books on Aliens, Alien abduction, and Native Americans. He'd also been doing a lot of searching online. The Native American you and I saw on horseback running across the road, and all the people in town being taken; this has to be something from the stars. No way our own government could do something like this. What about you?"

Feeling confident, before Cindi could respond, Junior felt compelled to say something else so he did.

"Cindi, you have the most amazing eyes. They're so clear. I've always had a thing for green eyes."

Cindi squeezed J.J.'s hand. She really hoped things worked out with him. He was so handsome, talented, and from her hometown. With his pro baseball career, they'd travel and live wherever they wanted.

"I think it's Aliens, J.J. There is too much crazy stuff going on that humans aren't yet able to do. Right?"

Delilah sat out of habit as the couple reached the side door of Jasper's garage. Junior looked down at Cindi and felt his heart flutter as he looked into her beautiful face. Her eyes were like nothing he'd ever seen before; so clear, and surrounded by her beautiful face, holy shit.

Cindi, flushed with warmth, patted Delilah on the head.

"Good Delilah, you are such a good girl. You need to stay outside and wait for us, okay? We shouldn't be too long."

Junior gave Cindi a soft kiss on the lips, then knocked on the door.

Chapter 76

The Guests

"Okay, now what, DeeLoreUs?"

Jasper annunciated her name in an effort to irritate her. He realized he was losing all the battles with her and had no chance in the war. She was one step ahead of him at every turn. With his weapon neutered, at least in the bedroom, he was going to have to figure out a way to isolate her or get away. But getting away meant leaving the kids across the street vulnerable. Hell, there had to be something he could do. He had other weapons stashed in the living room and the garage. Perhaps he could make one more attempt.

Delores walked over to Jasper and condescendingly put her arm around his shoulder. She took the gun from Jasper's hand and threw it on the bed with the bullets.

"We're going to go into your garage of paranoia, sit down and come up with a reasonable plan to grab Cindi, and get to the rendezvous point. You can help me as I wish you would, or I can knock you out again, and when you wake, you'll be tied up. Your choice at this point, old man."

'Old man' coming from this bitch stung Jasper. He couldn't stand this woman and what she was asking him to do.

Delores followed Jasper through the door of the bedroom, down the hall, and back into the garage. As they walked, she talked softly.

"I'm pretty sure I found most of your weapons while you were out the first time, so don't waste your energy. The one under the table in the living room is empty. The one in the crawl space going into the attic has been disabled, and all the ones in the garage are out of commission. I put them all in a duffle bag and hid them in your house. You can search for them when this is all done, and I'm long gone."

Jasper laughed in defeat. Realizing weapons were out and wondering how she could possibly have found all of his stash spots pushed him to focus on alternative solutions.

Jasper asked, " Why didn't you hide the gun in my closet?"

Delores smiled, "I wanted to keep things interesting Jasper."

In the garage, Delores grabbed a stool, slid it up to the table and reached for a map she'd already studied and highlighted the immediate area. She pointed at the map.

"Come over here, Jasper."

Jasper moved to the table and stood with his hands at his side and his back straight. He wouldn't speak. He decided he would cooperate as little as possible, doing only what she asked so he wouldn't be tied up. He needed to stay upright and thinking. An opportunity might present itself, and he had to be ready.

"Once we get Cindi, you're going to drive the two of us to this spot on Evens Creek Road. You'll drop off the girl and me and then leave. If you stay around, they'll take you as well. Or because of your age, they may just kill you. They don't like older people because you're weak and need to be cared for at some point; those characteristics aren't something they cope with very well."

"They sound like assholes, if you ask me."

Jasper was getting increasingly upset with his inability to come up with any kind of plan. There wasn't anything decent lying around in here he could use to immobilize her. A keyboard wasn't going to do it.

The stools were too awkward. He made a mental note to plant a baseball bat or two in here when this was over. A pipe lying against the wall would be useful as well.

"They're most definitely assholes, Jasper. But they're stronger and smarter than we are, and right now they have a huge technological advantage, so we have to do what they want. Now, back to the map. If I'm calculating this right, I think it will take us about forty-five minutes to drive up Evens Creek Road to this meadow off Rock Creek Road. The coordinates are 42.656479, -123.051225. We can put them into the GPS I have and be on our way."

Jasper was wondering if there was a way he could get to his Jeep and the gun he had under the driver's seat. Or perhaps he should wait and pull it out sometime during the drive. He could dump her on the side of the road and hightail with Cindi.

Delores took the map and folded it up, sliding it into her pack. Jasper had noticed she had the pack at the coffee shop but didn't pay any attention when she brought it in here. He wondered what, besides her GPS device, was inside.

Delores stood, turning away from the table and the monitors to look directly at Jasper.

"Okay, here's how it's going to go down. We'll go across the street to Mitch's home. I'll explain that Jack took off to meet Mitch. Let's see if we can get Cindi and Junior to come back here with us. I'll think of some bullshit before we get there why those two need to return with us while the rest of them stay put. Let me worry about what to say. Then when we get back here, we go straight to your Jeep and head out."

"Oh, this sounds like a brilliant plan. Good luck prying Cindi away from her mother under these circumstances."

"Again, old man, not your worry."

Jasper looked over Delores' shoulder at the security monitor showing the outside of the garage. He saw a couple of people approaching with a dog. The closer they got, he realized who they were. He swallowed, as his eyes betrayed his visitors.

285

Delores turned to see what Jasper's lying eyes had seen. There on the monitor, showing an image less than ten feet away from the door, was her prize. This just keeps getting better and better, Delores thought. Jasper, on the other hand, was thinking, 'un-fucking-believable!' Is anything going to break in their favor?

There were whispering voices outside the door followed by silence and a confident knock. Delores was all too happy to go to the door and admit the guests.

Chapter 77

Fear and Confusion

Delores answered the door, unable to disguise the devilish smile her face wore. Junior noticed. Cindi did not.

"Cindi, Junior, so good to see you both. Come in. Jasper is studying a map. We think Mabey might be near here, and Jasper's trying to pin down the location. We're thinking of driving up there."

Jasper rolled his eyes in disgust at Delores' bullshit. He contemplated saying something but was fearful for everyone right now. He didn't want to jeopardize anyone's life trying to be a hero. He decided to bide his time and look for an opportunity.

Cindi came through the door and reminded Delilah to stay outside. Junior followed Cindi inside after patting Delilah on the head and telling her, "Good Girl."

Junior felt heaviness in the air. He'd never been in Jasper's place and didn't know the old guy very well, but the stress in the room wasn't something he expected. Throw in the weird manipulative greeting and odd looking smile from Delores, and he was apprehensive about what she'd said.

"Hey, we brought you guys some food, Jasper. Thought you and Dad would be hungry. Where is my dad and Mitch, by the way?"

"Hey, Kid, your dad…"

Delores interrupted Jasper without the slightest bit of hesitation.

"Your dad took off after Mitch. Right after we got back from the diner, a Native American on a white horse showed up out front. Mitch climbed on board, and they took off."

Cindi looked at J.J., and each knew what the other was thinking. Their near-crash experience driving to the movie included a Native American on massive white horse.

Junior jumped in, cutting off Delores.

"Okay, so Mitch is accounted for. What about my dad?"

Jasper responded without missing a beat. "We, the three of us here, that is… Hell, your dad and I were actually talking about what's happened so far and what we could do."

"So your…"

Delores tried to interrupt again, but Jasper talked over her. He looked at her as condescendingly as he could without pushing it too far. Delores was confident in his submission overall, so she decided to let him run with the discussion, for a time.

"As I was saying, your dad stands up at one point in the conversation. He tells us a very personal sad story about your mother and says he thinks Mitch is in trouble. He says he won't forgive himself if he stands by and does nothing. The next thing I know he's fading away and flat out disappears."

Cindi looked at Junior. Her gorgeous green eyes relayed fear and confusion.

"Disappeared?" Junior questioned. "As in poof, gone?"

"Exactly. Your dad, I can only assume, took off after Mitch with his arrow-laden place-jumping ability." Jasper said.

Junior responded without hesitation to Jasper. "What was he saying about my mom?"

Delores cut everyone off.

"We really should look at this map together and get going. Mitch and your dad could be in serious trouble."

Standing, Jasper ignored her.

"I won't go into all the details. Junior; you know the story, I'm sure, but suffice to say, your dad was second guessing himself about your mother's death. It was easy to tell after listening to him that he felt responsible for her death in some way."

Junior nodded. He thought about how many times in his life, thousands he was sure, he had wished he or his dad had taken out the trash as they were supposed to. Had they done the simple chore, his mother would be alive. Or, was the age-old adage true that when it's your time, it's your time; your demise is assured, no matter what anyone else does or doesn't do?

Cindi felt sadness radiating from Junior. She was familiar with the feeling of a lost parent. Her heart welled-up thinking about her father for a moment, and then she redirected her attention to Junior. She put a hand on his back and moved it back and forth with gentle pressure and empathetic care as Jasper continued.

"Listen, Kid, I don't know with certitude what you're thinking, but let me say this: fate has a way of working itself out no matter what we do. Everything is meant to be, every decision, every action. They're all mapped out. Sure, we can make educated and calculated decisions, but in the big old grand scheme of things, it doesn't matter. What the clown has in store for us will happen, either now or the next day regardless of the actions we take. Your mother was meant to move on to the next chapter in her existence, son."

Jasper watched Delores and could tell she wasn't listening to anything they were saying. He tried using his body, not words, to say as much as he could to Junior. He moved his eyes and shook his head towards Delores in an effort to let the kids know something was amiss. The looks Junior and Cindi were giving back to him were ones of complete sadness and confusion. He walked up to Junior and put his hand on his shoulder to comfort him. He squeezed hard to get his focused attention. Jasper started to whisper in the kid's direction, hoping Delores might still be zoned in on the map.

When he started to speak, he saw Cindi's eyes show instant fear. The soft shade of green had darkened the slightest bit. It didn't take Jasper any time at all to see her eyes weren't looking at him, but past him. He knew what caused the fear in the youthful eyes without turning. Jasper recognized the all-too-familiar sound of metal scraping against metal as Delores positioned a bullet in preparation for firing.

Jasper looked at Cindi and spoke with calm deliberation in an effort to soothe her.

"Not to worry, kids. The damn clown always shows its disgusting true intentions, but it can be beaten."

Chapter 78

Is he Alive?

Mitch enjoyed this quick ride more than the last. He knew what to expect, so he tried to absorb the full experience. Perhaps his enjoyment made the trip shorter as the time went excessively fast for his liking. Mitch wondered where they were going. He'd forgotten to ask Wise One prior to the beginning of their journey; they departed the dark and dank smoke-filled cave. Mitch felt stress and apprehension exuding from Jack. He thought it was similar to the feelings he had on his first ride atop Shadowfax. Perhaps not, on reflection: Jack had moved through space a number of times already, just not on the massive white horse.

The beautiful beast glided to a slow trot, and the surroundings came into focus. These recognizable surroundings were comforting, even amid the chaos. His and Jack's neighborhood, home for so long, had a soothing effect on him, no matter what the circumstance. His heart flickered, and he hoped that inside his castle would be Mabey. He knew, though, and could feel deep down in the depths of his DNA, this wasn't the case. He also felt Mabey was okay, but that others needed him right now. He wasn't sure who, and it irritated him.

Wise One brought Shadowfax to a stop in front of Mitch's residence. The great horse knelt, and Mitch jumped off, followed by

Jack. Wise One stayed on the steed, patted his neck, and the horse rose with little effort.

"Aren't you going to come in with us, Wise One? You're welcome in my home anytime."

"Thank you, Mitch Wilde, but I will stay here. I may need to leave soon, with or without you. I feel as though we are not where we need to be at this very moment. I felt something during the journey, but not strong enough to think of a new course. So we are here at this place and time. Please go inside, and see what you can learn."

Jack had already started walking up the sidewalk to the front door. Mitch nodded to Wise One and jogged to get in front of Jack. Mitch grabbed the door and tried to turn the handle. The door was locked. Mitch rang the bell and heard a familiar scuffle and bark between him and the heavy oak door.

Mitch turned his head toward Jack who was gazing around the neighborhood.

"Who do you think will answer the door, Jack?"

"How the hell would I know, Wilde?"

"Damn, Jack, a bit testy, aren't you?"

"I wonder why, Mitch."

"Does the ride on Shadowfax have you out of sorts? Don't worry; you'll get your belly and legs back pretty soon. The first time I rode, it took me a few minutes. You'll be fine."

"No, Mitch, I'm fine. Nothing at all to do with the way I'm feeling. Something's wrong beyond the shit storm going on. I have a fucking bad feeling, okay? Let's go through the garage since it appears no one is home. They could be over at Jasper's or at my place."

The door creaked open, and Debbi beamed.

General pushed her aside and bounced up and down working to get Mitch's full attention. Mitch knelt down and greeted his four-legged friend. General's whole body twisted back and forth like a piece of licorice whipping around. Mitch talked to him, let him lick his face, and hugged him mightily before he rose to his feet and hugged Debbi.

"Get in here, you two. The radio says to keep all the lights off and the doors locked."

Debbi stood aside, letting Mitch enter with General at his side. She grabbed Jack's hand and pulled him in, then closed the door and locked it.

Mitch headed to an empty kitchen. He popped his head inside the family room and saw Shontey asleep on the couch. No one else was there.

"The kids asleep? I don't suppose I'm so fortunate as to have Mabey in a bath or bed, am I?"

Debbi sighed with regret.

"No, Mitch, we haven't seen Mabey or heard anything either. The kids are across the street at Jasper's. Isn't that where you both came from?"

"Long story, Debbi, but no. Why?"

"I sent Cindi and Junior over to Jasper's to take some food to you guys. I thought you all were over there trying to make plans. Isn't that what we decided when we left downtown earlier this afternoon? I can hardly keep events straight in my head anymore. So much chaos."

Jack jumped into the conversation.

"You're right, Debbi. That's exactly how we left it. However, Mr. Wilde here decided to take a ride on a horse with his Native American friend, so Jasper and I were left alone with Delores to try to figure out what to do."

Mitch grabbed a glass from the sink and then bent over to smell one of the vanilla candles burning on the kitchen island. The vapor soothed part of his mind with a memory of Mabey. She loved vanilla-scented candles, and he loved them because of her. He filled his glass and then downed it. He filled the glass again and downed it again. Filling it one more time, he walked over to Jack.

"Drink this whether you want it or not, Jenson."

Jack took the glass and started to set it down on the counter out of resistance to Mitch's command. His mind argued, reminding him he was actually quite thirsty. He fought his stubborn resistance and drank the glass of water.

Mitch smiled and patted Jack on the shoulder.

"Sorry, bro; I don't mean to be bossy, but I can tell you're worried about Junior, and I figured you were probably as thirsty as I was. Let's go across the street and see what the kids and Jasper are up to. General, want to go over to Jasper's with us?"

General let out a huge bark and ran for the front door.

"Mitch, would you mind if General stays here with me? I like having him around. I feel much safer."

Mitch realized for the first time since returning that General's sister Delilah wasn't around.

"Where's Delilah, Debbi? Can't she stay with you?"

"She went across the street with the kids. I thought it was a good idea for them to have her with them on the walk over."

"Oh, okay."

Jack went to the front door joining General.

"Come on, Wilde; let's go."

Mitch nodded and turned to Debbi.

"You better follow me then. You're going to have to hold General. He isn't going to like my leaving without him. He'll be okay, though."

When Mitch got to the door, Jack grabbed the door knob.

"Wait a second, bro. Let Debbi get hold of my dog first, or he'll bolt outside."

Debbi got to the door and for some reason gave Jack a kiss on his cheek. She couldn't figure out what the hell had come over her, but she was drawn to him more than ever right now. Perhaps it was a new bond because of their kids that drew her in. She blushed and expected a bad reaction from Jack for her bold action.

Mitch watched, surprised at Debbi's touching action toward Jack, as Jack relaxed. He could see his shoulders loosen up and saw his back straighten. It was the tallest Mitch had seen his friend look in a long time. He continued to soak in the moment as Jack put a hand on Debbi's shoulder with affection and spoke to her in a voice Mitch hadn't heard since Jack's wife died.

"Thank you, Debbi. I'll go get the kids and get them back over here with you. Everything will be okay."

Jack opened the door and stepped outside. Mitch, beaming now, patted Debbi on the back and whispered to her.

"Well done, you tease."

Debbi smiled and slapped Mitch on his back.

"Get the hell out of here, and get my daughter back. Tell her to bring the plastic container back, okay?"

"God, Debbi, you are bossy just like Mabey. You sure you two aren't sisters? Oh hell, where is Michelle?"

"Drunk and asleep upstairs, Mitch. She's fine. Just too much wine. She apparently doesn't cope with stress as well as Mabey."

Mitch laughed and nodded in agreement. He patted General on the head.

"I will be back in a bit, bud. Take care of the ladies and the house."

Mitch left the safe doorway, heard the door close and lock behind him. General continued to bark, he could hear, but he knew it wouldn't last long. His canine companion would listen to Debbi and quiet down in short order. Mitch jogged to catch up with Jack who was already halfway to Jasper's place. He was at his side by the time Jack reached Jasper's door. Jack started to knock when Mitch grabbed the handle and entered.

Mitch stepped inside, and Jack followed, closing the door behind him. The room was dark except for the glow of the computer monitors. There appeared to be no one in the room. Jack turned on the light.

Mitch gave his eyes a second to adjust as he walked to the middle of the room. His heart pounded as his mind commanded him to drop to his knees.

"Fuck!"

Mitch put a hand on the body that lay face down in front of him. Blood oozed from the back of the head. Not a lot, but enough to dampen the hair.

"Jack, can you go inside the house and find a towel, please?"

"Is he alive, Mitch?"

"I think so. Get me a towel and some water, Jack."

Jack took off into the house as Mitch rolled the body over.

Chapter 79

You Too, Wilde?

Mitch held the towel on the back of Jasper's head and lowered it to the floor. He could see the old guy breathing but knew he was unconscious. He felt for a pulse just the same. Jasper's body couldn't hide the life pulsing through the veins. Mitch knew it would take much more than a knock to the back of the head to take out the cantankerous old coot.

"How long until he comes around, Mitch? We need to figure out what the hell is going on."

"It won't be long. This is the toughest guy you or I will ever meet."

On cue, Jasper's eyes danced inside their sockets.

Jack fumbled around the tabletops and started looking at a map with highlighted markings all over it.

Pointing, Mitch barked at Jack.

"Jack, hand me the bottle of water, will you?"

Jack grabbed a bottle of water off the table and handed it to Mitch.

"Thanks, Jack."

Mitch turned his attention back to Jasper and helped guide the old guy into a sitting position. Mitch kept his hand against the towel on the back of Jasper's head.

"That damn squaw bitch cold-cocked me! Goddamn, my head hurts."

Mitch cringed over Jasper's reference to Delores. Then he smiled in thankful relief as his friend seemed to be normal as he came around.

"Jasper, drink some water, and then get your lazy ass off this floor. We need to know what the hell is going on."

Jasper smiled at Mitch being a smart ass. Mitch figured it was the only way Jasper would respond. He was correct.

Jack took his gaze off the map, walked over and stood next to Mitch.

"Where are the kids, Jasper?"

Jasper took a couple of drinks of the water Mitch handed him and felt the back of his head. He noticed some blood on the towel. Not a lot but enough to be recognizable.

"You are going to be fine, old man. It must be less painful than a crushed pelvis."

"You got that right, Wilde."

"Jasper, the kids! Jesus, you two! Where is my son, Jasper?"

Mitch helped Jasper to his feet.

He watched as Jasper glared at Jack. Mitch figured something non-productive was about to come out of Jasper's mouth, so he cut him off.

"So Delores cold cocked you, old man? Do you know why? Did it have something to do with the kids?"

Mitch grabbed a stool for Jasper and then one for himself as he plopped down on it, waiting for Jasper's reply.

Jasper stood next to the stool, removed his hand from the back of his head, and examined his fingers: dry.

"She wants to turn the girl over to the invaders. Something about her being able to stay on earth if she finds a suitable birthing replacement to take her place in whatever fucking time or place she comes from. She claims she was taken years ago, or rather given away by her grandfather, to keep his tribe from further abductions – a hundred years ago or some ridiculous unbelievable number. We didn't chat too much. She was busy tying me up and knocking me out so I wouldn't scalp her sneaky ass."

Mitch stood and walked over to the map spread out on the table. Jack joined him.

"Does this map show where they're going, Jasper?"

Jasper walked over and pointed to the orange highlighted circle on the map.

"Yep. A meadow or open field: it looks like up Evens Creek Road. From what I understood from her devious ass, this place is where the ships will pick up all the abducted people. It's where she plans to turn over Cindi."

"Why did she take Junior with them? Do you have any idea, Jasper? Was he okay the last time you saw him?"

"He was fine, Jack. I'm not sure why she took him but probably to drive and to help keep Cindi under easier control. That's what I'd do anyway."

"Do you know how long they've been gone, Jasper? I know you've been out."

"Not exactly sure, Mitch but my best guess is thirty to forty-five minutes."

"Shit, Mitch, that's enough time to get up there, unless they drove really slow."

"What'd they drive, Jasper, do you know?" Mitch felt he was grilling Jasper, but there was no other way to get the information they needed.

"Best guess: they took my Jeep. She probably told the kids some far out lie about how I was slowing them down, wouldn't agree to go, blah blah blah, and it was better to try to go find Junior's dad without me. Some shit like that. Or she scared the shit out of them by knocking me out and then leveling the gun at them. Either way, they're gone. What are we going to do about it?"

Jasper looked at Mitch, then at Jack.

"Oh, there he goes again, Mitch. Last time his eyes looked like that, he left my ass alone with an evil Indian bitch named Delores."

Mitch looked at Jack and watched as he started to fade away. He heard Jack's last words.

"Follow me if you want, Wilde. I'm going to get Junior and Cindi."

Watching Jack disappear made Mitch think about Wise One. It occurred to him he hadn't seen him outside his house when he and Jack walked over here. He remembered Wise One's saying something about possibly not waiting for the two. Mitch moved out the side door without hesitation to peer across the street. Jasper followed him.

"Where you going, Wilde?"

"The Native American chief was out here on the white horse waiting for Jack and me. I guess he left. He said he might. I didn't notice when we were walking across the street. Somehow he's more involved in this than we originally thought. Putting the puzzle together the last couple of minutes, based on what you said and the stories he was telling me, I think Delores is his granddaughter. "

"I don't care who the hell she is, Mitch. She all but tortured me today, and I want to stop her from giving Cindi to the damn intruders. What do we do?"

"Well, Jasper, I know what I have to do."

Mitch concentrated on the map location he just saw circled in orange. He repeated the numbers over and over to himself. He knew they were latitude and longitude and hoped they were the meeting place. He was about to find out.

"Ah, shit, you too, Wilde?"

Jasper watched as Mitch's eyes bobbed and danced. Mitch's last words before he disappeared, leaving Jasper standing in his driveway:

"I have this feeling Mabey is going to be in the same place."

Chapter 80

The Shadowy Figure

Mitch's journey was almost instantaneous. He landed a little harder than he would have liked and wondered why before he picked himself up and brushed off his shirt and jeans. He looked around and saw he was in thick woods, lots of tall pines; ahead, a hundred yards or so, were bright lights in the sky. He wasn't sure, but it looked as if someone was walking ahead of him through the trees toward the light.

"Jack!" Mitch yelled. The body stopped and turned. Mitch took off running and was with Jack in no time at all.

"I was hoping you'd follow me, Wilde."

"Why didn't you tell me you were going? We could have gone together, dumb ass."

"Because you and Jasper were carrying on like a couple of cackling hens, and my son and his girlfriend are in danger."

Mitch nodded in agreement and smiled. He patted Jack on the back.

"Point taken, Jack. Let's go see if we can find them. I have a feeling Mabey is around here too."

Mitch moved toward the lights and what he assumed was an

open field. He half expected to see a scene similar to the one he saw in *Close Encounters of the Third Kind* as he approached the edge of the woods; he prepared to step into the meadow leaving the protection of the trees.

Jack moved to the left away from Mitch, surveying the landscape as he walked. He hoped there was a road nearby since Junior drove here. He figured there had to be one near the meadow if the map was accurate. Jack turned back toward the meadow to catch up to Mitch when he heard a shout. He turned back away from Mitch in the direction of the shout.

Mitch pressed forward unaware Jack had left his tail.

"Don't you fucking move, Wilde!"

Mitch slowed his walk and came to a stop. He recognized the voice and thought, 'Of all the times this inevitable confrontation could happen, did it have to be right here and now?'

"Put your hands up, and turn around. Make it slow. Anything funny from you, and I will not hesitate to put a bullet in your chest. Do you understand?"

"Things a little slow in town, Sheriff, so you felt the need to come up in the middle of nowhere to harass me?"

Gunther laughed a Jekyll-type laugh, one Wilde had never heard before. The sound made him pause as a chill ran down his back in the warm night air. He tried not to get distracted by the noises coming from the meadow: noises that included screams and electrical humming. Mitch turned to face his childhood nemesis, Sheriff Gunther, who was decked out in his uniform with creases in his pants even President Obama would envy.

"What are you going to do, Gunther? Shoot me right here where I stand?"

"You aren't as stupid as I thought, Wilde. Shoot you in your chest where you stand is exactly what I'm going to do. I had to in order to protect myself from your attack. 'It was the darnedest thing, your honor. Mr. Wilde had attacked me once already in the café in town, completely unprovoked. I went up to Evens Creek Road to search for and arrest him after I got a tip he was there. I tracked him into the woods and told him I had to take him in when he came at me and tried to get my gun. We wrestled briefly, and Wilde hit me on the head with a rock. I was dazed and tried to get away, but Wilde kept coming at me. I had no choice but to defend myself, your honor. It's such an unnecessary tragedy.' "

Mitch laughed eyeing his surroundings wondering where in the hell Jack was. He figured he could place-jump somewhere else, but where? He felt Mabey was near, and whether or not she needed him, he didn't want to take any chance of losing her by leaving.

"And you think the judge will believe you, Gunther?"

"Of course he will. Plenty of witnesses saw you attack me at the coffee shop, and the rest of the story is your word against mine. Oh wait, that's right; you won't have any words. You'll be dead."

Mitch stared in disbelief as Gunther threw his head back and laughed like a crazed soul. As twisted as the S.O.B. was, Mitch had never seen him like this. Mitch took a couple of steps backward while Gunther's head was back. He wanted to increase the distance from him and decrease the success rate of the Sheriff's shot. He wondered how good a shot he was.

"All because I beat you out for quarterback in high school and stood up to your old man, Gunther? Really? We're grown men now, and that was thirty years ago."

"You shut up. It was yesterday, you asshole. God-damned-fucking yesterday. My mom drank herself to death because of you, and my dad never liked me after you hit him with the football."

Mitch saw a shadow moving behind Gunther in the trees. He hoped it was Jack.

"Listen, Myron," Mitch used Gunther's first name trying to calm him. He didn't know if it'd work but felt it worth the effort.

"Myron, your dad hated you because you're gay, and you know

it. It had nothing at all to do with me. I was just an excuse and I was someone you could hate other than your old man. You know I'm right."

Gunther's voice rose, almost to the level of a scream.

"You shut your mouth about my father, Wilde. You know nothing about him. He was a good man and wanted to love me, but he couldn't. He just couldn't. You are right, it's because I'm an abnormal gay freak, Wilde!"

Mitch knew he needed either to make a run for it now, or disappear. Gunther was over the edge, and there was no hope of pulling him back. Mitch could see it in his face and hear it in the eerie tone of his voice.

"I tried to be your friend, Myron, and you turned on me. You had no reason to turn on me other than the hatred you had for your father. It's called projecting, you asshole. You've been doing it ever since I hit your father in the face with that damn football. And you aren't any freak, you idiot. You're gay. Like millions of other people in the world. Big fucking deal. You seriously want to kill me because you hate your father and you're gay? Listen to yourself."

The shadow reappeared behind Gunther. Mitch could tell it was human. At least in the moonlit night, it looked human. At this point he didn't care. If it could distract the sheriff for a split second, Mitch could get away, stay in the area, see if he could help Jack find the kids, and he could find Mabey.

"Where the hell are you, Jack?" Mitch whispered to himself.

Mitch wasn't sure; the distance was too great for him to make out Gunther's face with any clarity, but it sounded like Gunther was crying now. For the first time, Mitch realized how much help Gunther needed. He wasn't just a bitter sheriff; he was a very flawed man with deep issues. Mitch decided to make his break when the shadow appeared again. This time it was within feet of Gunther. Mitch couldn't make out who it was in the moonlit sky. Dirty and disheveled, he could tell but the shadowy figure was unknown, until he heard the voice.

Chapter 81

A Recognizable Voice

Mabey took the safety off as she approached Outlaw River's Sheriff from behind. She recognized the voice of the sheriff's conversation partner long before seeing the face. The trees were doing a great job of blocking the moonlight. Electrical noises from the meadow, along with intermittent screams, helped cloak her approach. She lifted her hand with the steady calm of a seasoned law enforcement agent.

She could hear Mitch out there, but she was having a hard time seeing him. Gunther was between the two of them. Mitch's voice was so soothing for her. She knew she could let her guard down only when she was in his arms. The hours seemed like an eternity since she had last seen him. A flood of emotions and thoughts fought to break from her mind as she approached the Sheriff. The chaos in the meadow helped her in the approach from behind. Gunther was so intent on harming Mitch that he'd become oblivious to his surroundings.

"Drop your gun, and put both hands in the air. If you make one wrong move, I'm going pull the trigger of this gun I'm holding and put a bullet into the back of your head. I'm sick of you messing with my husband. Do you hear me, Sheriff Gunther?"

Mabey's only mistake over the day's events almost cost her. She realized some distance between Gunther and herself would have been best. However, it was as if he were a magnet, and she couldn't stop. What happened next surprised Mabey. Sheriff Gunther spun without hesitation and crashed the back of his left hand against her head. Whether she was near exhaustion or too confident from her recent undefeated record with death, Mabey went down from the Sheriff's blow. Somehow she kept a grip on her gun, and it fired. The noise of the shot was swallowed by the outdoors and the meadow's madness.

Sensing things were about to go awry at the moment Gunther started his spin towards Mabey, Mitch took off on a desperate sprint. Panic left his body as adrenaline kicked in; he moved with the speed of his youth. Gunther pointed his gun at Mabey, now on the ground. Mabey leveled her gun at Gunther towering over her. Mitch leapt for the Sheriff as a shot rang out. He tackled Myron Gunther in a similar fashion as he had some thirty years ago on the football field after he'd blindsided Mitch in practice. This time was different. Despite all the rage Mitch carried at that moment against the Sheriff, and with the fear of losing Mabey, a rush of sadness flowed through him when he realized the body he now tackled was lifeless.

Mitch released his grip and rolled over to face a tattered and torn-to-hell Mabey: she was hardly recognizable. If not for her voice and eyes, Mitch wouldn't have known who she was. Her head was shaved; her feet and hands were swollen and cut up. Dried blood covered the areas fingernails and toenails once occupied. She was in some kind of grayish jumpsuit covered in dirt and filth. Mitch grabbed her shaking hand and lowered the gun to the ground. He pulled her in tight to him and held her as he had never held her before.

"Thank you, Mabey; you just saved my life, my lady."

Mabey fought back the tears. She was spent. She had nothing left. There was no safer place she could be right now, and she knew it.

"Are you shot, Mabey?"

"I don't think he fired, Mitch. Is he dead?"

Mitch looked at Gunther who lay in a horrific pose. He turned back to Mabey.

"Yes, Mabey. A bullet between someone's eyes like that is almost always fatal."

"Mitch, I didn't mean to kill him. I just didn't want him to shoot me."

Mitch stood and helped Mabey to her feet. He took the gun from her hand, put on the safety, and slid it in the back of his pants.

Mabey went over and rolled Sheriff Gunther on his back. A small bullet entrance slightly off center and above the bridge of the nose was noticeable. The sheriff's eyes were as clear and bright as Mabey had ever seen them. Somehow he had a smile on his face. Mitch came over and lowered the sheriff's lids over the lifeless eyes.

"A sad waste. He took his bitterness and anger with him to the very end."

"What are we going to tell people, Mitch? Am I going to go to jail? Will anyone believe us?"

Kala and Aaron approached.

Mitch spun toward the noise, pulling the gun from his pants and leveling it at the two strangers.

Mabey reacted with speed and regained focus.

"Mitch, it's okay. They're with me."

Mitch hesitated before the words sank in. He put the gun back in his pants and turned to face Mabey. He grabbed her and held her.

Aaron had his arm slung over Kala's shoulders and was keeping as much weight as he could off one foot.

"We heard and saw the whole thing, girlfriend. You aren't going anywhere but home when this is all done. We'll swear to the whole thing in court if it gets that far."

Mitch let go of Mabey as the couple approached.

"Mitch, this is Kala and Aaron, Shontey's parents. We've been surviving and helping each other since we were taken."

Kala laughed.

"More like Aaron and I have been riding Mabey's coattails staying alive, thanks to her. You have one awesome woman there, Mitch. I hope you know it."

Mitch shook hands with both Kala and Aaron.

"Nice to meet both of you."

He turned to look at Mabey.

"Yes, I do, and I've never once thought anything else the whole time I've known her – how awesome she is."

The foursome stopped talking and making any noise as they all heard someone scream "MITCH" through the woods.

Chapter 82

Unabated Moonlight

"Mabey, that sounds like Jack! Get the Sheriff's gun, and the three of you stay put. Don't leave unless you absolutely have to. I'm going to go help Jack. Junior and Cindi have been brought here."

"Oh my God, you've seen Cindi, Mitch? Was our Shontey with her?"

"No, actually I haven't seen Cindi or Junior. Jasper said Delores planned to bring them here against their will. Shontey, though, I have seen. She's asleep on our family room couch with Cindi's mom and Mabey's sister. She's fine."

Kala turned and hugged Aaron. He almost fell but caught himself on his swollen and badly sprained ankle. Mitch noticed the grimace on Aaron's face, impressed he didn't cry out. He held it in for his wife, seemingly on the verge of a breakdown, probably from exhaustion and the relief in knowing their daughter was safe.

"Mitch, I know you have to go, but don't you dare take too long. I am out of fight. I just don't have any energy left."

Mitch moved to Gunther, grabbed his pistol from his already-cold hand and gave it to Mabey. "A thirty-eight, Mabey; you know how to handle it. You all sit down with your backs to a tree. Face in three different directions. If you have to use the gun, don't hesitate. I'll be back as soon as I can. Junior and Cindi are in danger.

Mitch gave Mabey a gentle kiss on her swollen mouth. He then kissed her forehead, probably the only part of her body not swollen. He reflexively wiped the dirt from his lips after kissing her and pointed to a tree for them to get around.

"I will be right back, babe. I can't even begin to describe how glad I am to see you. By the way, you can totally pull off the bald look.

"Hah! Get out of here so you can get back, Mitch."

Mabey turned and plopped on the ground, scooted her butt against the base of the massive pine and leaned back. She put Gunther's gun in her lap and sighed. Kala and Aaron followed suit so all three were looking in different directions. Mitch took off at a dead run toward the sound of the voice which moments earlier had called out his name.

Mitch was just inside the tree line bordering the meadow. He could see large groups of people in tight circles being sucked upwards one by one into large ships. The ships were difficult to see. He could make out only the outlines and pick-up movements as they rocked from time to time. Mitch realized they had some type of invisibility engineering. Flashing through his mind was the question of whether they were Alien or government. He chuckled to himself thinking about next summer's barbecue, and Jack's going on and on about the U.S. Government's making some kind of deal with these foreigners in order to keep D.C. whole. Mitch smiled thinking Jack would have enough conspiracy stories to last a lifetime.

"MITCH!"

Mitch heard the voice again and redirected his path. The humming noises coming from the ships and the screams of people being taken were loud and distracting. Mitch didn't understand why the people weren't trying to escape until he saw several making attempts to break free by running away from the inner circle of people. Each time they did, there were loud hissing noises, and their bodies were thrown backwards, away from the outer edges of an invisible barrier. As he ran, he wondered what he would do if he were inside one of those circles. He figured there must be a weakness of some kind.

"MITCH!"

Mitch thought he saw a horse ahead in the woods. The scream was coming from there, less than a hundred yards away. He traversed the distance in seconds, flashing back to his first timed fifty-yard dash in fifth grade. He wondered why he would think of the dash right now. Mitch slowed as he approached of a group of people, placing the gun he got from Mabey in his pants against his back. He wondered how many bullets were left. Mabey had fired one accidentally and one intentionally between Gunther's eyes. But had she used it at all prior to then?

Wise One, Jack, Delores, and Junior were in a combative arc opposite Delores and Cindi. Shadowfax was outside behind Wise One in what Mitch thought was an aggressive and protective posture. Mitch wished he had General with him. He approached with caution. Jack saw him first and then Wise One. Delores had Cindi in a hold around her throat with a gun pointed in the direction of Junior and Jack. Cindi's back was to Delores, and she was crying. She looked terrified. Not that Mitch needed any incentive to try to save her, but seeing her in that state of distraught fear made him angry. He wondered if the anger could be any more intense if Cindi were actually his child.

Delores spoke first on Mitch's arrival.

"Don't come any closer, Mitch. All of you let me pass and get into the meadow with Cindi, and no one else will get hurt. We don't have much time. If you don't do as I say, I'm going to have to shoot each of you. I'm not going back. I paid my time, and I'm not going back."

Wise One spoke.

"Daughter of Sorrow, you cannot do this. Please leave the girl and these people alone. There must be another way. You can leave with me; I will talk with the Star People. You are right: you have sacrificed enough."

Delores screamed directly at Wise One while tightening her grip on Cindi. She had the gun leveled at Junior, who was closest to her.

"How could you, Grandfather? How could you give me away to those freaks? Your own granddaughter? I HATE YOU!"

Mitch watched as Junior inexplicably started moving backwards. He was now behind his father and continued to retreat. Mitch thought the kid had something in mind, but he couldn't for the life of any of them figure out what.

"You are right, Daughter of Sorrow. I live each day of my life with regret. This is not these people's problem, though. The struggle is with you and me. Let the girl go. You and I will leave, and the Star People will do nothing."

Delores fired the gun. Wise One dropped to his knees holding his left shoulder. Mitch started to make a move towards him when Delores repositioned the gun on him. He knew she wasn't reluctant to use it, so Mitch stopped.

Mitch watched Junior bend over and pick up something off the ground. Delores was focused on Mitch, so she didn't see Junior's action.

"Look, Delores, I am not sure what the hell is going on, but hurting any of us and taking Cindi is not going to solve your problems. In fact, it will create more problems, unless you kill all of us."

"THEN THAT IS WHAT I WILL DO."

Mitch moved his right hand with deliberate care toward the small of his back. From his position he felt he could get a decent shot at Delores's right shoulder. It would be a tough shot, but he knew he could do it. If he missed wide, he risked hurting Cindi, but it would have to be way wide to hurt her seriously. He decided if he was going to miss, he would miss to her left. He hoped the surprise would throw Delores off her guard, and then Cindi could break free exposing Delores completely. Mitch would then drop her without hesitation. If he had another bullet.

Mitch froze when he saw Junior make a sudden move. He stopped pulling the gun from his pants. Whatever the kid had picked up from the ground left his hand with amazing speed and accuracy and in an instant, found its intended target. Mitch heard a sickening thud, distinguishable over the loud sounds still coming from the meadow. The gun Delores held in her hand fell to the ground. Her head rocked back, now grotesque. The grip of her left arm tightened around Cindi as the two bodies fell backwards. Cindi screamed and reached out to grab something to hold her up. Jack made a break for the young girl, and Junior followed. Mitch finished taking the gun from his pants and spun around half expecting to see another force wanting to hurt them. He breathed a sigh of relief as all he saw was Shadowfax standing over Wise One, now on his knees weeping.

    Mitch let his hand relax as he repositioned the gun in his pants. He thought of Mabey and getting back to her as the meadow lights dimmed. The humming noises faded, and the moon pierced through the pines unabated for the first time all evening.

Epilogue

A Wilde Entry

It has been a month since I've written in my journal. Things are starting to settle, and Mabey and I are not as stressed after the judge's gavel came down today following his words, 'due to the testimony of several witnesses, and a clear-cut case of self-defense, the court, if it pleases the district attorney, dismisses any and all charges...' The Mayor kept telling Mabey and me there was no way she would be charged with the murder of Sheriff Myron Gunther after our accounts of events, along with those of our new friends Kala and Aaron, were recorded.

I wonder if normal will ever again exist for us. Everyone in town, those of us left anyway, look up into the skies and down alleyways as never before. The official count is thirty-seven Outlaw River citizens missing, all presumed taken by the Star People, whoever they are. Jack, of course, says they were government operatives all along, and the missing people are destined for a life of experimentation in the deepest darkest secret places in America. Jasper has his own theories, none of which include our government's taking anyone. He does think the government has turned a blind eye hoping the problem would go away, but the people weren't taken to secret government facilities. Listening to Jack and Jasper argue about what did happen should be entertaining for years. As for me, I think they are us in the future. Call it a parallel universe or future earth if you want. I don't know enough about physics no matter how many times I watch What the Bleep Do We Know? *on video to write down a definitive explanation. My theories are in my own head, and I share them with Mabey and no one else, to the dismay and frustration of Jasper.*

Mabey's nails on her feet and hands are starting to grow back. She has a ways to go before they're fully healed. Her feet took almost three weeks before she could get back into her regular shoes. Her hair is coming back in, and what was once a deep auburn now appears to be a lighter red. No idea what this is all about. The doctor says it isn't all that uncommon for hair color to change. Most likely it has to do with the extreme stress Mabey was under. Mabey is fascinated and wonders if it will stay light or go back to deep auburn. I don't care. I told her she can leave her head shaved. I will love her no matter what. I do tell her I hope she will wear a hat when we go out into public, though. She hits me, of course and then thanks me for shaving my head along with her in a very selfless act of solidarity.

Mabey is slowly working back into her physical-training practice. Clients are eager for her return. The Mayor says he wants to up his training with her and asks Mabey if she's ever thought of doing some outdoor survival training exercises. Kala has asked her the same thing. Mabey is thinking about it. I encourage her to do what her gut tells her. The stories she shares with me about what she went through during her capture and escape, are the stuff from which legends are made. She has always been confident, but now she has this super-sexy, calm, steel reserve about her. As if she needed to be any sexier to me. I call her Lara Croft as often as I can and ask her if she will train me in the art of outdoor survival too. I no longer feel the need to roll up my shirt sleeves when out with her. Let's just say that any person dumb enough to mess with Mabey Wilde is going to be in for the surprise of his life.

Neither Jack nor I can place-jump anymore, and both of us have tried. I wonder if those damn star people come back, whether I will regain the ability. I wanted to ask Wise One, but after the meadow incident, I couldn't. All of us stood by and watched as he stoically walked over, picked up his granddaughter, then got on the back on his magnificent horse and disappeared. I thought I saw him the other day near the river trail while I was out cycling with General at my side. I would like to see him again, but I suspect I never will. I feel bad for him and what he must be going through in regards to Delores. When he was carrying her and climbed on his horse, I have never seen a sadder face on a human being.

When Delores fell back after Junior's rock-fastball found its mark, her muscles flexed giving the impression she'd survived. But when her back hit the ground and Cindi fell on top of her, the arm relaxed, and Cindi scampered to her feet and into Junior's arms. None of us really know with certainty if she died. We all like to think she didn't. It would be nice to think of her and her Grandfather Wise One having an opportunity to reconnect and heal their terrible emotional wounds.

Junior and Cindi appear destined to be together. Not sure I ever believed in destiny before all this, but some part of me does now. Junior is pitching for the Los Angeles Dodgers this weekend. They had a rash of injuries to their starting staff and called him up for a spot-start to see if he was ready for the big leagues. It's all Cindi talks about. There's a booth – shit, a shrine – down at the Coffee Shack now with his photos, a baseball, and a Dodgers cap. Everything is autographed, of course. There used to be a rock in a plastic case as well, but Debbi made Cindi take it away. She said death should never be celebrated no matter the circumstance. Plus, none of us know for certain if Delores died. Cindi is already applying to colleges in Los Angeles. She has a wedding in mind as well. Jack says Junior is actually excited about it. He tells his dad he's found his 'Ginny.' Jack loves to tell Mitch the story of the homage to his deceased wife and Junior's mother, Ginny.

Jack and Debbi have started dating. They've had a few dinners at her place and a couple of times here. It's a good fit. Both of them have suffered terrible and unexpected losses in their lives, and both deserve a good partner. Not sure where it will end up, but for now they're enjoying each other's company. It is great to see Jack laugh again with a woman.

Mabey's partner in crime, Kala, and her husband, Aaron, have been here to dinner once, and we've been to their house once. Mabey and I like them a lot and have much to talk about and more to learn. It's nice to have new friends Mabey and I both enjoy. Mabey is already thinking about next summer's barbeque saying we should scale it back and invite a smaller core group of friends; I'm all for that. She wants to try to figure out a way to include Junior. Good luck with scheduling, I tell her. I hope Junior is going to be busy during his summers for years to come.

Michelle has started working for Jack at his sporting good's store in Medford. Jack has already promoted her to assistant manager and says she is one of the best employees he has ever had. She stopped drinking and has a new boyfriend she met in the camping section of the store. Mabey is thrilled with her change. We both wonder exactly what happened but don't question Michelle for fear she will revert to her old ways.

Sheriff Gunther was laid to rest without ceremony in Outlaw River's lone cemetery. The Mayor, the remaining members of the Sheriff's office, Mabey, Jasper and I were all who attended. Both Mabey and I did it out of respect for the Mayor who has been amazing in working towards getting Outlaw River back on her feet. Something happened in the whole ordeal, making him a better human. Mabey and I often talk about what really caused his change. We always end up deciding it doesn't matter. Mabey says she prays it stays this way because she doesn't want me running for mayor. I always smile and say, yeah yeah, whatever.

Old man Jasper is as spunky and determined as ever to resolve exactly who came, why they came, and will they be back. He says it isn't a will, but a when. He's opened up quite a bit, and I regularly see him talking with others down at the Coffee Shack where he has a regular booth reserved for him at all times. It's the same booth with Junior's paraphernalia hanging on the walls. Jasper goes hiking with General and me a couple times a week down on the river bank. They are some of my favorite days. He reminds me a lot of my father. We have many unspoken moments of meaningful affection. We have an open-door policy for him now. I often come home to find him in the family room with his feet on the coffee table drinking one of my craft brews and talking with Mabey while she has a glass of wine. Jasper and I returned to Crater Lake, with Mabey and General this time. I took them all to my photo rock. My bike was still locked to the tree right where I left it. I couldn't believe it was there! Mabey couldn't believe how excited I was to find it. I have tried to explain to her a number of times how a relationship with a bike is a bond. When you find one that fits you just right, you will hold onto it for life. She makes a smartass comment about boys and their toys. I always tell her the choice would be easy between her and the bike. She would win nine out of ten times. :-) I also found some of my camera gear, but it was ruined from the weather. Jasper had recovered the camera body when he found my clothes, so those great photos I took were saved. I sold the video footage at Applegate lake through my buddy Ron who requested the Crater Lake photos initially for the Portland Tribune. They somehow came up with a hundred thousand dollars for the video. This should keep Mabey off my back for at least a couple of months about 'not bringing in any money'. The Tribune is in court right now battling with the federal government who had the footage yanked from the internet shortly after it aired. Something about national security. I have a copy, of course, and Jasper and I look at it from time to time. Jack uses this as fuel for his government-conspiracy argument.

    Mabey doesn't like me going off on photo shoots anymore. I am hopeful her reluctance will fade with time. I have promised her I won't go anytime soon, and when I do go around Outlaw River and her banks, I always take General with me. Mabey is convinced if General had been with me, I would never have been hit over the head and put into the Lake. I argue it would have happened regardless, and they probably would have killed General.

    Needless to say, I'm a bit bored now. I got so used to going on my photo shoots. I'm considering writing a novel. I tell Mabey we could write one together and explain how women would love to read her take-charge chapters. She is flattered but hasn't warmed to the idea. In her modesty she doesn't like to talk about what she accomplished. I think it brings back scary memories, and she isn't ready to talk about them. I will patiently keep working on her. I tell her we could call it A Wilde Journey, to Hell and Back. She always smiles and tells me she *can't believe how infatuated I am with my last name. It is a Wilde name.*

General is barking downstairs, and Mabey is calling me about dinner, so I will do my part as Lord-of-the-Manor and partake in some earthly sustenance. It is awesome to be married to such a strong queen I hope she doesn't try and get rid of the king. Until next time…

Thank you for taking the time to read The Outlaw River Wilde. If you enjoyed it, please consider telling your friends and posting a short review. Word of mouth is an Indie author's best friend and much appreciated. You can post a review on Amazon, KOBO, NOOK, Smashwords, iBook, or Goodreads. If you didn't like it, well it can be our little secret.

Author's Notes

I would like to say thank you to my editor, Jill Foltz, for her passion and professional approach in making Still Wilde in Outlaw River a better piece of fiction. There were a number of times throughout the process when she would challenge me, pushing me to clarify my thoughts. Many times I received notes from her questioning my characters' attitudes and their choice of words. This improved the clarity of the dialogue in numerous situations. It was as if she were in my head, which helped tremendously when I was struggling for the right thoughts. Having her come back into my life at this stage in my writing is something I think the Star People had a hand in. :-)

Finally, thank you to my first reader, Helen. I have heard Stephen King make reference a number of times to the importance of a quality first reader; now I understand why.

Thanks to the Native Americans, specifically the Klamath Tribes, for pointing me in the right direction for using some of their language in this novel. Any Native American words and phrases are those from the Klamath Tribes and were taken directly from their website:

http://www.klamathtribes.org/mobile/sentences.html

sat'waaYi ʔis - Help Me

san'aaWawli ʔan ʔambo - I want some water

Mike's Social Media Presence

Web Site: **MikeWaltersNovels.com**
Facebook: **https://www.facebook.com/MikeWalters24**
Twitter: **https://twitter.com/MikeAWalters**
Pinterest: **https://www.pinterest.com/MikeAWalters24/**

Made in the USA
Charleston, SC
26 September 2016